"I need an answer, Alex...

"If I work on your place, I'll be here while the gate's open," Nick added. "You won't be alone. The gate will be locked every night. I'll handle that."

"I..." Alex let out a soft sigh, pressing her lips together. "We'll negotiate as we go."

"I know this isn't easy."

"The gate *has* to be locked at night. That's my... difficult...time."

He hated the thought of her—of anyone really— having difficulties getting through the night. He knew what it was like to lie awake, haunted by thoughts, wishes, regrets.

"I'll see to it."

Neither of them moved from where they stood.

Finally she said, "Should we sha‌k‌e ‌ ‌ ‌ ‌ ‌or something?"

Nick's lips tw‌

She took a sm‌ ‌ ‌ ‌ ‌ ‌ed to get back to m‌ ‌ ‌ ‌ ‌ ‌t."

"I need to get t‌ ‌ ‌ ‌ ‌ ‌ ‌. He smiled, wishing that they both fe‌.. good about this deal. "Thank you, Alex." *I won't let anything happen to you...*

Dear Reader,

When I was young, *The Waltons* was one of my favorite television shows. I love stories that involve members of a family working their way through life, overcoming obstacles, learning life lessons, finding love and dealing with personal growth as it relates to the family.

This is what inspired me to write the Sweet Home, Montana series. I wanted to write about a family with multiple generations, so I created the Callahans—a family that consists of widower Nick Callahan, his two young daughters, his sisters and his grandmother. Each of the Callahans have their own personal challenges and each find love in their own way—including the grandmother. Yay, late-in-life romance.

I hope you enjoy this series and the journeys of the tightly knit Callahan family.

I love to hear from readers and I am available on Facebook, Facebook.com/jeannie.watt.1, and my website, jeanniewatt.com, where you can sign up for my newsletter.

Happy reading!

Jeannie Watt

HEARTWARMING

Montana Dad

———

Jeannie Watt

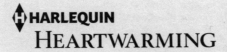

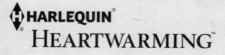

ISBN-13: 978-1-335-88959-1

Recycling programs for this product may not exist in your area.

Montana Dad

Copyright © 2020 by Jeannie Steinman

This edition published by arrangement with Harlequin Books S.A.

For questions and comments about the quality of this book, please contact us at CustomerService@Harlequin.com.

Harlequin Enterprises ULC
22 Adelaide St. West, 40th Floor
Toronto, Ontario M5H 4E3, Canada
www.Harlequin.com

Printed in U.S.A.

Jeannie Watt lives on a small cattle ranch and hay farm in southwest Montana with her husband, her ridiculously energetic parents and the usual ranch menagerie. She spends her mornings writing, except during calving season, and during the remainder of the day enjoys sewing, doing glass mosaics and fixing fence. If you'd like more information about Jeannie and her books, please visit her website at jeanniewatt.com, where you can also sign up for her newsletter.

CHAPTER ONE

ALEX RYAN CLIMBED out of her car and stretched the kinks out of her back before swinging the door shut with a satisfying slam. Two thousand miles, three nights on the road, four days of checking the rearview mirror for familiar-looking cars, and she was finally here.

And she was alone. She was sure of it.

She'd had the highway to herself as she left the Gavin, Montana, real-estate office where she'd picked up the keys to both the house and the gate closing off her isolated home from anyone who accidentally started down the road. The graveled lane leading from the highway to the ranch turnoff had been equally empty, and when she'd gotten out of the car to unlock the gate, the only sign of life had been a flock of geese flying toward a distant river.

Yes. Alone.

She let out a long breath and rolled her

shoulders as she took stock of her purchase. The two-story house was smaller than she remembered. More run-down. The paint was flaking and one of the shutters hung at an odd angle. Behind the house, the garden shed was losing its roof, and the barn didn't look as if it was in much better shape and the low hanging rainclouds made everything look just that much drearier. But it was home. Alex pulled the keys out of her raincoat pocket and crossed the weathered porch to the equally weathered front door. The house and her life had a lot in common. Both needed work.

The old bolt slid sideways, and Alex pushed open the door. A wave of musty air rolled over her and then a sharp gust of wind blew in from behind her and dissipated the nasty smell. She hunched her shoulders against the cool air and stepped inside, letting the door swing shut behind her.

The house was totally, utterly silent. The kind of silence that pressed in on the ears… the kind of silence Alex relished. She stood for a good minute, straining her ears to hear anything over the sound of the breeze lightly rattling the shutters.

Not so much as a creak inside the place.

She didn't know what she would have done had she heard a creak. Investigate? Dash for the door?

She was tired. And jumpy. A rotten combination and one she'd been living with for over two months. But a faint stirring of excitement began to bloom inside her as she stood in the center of the empty living room, wrinkling her nose against the musty smell that resurfaced now that the door was closed.

This was her house. A place to rebuild. A place to start a new life, far from the disaster that had been her old.

Nobody here would look sideways at her when she entered a store, or suddenly stop talking when she came into a room. No one would be caught creeping around her property. The encounter with the person in her living room a few days after she'd been cleared of criminal charges might have been unrelated to everything else that had gone down over the past several weeks, but she was taking no chances. She'd moved in with her mother after the break-in and endured almost three weeks of "I told you so" before closing the private deal on the house and heading across the country.

Alex walked through the living room and

dining room to the smallish kitchen with its painted beadboard walls and limited counter space. There was work to be done here—painting, if nothing else. She tilted her chin up to study the grease-stained ceiling above the stove. A ventilation fan would be a wonderful addition to the room.

Funny that she didn't remember the place being this small and...greasy.

She'd spent a summer in this house during her early teens, reading, making cookies and riding horses while her parents traveled Europe. At the time she'd had no inkling about what made a workable kitchen; she and Juliet had turned out sheets of chocolate chip cookies and whipped up batches of fudge using the kitchen table and a rolling cart for additional workspace.

There was no longer a table or a rolling cart—only about twenty-four inches of counter space on either side of the enameled cast-iron sink, which would be adequate space for Alex's needs, because she didn't see herself doing a lot of entertaining.

A choked laugh escaped her lips. Had she really given up her new apartment with the state-of-the-art kitchen that she'd loved so much for this?

Yes. And you are fortunate to have this place.
Agreed.

Things weren't perfect, but buying this house from her aunt Juliet gave her a place to land far away from the drama she'd been facing at home. A place where she had a passing familiarity, yet no one knew her. But it almost hadn't happened.

Less than a week before Alex contacted Juliet about buying the place, a neighbor had made an offer on the property, which Juliet had been in the process of accepting, pending loan approval. Alex had pleaded with her aunt to sell to her instead, digging deep into her savings to outbid the neighbor.

Juliet allowed herself to be swayed, and they'd closed the deal days later, signing a private contract. No mortgage. No paper trail. Juliet's name was still on the deed, for the time being, and she carried the loan—which she could afford to do, having outlived three relatively wealthy husbands. The trick, she'd confided to Alex during their cookie making, was to marry a much older man. They appreciated younger women, expected less and gave more.

At the time the advice had seemed callous, but Alex had thought maybe she'd understand it better once she grew up. And now she did. Her aunt Juliet used people, but she'd also come to Alex's rescue—for a price—so she wasn't going to get all judgy.

The important thing was that she had the house, and here she would be Alex Ryan, newcomer, self-employed technical writer if anyone asked about her occupation, rather than Alex Ryan Evans, private investment firm accountant and embezzlement suspect. Technical writing seemed like a believable pretend occupation—one that didn't invite awkward questions, because it wasn't all that exciting.

She would have loved to have landed a job related to accounting or finance while living in Montana, but there was no way she'd make it through a background check without a sea of red flags popping up, thanks to Jason Stoddard, her former boss. She'd left behind a lot of things she loved, including a career, because of that man, who was now probably living the good life on a beach in Rio.

Alex tamped down yet another wave of impotent anger. It did her no good to mentally rail against Jason. The guy had played her and that was that. She was still suffering repercussions, but here in Montana, as long as she kept to herself, her past should stay where it belonged—in an upscale Virginia community.

She walked through the dining room to the staircase leading to the three upstairs bedrooms, and automatically went to the room that had been hers during her summer visit. She crossed to the window and looked out over the fields and river. This would be her office when she decided it was safe to resume her accounting career, but that time, she feared, might be a long way off. She had to be certain that all repercussions of the nightmare phase of her life were over and done. That no one was looking for her, believing that she knew more about Jason's whereabouts than she did.

As she opened the closet and took in the unexpected stack of cardboard boxes and plastic storage bins, the distinctive sound of water hitting wood brought her up short.

No.

A quick look into the room that had once been her aunt's crafting room told her *yes*. The roof had a leak. A persistent one, judging from the size of the stain on the ceiling.

She needed to find a towel and a container to catch the drips.

But if the biggest problem she had in her new life was a leaky roof, she could live with it. Such things were to be expected in an older house—especially one that had been bought sight unseen and hadn't been inhabited for almost two years. The only thing that bothered her was that she'd really hoped to lay low for a few months. Assure herself that she hadn't been followed. That the ski-mask-wearing guy who'd broken into her apartment and slammed her up against the wall hadn't been one of the people Jason had screwed out of a fortune before taking off to parts unknown.

No one believed she was clueless as to his whereabouts, but there was no evidence that she was involved, either. Some of her former neighbors and the people associated with Stoddard Investments would probably take her disappearance as proof positive, but she couldn't keep them from thinking that, so she wasn't going to worry about it. She'd leave that to her mother, Cécile Ryan Evans.

Alex watched as another drip slowly built, the droplet growing so slowly that it would probably be several minutes until gravity took hold and pulled it from the ceiling. A slow leak. Which meant she would have time to find someone to fix it, as much as she hated having anyone on the property just yet. She was still too raw.

But leaks did tend to grow, so she was going to have to rein in her paranoia and seek out a handyman.

Not a problem. You're in Montana. Thousands of miles away from the people who believed she knew more than she did. She controlled access to the ranch via a locked gate, and she was about to get a very big dog.

She was going to be okay hiring a roof-repair guy. But she was going to settle in, get her bearings first.

"Do you want me to come to the Dunlop ranch with you?"

Nick Callahan hadn't told his sister, Katie, where he was going that morning, but she was pretty good at putting two and two together. "I can handle it," he said dryly.

"Be tactful."

As if he wouldn't be tactful. He wasn't exactly the laid-back guy he'd once been, but he could still finesse a situation. "Thanks for the suggestion."

"Daddy!"

Nick's youngest daughter, Bailey, came

barreling out of the kitchen at a dead run. He swung her up in his arms.

"What's up?"

"She thinks that you need to stay and make cookies with us," Kendra said from behind him.

"I'll be back to frost them," he promised his five-year-old as his almost-three-year-old patted his face with her hands.

"More like to eat the frosting," Katie murmured.

"I do my part."

She rolled her eyes and reached for Bailey, masterfully transferring the toddler into her arms and then balancing her on one hip. Nick gave Bailey a quick kiss on top of her curly head as his grandmother Rosalie came out of the kitchen, wiping her hands on a towel.

"Are you going to the Dunlop ranch?"

Was every woman in his family a mind reader? "Yes."

His grandmother nodded but had the good grace not to remind him to be tactful. "I have to head back to town as soon as the cookie dough is finished, but I want to know what happens."

"I thought you were staying for the day."

The ranch was now Rosalie's home away

from home. She'd lived there for most of her life, but after the death of her husband, she moved to town where she and her best friend, Gloria Gable, bought a house and started a gift and garden business.

"Gloria called a little while ago. We're meeting with a local artisan this afternoon to see if her creations are a good fit for The Daisy Petal."

"I'll keep you in the loop," Nick promised.

"Thank you." Rosalie turned to the girls. "Who wants to turn on the electric mixer?"

"I do!" Kendra gave Nick a quick hug. "Hurry back, Daddy." She followed Rosalie into the kitchen as Katie hefted Bailey a little higher on her hip.

"Good luck. And remember, you catch more flies with, well, you know."

"I will be tactful."

Katie raised an eyebrow as if she didn't fully believe him, and he couldn't really blame her. Two weeks ago, when he'd discovered that his offer on the property next door—property his family needed for access to their ranch—had been rejected, he'd pretty much gone ballistic. He'd been outbid at the last minute and the seller hadn't given him

a chance to bid again. Juliet Dunlop simply
told him the deal was off.

Since that time, he hadn't managed to get
much information on the new buyer, except
that she'd paid cash and was from the East
Coast. That smacked of entitlement, but he
told himself not to jump to conclusions. He
needed very much to get along with this
woman.

"Hey. I used to be charming."

Katie smiled a little. "Once again, good
luck."

Nick left the house to a chorus of "Bye,
Daddy," and got into his truck, drove over
the cattle guard, then took the bumpy side
road that led from the Callahan ranch to the
old Dunlop place. The gate that separated
the two properties was constructed of three
strands of barbed wire connected to thin
posts. He unhooked the latch and dragged
the wire across the road, drove through and
left the gate lying beside the road. He'd be
back soon enough, and the cattle were on the
river pasture, so they wouldn't be straying
through the gate.

Losing the bridge two months ago during
a series of spring floods had hurt, and now
the family had to jump through hoops to get

it rebuilt. Permitting regulations had changed since the original bridge had been rebuilt in the 1960s, and the process was moving forward at a glacial pace thanks to a county commissioner who kept throwing roadblocks into the process and Nick suspected he knew why.

He realized then that his fingers were tight on the steering wheel and forced himself to relax. He really didn't want to fight with anyone. He just wanted to raise his daughters in peace on the ranch where he'd grown up. And to do that, he kind of needed easy access to the place.

He needed to make a deal with the new owner of the Dunlop place.

ALEX NEARLY DROPPED the dishes she was in the process of unpacking when the sound of an engine hit her ears. The gate across the road was locked—she knew because she'd double-checked after driving through. There was no way anyone should be able to drive into the place.

Unless they had a key.

Or bolt cutters.

Her insides went cold at the thought.

Do not jump to conclusions. Breathe!

Carefully, Alex set the small stack of plates on the freshly washed countertop and then made her way to the dining room, heart pounding. Sure enough, there was a pickup truck parked just outside the picket fence. Montana plates. Okay. That was good. Not terrific, but better than Virginia plates. Or rental car plates.

Alex automatically drew back as the man glanced toward the window, even though she wasn't close enough for him to spot her standing near the kitchen doorway. He was tall, dark haired, and he moved with athletic grace as he sidestepped puddles and headed for the walk leading to the front door. That was when Alex noticed that his truck was pointed the wrong way. He hadn't come from the county road—he'd driven in from the back of the property.

Great. Now she was going to have to buy another gate lock.

Alex pulled in a breath and squared her shoulders before crossing the room to meet the stranger at the door. She should have gotten the dog she planned on adopting sooner.

No. You should get a grip. The guy's wearing a cowboy hat, for Pete's sake. A black one, true, but good-guy white probably got dirty too quickly in this country.

At the sound of boots on the porch, she pulled the door open and attempted a cool smile. Not an easy thing to accomplish with her heart hammering.

Just a local cowboy. No big deal. She'd just hear him out, then send him on his way and see about getting another lock for the rear of her property.

"Hi," she said. "Can I help you?"

He took a moment to study her face before he answered, making her wonder what he saw. A nervous woman who didn't want strangers lurking about? Or a confident woman who could hold her own if push came to shove?

She knew what she saw. One good-looking guy with an almost straight nose that had obviously been broken, an amazing jawline and dark, unreadable eyes. And he looked...nervous.

Huh.

Nervous because he was planning something?

Before she got too far down that track, he said, "Hi. I'm Nick Callahan. I live next door."

Alex frowned. "I didn't know there was a next door."

"Well, two miles next door."

"Two miles isn't next door."

He gave her an odd look, telling her that she was coming off like a city girl. "I know you just arrived and are settling in, but there's a matter that's kind of important that I need to discuss with you."

Alex politely lifted her eyebrows, clueless as to what he might want to talk about, but relieved that he seemed harmless. So far. "What's that?"

"The bridge to our ranch washed out last month. The only easy access to our place is through your ranch, and I'm here to ask permission—"

"To drive through my...place?" She couldn't exactly call it a ranch. For one thing, she wasn't the ranch type. For another, it would never be a ranch again.

"Exactly."

Alex pulled in a breath, telling herself to get more information before she panicked. "Who would be driving through?" The road went directly between her house and the barn. It wasn't as if she wouldn't notice the traffic.

"Me and my family. The ranch hands. When bridge construction begins, the bridge builders."

"For how long?"

"The way things are moving, I'd say six months. Maybe a few months more."

Alex's cheeks tingled as the blood left her face. Six months or more of strangers driving through her property? Six months of not knowing who was *on* her property?

No. She didn't see that happening. Not when she was still uncertain as to whether the people who so desperately wanted the money Jason absconded with were going to follow her across the country.

He seemed to sense her uncertainty. "It wouldn't be a lot of traffic."

"You must have another means of access."

"Almost ten miles of unmaintained road."

"Which I assume you've been using to this point."

"Yes."

"And could continue to use. It's not like I'm locking you out of your property. It's more like I'm saving you time if I granted access."

"Time is an important commodity." He shifted his weight, pressed his very nice lips together and stared down at his boots. When he looked up again, she read the light of challenge in his gaze and steeled herself. "It isn't like everyone and his uncle would drive through. It would just be my family and me. If you want to keep the gate locked, we could share a key."

"What about the bridge builders?"

"They would need to share the key, too. Otherwise, I'll be paying them extra to travel the unmaintained road."

Alex shook her head. "I'm sorry, but I moved here for privacy." She instantly kicked herself for saying that. What if he did an online search for her? Even though she was going by her first and middle names, it might be enough to pin down her identity, given the coverage Jason's story had received when he first skipped town with all that money.

"It's not like we're going to stop and chat as we drive through."

"I don't want people driving through my place, even temporarily." The next few months were crucial to her as she determined whether or not she was going to continue to be targeted as Jason's accomplice. "I don't think that's unreasonable, given what I spent to buy the property."

Something shifted in his expression. Something she couldn't read...and then it struck her. "Were you the other bidder?"

He gave a nod.

She didn't even think about saying sorry for outbidding him. This was the way business worked—sometimes people got outbid and had to live with the consequences— but there was no way she was voicing that thought to the guy standing in front of her. Once again, she wished she had a big threatening dog standing beside her. Something to kind of hurry this man on his way.

"I apologize for not being able to help you, but I can't have open access to my property."

Once again, his mouth tightened, as if he was making an effort to hold back words. As far as Alex was concerned, he could let them out. It wasn't like it would hurt her feelings or cause her to change her mind.

"We'll pay for access. Write up a contract."

"No." She gripped the edge of the door more tightly. At any other time in her life she would have said yes. But not now, while she was still jumping at shadows. Another apology teetered on her lips, but she held it in. This was her property. Her right.

"Fine." He pushed the brim of his hat up,

allowing her a better look at his chocolate-brown eyes. "If you change your mind and want to discuss matters…" He reached into his back pocket, pulled out a wallet and handed over a card. "That's my cell number."

Alex took the card and palmed it without looking at it. "I don't want to be a bad neighbor." The words slipped out of her mouth before she could stop them.

"Excellent goal. Poor execution." The man turned and walked down the uneven sidewalk toward his truck.

Despite a desperate need to have him leave her property—now—Alex lifted her chin and called after him. "Do not judge me when you don't know my circumstances."

He swung around. "Lady, we all have circumstances. If I could help you with yours, I would." He curled his lips into an ironic smile before adding, "You have my number. Call anytime."

CHAPTER TWO

KATIE WAS AT the kitchen table studying a spreadsheet when Nick walked in the door. She glanced up, a clear question in her eyes, and he shook his head.

"I *was* tactful." He jammed his hat onto the hat hook next to the door as he spoke.

"She said no?"

"Unequivocally." Nick headed for the coffeepot. "Where are the girls?"

"Grandma has them out in the greenhouse."

His sister was starting an herb business, and his girls loved playing in the greenhouses. Katie slid her empty coffee cup across the table and he picked it up on his way by. After filling both cups, he sat down opposite Katie at the table he'd made when he'd first started his carpentry business.

"She wasn't very reasonable."

"I should have gone with you."

"I don't know if your human resources magic would have worked on this one."

"Do not underestimate my abilities," she replied with mock sternness. Katie had headed the HR department of a decent-sized corporation in the Bay Area before returning home to the ranch. "I might have been able to read her and judge the best way to approach the situation."

"I read her. The lady is nervous."

Katie settled her elbows on the table. "Like new-to-the-neighborhood-strange-man-shows-up-at-her-door kind of nervous?"

"Maybe." He'd considered that on the drive back to the ranch, but while he was certain that may have added to the woman's demeanor, he wasn't certain it fully explained her attitude, which had been an odd mix of superiority and jumpiness.

"So what now?"

"I guess we deal with a long drive to Gavin and to paying the construction crew extra travel."

"G-r-eat." Katie picked up her cup and leaned back in her chair. "Maybe I can talk to her."

"I'd give it some time. If you show up today, I think she might call the sheriff."

"Don't want that." Katie sipped her coffee.

"Any idea where she's from or how she happened to buy the property out from under you?"

He'd been digging for that information, but no one—not the real-estate agent or any of the local gossips had any light to shed on the subject. "Not one clue. And trust me, she wasn't about to let go of any information."

"What's she like?"

Nick frowned at the question, and Katie gave a faint shrug. "Is she young or old? Rural or urban?"

"She's youngish. Your age. Maybe a little older. Nice looking. Unfriendly." Actually, *nice looking* was an understatement. She was model pretty, which had instantly made him think that she was used to getting her way because of the way she looked. That wasn't a fair assumption; he didn't know enough about her to jump to that conclusion, so he'd stick with what he did know—he'd had a deal to buy the property and she'd somehow zeroed in on said property and finagled the owner to take her bid instead of Nick's.

Why?

What was so special about the run-down Dunlop place that made her have to have it?

And while he couldn't say for certain that the woman got her own way because of her looks, he could say with a fair amount of certainty that she *was* used to getting her way.

Privileged people drove him nuts. As an artisan carpenter, he'd dealt with his fair share of them, and now that the wealthy elite were snapping up ranches in the Gavin area, they were seeing more and more folks who felt they were just a little more special than everyone else because of the size of their bank accounts and portfolios.

"I'm curious to see what happens if she ever needs help from a neighbor," Katie said in a musing tone.

"We aren't neighbors," he said mildly. Katie sent him a frowning look and he explained, "Two miles is too far away to be neighbors."

Katie laughed and set down her cup. "I guess that answers my urban-rural question."

Nick grinned at her. "I guess so."

"It's not the end of the world," Katie said softly. "We'll get past this."

"But it is annoying. And expensive."

"Yeah."

The sound of sneakers on the porch brought a smile to his face. He leaned back in his chair so he could see the door. Seconds later Bailey burst inside, wearing a coat that had once been lavender but was now brown down the front.

"Bailey took a tumble," Rosalie said as she followed Kendra through the door.

"I fell down." Bailey wiped her hands down the front of her muddy coat as Nick got to his feet.

"Let's get you out of that." He knelt to unzip the jacket and help Bailey pull her arms out of the sleeves.

"Lizzie Belle pushed her down with her head," Kendra said helpfully as she wiggled out of her own jacket.

Nick took hold of Bailey's shoulders and looked into eyes that were identical in color to those of his late wife. "You got pushed down by a little goat?" They had two goats on the property, but Wendell, who'd come from the neighboring McGuire ranch, kept a polite distance, while Lizzie Belle tended to make her presence known.

Bailey's lower lip came out as she gave a solemn nod.

"You know that goats like to push. It's how they say hello."

Bailey nodded again, looking none too happy about the communication habits of goats.

"Do you want me to launder it?" Rosalie asked.

Nick shook his head. "I got this. Some spray and a little scrubbing and it should be fine." He'd always done his own laundry, but having little girls had taught him a lot about stain removal. Kendra in particular did not like having spots on her clothing, so Nick had watched more than one YouTube video on tricky stain removal.

He got to his feet and smiled down at Kendra. "Did you get your seeds planted?"

"We did. And then we're going to sell flowers in Grandma's shop when they grow."

"Spoken like a true entrepreneur," he said, catching his grandmother's eye. "But maybe we can plant some of them in by the fence so that we have something nice to look at this summer."

"We can do that." Kendra tapped her chin with her forefinger in a thoughtful way.

"Just keep Lizzie Belle away from them," Katie said. "She loves to munch on flowers."

"Maybe Lizzie Belle will be back in town by that time," Rosalie murmured.

Lizzie Belle had been Gloria's pet until Gloria and Rosalie's next-door neighbor, miffed that the women wouldn't sell their property to him, had lodged a complaint about livestock within the city limits. Lizzie Belle came to live on the ranch then, but the neighbor, Vince Taylor, continued to do what he could to make life miserable for Rosalie and Gloria whenever possible. He was also close friends with members of the county commission, which Nick suspected was slowing down the permitting for the bridge that had washed out. Moral of the story? Don't mess with the privileged few.

Seemed to be something of a theme lately.

"You know that if Lizzie Belle goes to town, we'll have to do something with Wendell," Katie said.

Rosalie smiled. "I think we have room for two little goats in that big back yard."

"Just don't expect to have any flowers," Kendra said in a knowing voice.

"I'll keep that in mind." Rosalie waited until the girls had slipped out of their boots and went to the cookie jar before asking in a low voice, "How'd it go?"

"Not well." Nick explained the situation as he watched his grandmother's expression grow increasingly grim.

"I hate that long drive, but I guess we

should be grateful that we have a way here at all."

Nick wasn't feeling as grateful as Rosalie, because *he* hated his grandmother making the drive. As the weather warmed, however, she would be spending most of her time at her garden and gift shop in Gavin. "I can bring the girls into town on Sundays instead of you coming out here for the weekly visit."

"It will only be for six months," Katie said.

"Yeah. Doable." If Vince Taylor didn't continue to throw his weight around. The problem with dealing with hometown heavyweights is that they had ins with everyone—including the members of the county commission, who were now dragging their feet on the bridge permit. But Nick wasn't going to ruin his grandmother's day any more than it already was by questioning the six-month time frame.

The next day, Katie watched the girls while Nick made the trip to town to buy lumber and drop off a handful of business cards at Cooper's Building Supply and Contracting. He wasn't ready to hang out an official shingle yet. He'd made a decent amount of money selling his business in California prior to moving back to Montana to manage the family ranch, but he wouldn't mind the occasional small building or carpentry job. It'd keep his name in the game. He'd have to work around ranching, which was his number one concern now that he was back home. But, being something of a workaholic, he figured he could manage both ranch and carpentry if the right job came his way.

After ordering his lumber, he asked Emmie Cooper, daughter of the soon-to-be-retired owner of the establishment, if he could leave a few cards on the counter and put one on the bulletin board.

"Yeah," she said easily before she picked up one of his cards and flicked it with her forefinger. "But you know, it would be easier if you went to work for me full-time. Tater is quitting."

Nick smiled as he leaned on the counter. He and Emmie were old friends, having shared a storage area in shop class three years in a row. "I can't go to work full-time, Em—not until Brady gets done with his welding course, anyway." His future brother-in-law was completing a technical course before returning to the Callahan ranch, where he and Katie would be married, but even after he returned, Nick was more interested in being his own boss than working for someone else.

"I'm just looking for side gigs to bank some extra money. I have little girls I need to put through college."

"Are they leaving soon? Could you maybe spare me a year?"

He grinned. "Sorry. The ranch is my first commitment."

"After little girls."

"That goes without saying."

Emmie set his card back on the stack. "I heard the bridge has been delayed again."

"How'd you know?"

"I ran into Gloria in the grocery store. She blames Vince Taylor."

Gloria wasn't off base, but Nick wasn't going to verify that, even to an old friend. "They'll pass it after we get done jumping through hoops. I have to hire an ecologist that they approve of to certify that there will be no environmental damage downstream. That's supposed to be the last step, but I can't get anyone for a couple of months."

Emmie gave him a sympathetic look. "As soon as you have a time frame, let me know so that I can get my subcontractors lined out, okay?"

"Will do. They'll have to travel the back road."

"That'll cost you some man-hours."

"I know. The new owner of the Dunlop ranch has denied us access."

"Really? He's going to make you drive around?"

"*She* has a thing about privacy." Which he wasn't supposed to judge unless he knew the circumstances. Nick was judging, anyway. "She locked the gate and showed no interest in sharing the key."

Emmie shook her head and set the receipt that had just finished printing on the counter. "I'll see what I can do on my end, but I don't think I can do much."

"I know." Nick picked up his receipt and folded it before sticking it into his shirt pocket. "I still don't know how this woman managed to buy the place out from under me."

"Yeah. Something stinks there. I never did like that Juliet person. If you ask me, she married Dunlop for his money."

"I wouldn't have minded, if she'd sold the ranch to me," Nick said honestly.

"Touché," Emmie said with a half smile. "If you change your mind about full-time, let me know," she called as Nick headed toward the door. He raised his hand to indicate that he heard her, then stepped out into May sunshine.

Money and time. That was all this woman on the Dunlop ranch was costing him.

But he couldn't get past the fact that it shouldn't have been costing him anything at all.

"I'M CERTAIN I'LL be able to get internet service within the week." That had been the promise, anyway, after Alex had contacted the service provider. All of the utilities were still in Juliet's name, and while some things, like the electricity, had been turned on with a phone call, the internet provider had to send a repair person for a new and improved hookup. And they wanted Juliet there to sign. So, Alex was going to be Juliet. It bothered her, but hey. No paper trail.

"How will you work if you don't have internet?"

"I have everything under control, Mom." For now. She didn't have to work, thanks to her grandmother's trust, which dribbled enough money into her account every month for the essentials if she was careful with her spending. She wanted to work. Wanted to contribute to the world instead of organizing social events. She would eventually start her own business, working from home and doing contract jobs, but she wouldn't be doing it anytime soon.

Alex pushed the hair away from her forehead in a distracted gesture, then glanced at herself in the mirror she'd unearthed from one of Juliet's overstuffed closets and hung earlier that afternoon. Oh, yeah. Stress incarnate. And most of it was because she'd called her mother.

"I think you jumped into this too quickly. I mean, my goodness, if everyone who'd ever had their home broken into sold and moved to the other side of the country, well, then…" Her mother's voice petered out as she failed to come up with adequate words to describe the mayhem caused by such actions.

"I wanted to get away from the people who thought I aided and abetted Jason." *Duh.* "The situation was becoming untenable." She had no way of knowing whether the home invasion had been related to Jason's crime, but that had been the straw that broke the camel's back. Or maybe it had been the push she needed to make a move instead of standing paralyzed, afraid of looking guilty if she left the area.

"When they find this boss of yours and arrest him and clear your name, will you please come home?"

Home was such a funny word to come out of her mother's mouth—a woman who'd done everything in her power to keep Alex away from home. Boarding schools, summer camps, a trip to Montana to visit Aunt Julia.

"Are you worried about me, or how things look?"

There was a long silence, and then her mother said, "The guilty do not run."

"How do you know that?"

"Common. Sense."

Alex raised her eyes from where she'd been studying the floor as she spoke, caught another glimpse at herself in the mirror, then glanced away again. She looked awful. Two sleepless nights in her new house hadn't done much to improve either her disposition or her appearance. She needed to find a Laundromat, stock up on food and see about finding a repair person.

Even though she didn't want anyone in her fortress of solitude and safety, she had to do something about the leak in her roof and the other issues that were cropping up with her house. Her calls to her aunt Juliet had gone unanswered, which wasn't that strange for a woman who liked to disappear into the wilderness or lose herself in a massive metropolis when the mood struck her. But Alex needed information on the house, and Regina Hayes, the real-estate agent who'd initially handled the listing for Juliet, knew nothing about the wiring or the plumbing.

"It was bad enough when you were here, but at least you held your head up high, gave all appearance of innocence."

Appearance of innocence? Really? Did her own mother suspect she was guilty?

"Not that I think you had anything to do with it," her mother amended.

"Thanks, Mom." Alex did not attempt to hide the irony in her tone. She was tired and unsettled, and tomorrow she was heading into town, where she would hold her head up high and give all appearance of innocence.

She planted a hand on her forehead and looked up at the grease-stained ceiling as her mother launched into a description of what *she* thought *her friends* thought about the situation. Once upon a time, not all that long ago, Alex hadn't been snide in her responses or in her thoughts.

She'd been happy, working closely with

Jason at the office while dating him on the side—a situation that would have sent red flags flying, but Jason had charmed her into believing that they could make it work. And they had—until the day Jason hadn't shown up at the office.

She'd tried desperately to contact him before his first client meeting, which she'd ultimately winged herself. After the meeting, she'd continued the search, calling his brother, Lawrence, and his former business partner, whom she'd replaced, Blaine. No one had seen or heard from him. Finally, after a gut-wrenching night of worry, she'd contacted the police. A missing persons report became an investigation into the company when it was discovered that a large amount of money was missing.

She squeezed her eyes shut as memories of the insinuations and investigation that followed the discovery once again began looping though her brain. Lawrence had also been questioned but quickly cleared, and Blaine hadn't even been a blip on the radar since he was employed in another company in another state. The bull's-eye had ended up squarely on her. She clenched her fist. Hard.

"Alexandra. Are you there?"

Alex snapped back to the present. "Yes. You were saying?"

"I was saying that it would be nice if you flew back home in a few weeks and made an appearance."

"Let me guess—guilty people do not visit home."

"Alexandra."

Alex bowed to the warning note in her mother's voice. "Sorry."

"However, that is true. And it wouldn't hurt. Especially if that investigator continues looking into matters."

Alex went still. "What investigator?"

"You know. The person who was investigating."

"Is he still asking around?"

"No," her mother said impatiently. "I'm saying that if he decides he needs more information and starts stirring things up at some point in the future, it'd be better if you look as if you're not afraid to come home."

"That makes sense," Alex said. Even though she wasn't about to go back to that place where everyone was so quick to believe the worst about her.

Alex ended the call a few minutes later

and leaned back against the kitchen counter, gripping it on both sides. It creaked.

Of course it did.

But she'd rather put up with a creaking, leaking house than head back "home."

She let out a short laugh and pushed off the counter. She might not have a home, yet, but she had a house to live in. Here in Montana, where no one suspected her of a crime.

CHAPTER THREE

ROSALIE CALLAHAN QUIETLY let herself into the county courthouse meeting room just as the commission chairperson lowered his gavel and announced that the meeting was in session. She was late, but attendance was scanty that evening, so she was able to find a seat in a back-row chair with a minimum of fuss.

She unbuttoned her coat and pulled a small notebook out of her purse. Only then did she allow herself to scan the attendees. Vince Taylor, the man who owned the property on either side of her garden and gift shop, was not in attendance, apparently feeling that he had proper control of the situation via the commission members who owed him favors. Will McGuire, her former neighbor was there, sitting near the front, his full head of silver hair instantly recognizable. Will had been at every meeting she'd attended since having surprise permitting issues involved with the reconstruction of the bridge recently destroyed by spring flooding.

The bridge across the Ambrose River might be small potatoes to the county commission, but it was the lifeline to the ranch where her grandchildren lived. The ranch where she'd lived for almost fifty years with her husband, Carl, before moving to town to start her new business after losing him to a series of strokes.

Rosalie tipped up her chin and listened as the commission began discussing issues with a paving company that had not properly completed a project. The bridge was not on the agenda tonight, but since being blindsided by the additional requirements imposed on her family prior to bridge reconstruction, she didn't miss a meeting. She wanted these alleged pillars of the community to know that she was watching.

As was Will McGuire.

And she was watching him, even though she didn't want to be.

They hadn't had much contact since she'd told him off for interceding on her behalf with Vince Taylor a few months ago. That had been prior to the bridge issues, back when her only complaint was that Vince was being a very bad neighbor, due to the fact that he wanted to buy her property and she and her business partner, Gloria, refused to sell. So as things stood, her garden and gift store stood between the two Victorian houses he was renovating into upscale retreats. In her mind, they could have worked cooperatively. Vince saw things differently.

The meeting was short that night, and while Rosalie had doodled on her notepad, she'd taken no real notes. Just before adjournment, during the public comments part of the meeting, she gathered her purse and managed to slip out the door, only to be hailed by Martina Owens, whose husband owned Hardwick's Grocery. Martina had left a few minutes before Rosalie.

"Still no movement on the bridge?" she asked.

"We're waiting for the ecologist to finish the ecosystem study and to present the results to the commission."

Martina gave her a sympathetic look. "We had similar issues when we tried to buy the lot next door to expand the store. Small towns." She glanced out the door, then smiled at Rosalie. "My ride is here. Do you need a lift?"

"Thank you, no. I enjoy the walk." Rosalie followed Martina outside as the meeting room doors opened behind them and the attendees began making their way out, only to stop when she heard her name.

She automatically drew in a breath before turning to face Will McGuire. "Hello, Will."

"Rosalie."

"Not much of a meeting tonight," she said, needing to fill the air between them. The man put her on edge and there was no reason on God's green earth for her to be feeling that way.

"But you never know what might come up, so it's good to attend."

"Is that why you attend?" she asked, her curiosity getting the better of her.

"And it gives me something to do." He inclined his heads toward the concrete stairs as people began edging around them, and Rosalie started to descend. She sensed, rather than saw, his hand come to her elbow as if to steady her, then he seemed to catch himself and once again dropped his hand.

"Would you like a ride home?"

"I'll walk, thank you."

He nodded as if expecting that exact answer. "Then I guess I'll see you in two weeks at the next meeting."

"Probably so," she said. Then, she stunned herself by thrusting out a hand. "Goodbye, Will."

He took her hand, looking equally stunned. And his fingers closed just enough to send a small curl of warmth through her. "Goodbye, Rosalie."

He smiled and released her hand, then turned and headed in the opposite direction, toward his beat-up old ranch truck. The kind of truck Rosalie never had to ride in again.

She pulled her coat around her more tightly, despite the warm evening, and started the short walk home.

NICK WAS ALMOST asleep when the high-pitched wail brought him out of bed. He slept in sweatpants and kept a hoodie close by for moments like this. A second cry tore through the air as he pulled the sweatshirt over his head.

"Daddy!" Kendra called just as he pulled the door open. She was already out of bed, holding her bedraggled Foxy Loxy stuffed toy by the paw as she stood a few feet from Bailey's bed.

Nick reached down to hoist her up against his chest, and she buried her head against his neck as Bailey let out another shriek. Kendra understood that waking her baby sister when she had night terrors only made it worse, but that didn't stop her from burying her head in Nick's shoulder and dragging in her own ragged breath.

"I want her to stop," she whispered.

"Me, too, baby. But the doctor says she'll outgrow it." He hoped, anyway. He was a guy who fixed things, and it had been hard to accept that he couldn't fix this. Couldn't rock and soothe it away.

And he couldn't help thinking that, despite what the doctor said, he'd done something— or worse yet, hadn't done something—that in turn caused the night terrors to start. Had it been Kayla's death? Or the fact that she wasn't there? Or was he just doing stuff wrong?

"Do you want to sleep in Aunt Katie's bed?" he asked Kendra as he rubbed her back. Katie had spent the night in town with Rosalie, and sometimes the night terrors lasted a good twenty minutes.

"Bailey will be afraid if she wakes up alone."

"I can sleep in your bed."

He felt her smile against his neck. "Your feet will hang out the bottom."

Yes. They would. And they had.

"Maybe. But I'm tough. I can take it."

Kendra leaned back and put one hand on his cheek. "I'm tough, too."

His eyes started to sting, and he pulled his little girl back against his chest, cupping the back of her head. "Yes. You are very tough."

He swayed gently, just as he had when she was a baby and he'd held her, calming her when she'd had colic. Her little body relaxed against his, and about the same time Bailey gave the series of small whimpers that usually signaled the end of the night terror.

"She's done," Kendra said softly.

"Yeah. I hope this is the only one tonight."

"I'll call you if she has another," Kendra said matter-of-factly, as if he couldn't hear his youngest daughter shrieking the house down from his room across the hall.

"I appreciate that, but I think I'll sit here in Granddad's rocking chair for a little while."

"Then I'll sit on your lap."

Nick sat in the chair his grandfather Carl, the man who'd taught him the basics of carpentry, had made. Kendra locked Foxy Loxy close to her body as she curled up against him. Nick wrapped his arms around his princess and started rocking. If Bailey woke up, he'd get her, too, and rock both of his girls until they fell asleep. He tried not to think about the fact that his entire family could fit into one homemade rocking chair.

ALEX'S FIRST STOP in Gavin was not at the grocery store or the hardware store as she'd planned the evening before. Her third sleepless night in a row had convinced her that a stop at the animal rescue facility on the edge of town was a necessity.

When she opened her car door, a cacophony of barks and howls greeted her. It wasn't a huge facility, but every one of the ten or so runs extending from the cinder-block building was full of dogs of all sizes.

Slowly Alex walked toward the office, past the runs, her heart breaking at the hopeful expressions on so many canine faces. Every one of them seemed to be saying, "Pick me, pick me."

Before she reached the office, the door swung open, and a small, roundish woman with a beaming expression waved her inside. "Are you Alex?"

"I am."

"Not that many people call in advance, so I was taking a guess. I'm Wanda. Have a seat." She waved to a no-nonsense metal chair facing the desk. Behind her, the wall was filled with photos of dogs under a hand-lettered sign that read Adopted. "I have some paperwork you'll need to fill out."

"Can I…uh…shop…first?"

Wanda gave her a serious look. "Before you 'shop,' I need to know some things about you so that we can match the pet to the owner. For instance, I'm not going to send you home with a retired bomb-sniffing dog."

Alex leaned forward in her chair. "Do you have one of those?"

"Had." Wanda pointed to a photo of a police-type dog that looked as if he was either smiling or about to eat someone. "His original owner passed away, so I helped place him."

"Do you have any dogs that look like him?" Alex asked hopefully.

Wanda cocked her head. "No offense, but you look more like a poodle-mix person to me."

"No offense taken," Alex said. She picked up the paperwork and scanned the questions. There were a lot of them—three pages' worth—so she picked up the pencil and went to work. She hoped after filling out this packet, which was longer than her college application, that there actually was a suitable dog for her. She answered questions about her ability to feed, house and exercise her pet, her attitude toward pets, her expectations and reasons for wanting a pet. She paused at the point where she was required to state that she had a suitable enclosure for the animal. She did. It needed to be repaired, since the back gate was hanging on one hinge, but how big of a job could that be? She ticked the box. Yes, she had a proper fence—or would have one shortly.

When she was done, she passed the application across the table to Wanda, who took a pencil from behind her ear and started scanning the answers, her pencil hovering over the paper. Dear heavens, was she about to be graded?

Wanda nodded thoughtfully as she worked her way to the second page. "So, you have owned a dog before."

Alex almost said that she'd owned one that looked exactly like the bomb sniffer, but she'd never been a good liar, so instead she said, "Yes. A poodle mix. Teddy." And what a great friend he had been, but he was not chase-off-intruder material, and that was what she was looking for.

"Never owned a cat?"

Alex shook her head. "My mother was allergic." Her mother had sworn she was allergic to dogs, too, but she'd never been home enough to make contact with Teddy, so all had been well.

Wanda looked up at her, and Alex knew before the woman spoke that she was going to tell her that she looked like a cat person.

"I have nothing against cats. I simply want to start with a dog."

"Well, I was thinking, with you living out on the Dunlop place, that you might want an outdoor cat or two to keep down the mice."

Alex's eyes widened. Yes. She would like that. "Do you have outdoor cats?"

"We trap regularly on the surrounding ranches, and people will bring adult cats in when they find them."

Alex lifted her chin. "I will keep that in mind, but today I'd really like to meet some dogs."

Wanda pushed back her chair. "Let's do that."

Alex also stood. "I passed?"

"You did. It was Teddy that tipped the scales."

NICK SPENT THE morning reading articles on night terrors and discovered nothing new. No answers or strategies he hadn't read before and nothing stating that he was doing a poor job being both mom and dad to his girls. But he still wondered.

The last time he'd spoken to his dad, who'd left the country five years ago to join his Australian bride's veterinary practice, he'd asked about night terrors. To the best of his father's recollection, neither Nick, nor his sisters, had had any issues with nightmares... which left Nick with lingering doubts as to his parenting abilities. He'd simply have to do his best to be there whenever his daughters needed him.

Despite the disruption the night before, both girls were up and dressed by six thirty. Kendra liked to choose her own clothing and would have chosen Bailey's, too, but Nick knew what it was like to have a sister try to take over one's life. Every night before bedtime, he put a couple of seasonally appropriate tops and bottoms in a pink mesh basket, which was Bailey's "Choice Box." Sometimes she chose to wear two or three tops, squeezing one on top of the other, and he was good with it, but Kendra had a very hard time allowing her little sister to break fashion rules.

"Let's put Lizzie Belle in her pen before we go to town," he said to Kendra as she came into the kitchen. The little goat had a bad habit of dancing on the roofs and hoods of vehicles—particularly Brady's, Katie's fiancé and Nick's best friend. It was like she knew he was the only guy on the property who really cared about his paint job.

"I can do it."

Nick gave a nod. If the little goat fought her, she knew where to find backup. But just in case, he said, "Call if she gets stubborn."

"I will," Kendra said solemnly, and out the door she went, ready to wrangle a goat.

"Daddy, help!"

"Coming." Nick went into the girls' bedroom and found Bailey trying desperately to put on a hooded sweatshirt that was twisted in the back. She never showed any aftereffects of her night terrors. He was the only one who suffered the following day—as it should be.

"Won't fit," she complained, struggling to get her arm all the way into the sleeve.

"Well, let's just take this arm out, and give the shirt a little twist like this…" He straightened the sweatshirt and held it by one shoulder as Bailey slid her arm inside. "Just make sure it's straight before you start." He didn't know if she knew how to do that but figured she'd catch on. He picked up a shirt out of the basket and showed her straight, then twisted, then straight again.

Bailey nodded as if she fully understood, then said, "Shoes."

"Do not match."

She beamed up at him, lifting first her foot with the purple sneaker, then her other foot with the blue sneaker.

"Very nice. Don't let your sister talk you out of it."

She held up her arms, and he lifted her to his hip. "Ready to go to Grandma's?"

Bailey gave an emphatic nod, then hugged him. Nick's heart swelled. He would swim oceans and fight tigers for his girls. There were so many things he would do for them, and so many ways he could get it wrong.

Kendra did a perfect job of penning Lizzie Belle, and after both girls were strapped into their car and booster seats, they were on their way—their inordinately long way, thanks to a neighbor who refused to be neighborly.

What if one of his girls had an emergency?

No question about it, he would drive through the Dunlop ranch, neighborly demands be damned…or he would have if the gate wasn't locked.

Nick slowed to a stop at the turnoff he'd driven through a couple of days before. Sure enough, there was a bicycle cable wrapped around the post with a big lock attached.

Well, that was fast work.

"Do you see something, Daddy?"

He glanced back to see Kendra searching the brush for an animal. "I thought I did, honey, but I was wrong." He put the truck in gear and moved on, the truck lurching as it went through a rut he hadn't spotted in time.

"You guys okay back there?"

Bailey laughed. "Bump."

"That's right. A bump." And there were a lot more bumps and a bona fide quagmire ahead—thank you, New Neighbor, for adding an hour of travel time and a lot of mud and jolts to his trip to town.

Let it go. It's her property. Her right to lock the gate.

Except that it should have been his property—had been his property right up until the eleventh hour, when she'd skated in and somehow talked the seller into taking her not-that-much-larger bid.

Yeah. It was probably going to take him a while to let that go.

"Excuse me?" Alex stared at the woman on the opposite side of the tall counter at the building-supply store—the only store in Gavin in which she could buy the supplies she needed to fix the gate so that she did indeed have an enclosed yard for her soon-to-be adopted dog—a big, lovable golden retriever mix named Gus. It was also the store in which she'd hoped to get the name of a contractor to work on her roof and help repair the dangerously rotten porch steps.

"I said my guys are all booked for the next six months. I can put you on the list."

"Are there any independent contractors who might be available?"

The lady gave a sharp nod. "Nick Callahan." The words came out sounding like a punch line, which in essence it was.

"I see." She held the strap of her purse a little tighter. How much could she accomplish with YouTube videos? The gatepost hinge, but not the roof. The rotted steps… maybe. If this woman would allow her to buy the wood to fix them. And how was she supposed to get boards home? She'd turned in her rental trailer days ago. "Nick didn't happen to stop by and talk to you about me, did he?" As in, did he have her blackballed?

The woman made a mock shocked face. "Nick isn't that kind of guy." She leaned on the counter. "Why? Is there some reason he would have talked about you?"

Oh, yeah. This lady knew what had happened between her and Nick. She would bet money on it. So, what now?

"I'll pay extra if you can move me up on the list."

The lady laughed. And it was not a pleasant laugh. "Kind of like how you bought that ranch out from under Nick?" She shook her head. "I don't think so."

"I'm never going to hit the top of the list, even if I wait. Am I?"

The woman gave an eloquent shrug. "There are some excellent contractors in Dillon and the surrounding areas. Of course, you'll have to pay extra for travel." She gave Alex a look that clearly said, *"Touché."*

Fine. She turned to leave, startled to feel tears of frustration and anger stinging the corners of her eyes. She was not normally a crier, but she didn't normally live life on edge after moving across the country. Lots of stress building with no release.

Well, she wasn't going to release in front of this woman. She was going to get out of there as fast as she could without looking like she was running. She turned and marched toward the door.

"Do you want your hinge?" Which Alex had set on the counter before asking about hiring a contractor.

"No," Alex called as she reached the knob. "I'll buy one online."

"Yeah? How will the delivery truck get it to you with your locked gate? They don't deliver to post office boxes, you know."

Alex clenched her teeth together and pushed out the door. She'd moved here to live anonymously, to avoid having persons unknown be able to easily find her, and instead she was the object of gossip, rumor and speculation.

She and Nick Callahan were going to have a talk. She had no idea how to get to his ranch, but she did have his business card folded into fourths and stuck underneath a wobbly table leg in the kitchen. She'd drive home, get his number and then give him a piece of mind.

Or…she could pull in to the grocery store parking lot and have it out with him there, because if she was not mistaken, that was the man himself, climbing out of the truck parked right next to a cart-return area.

Alex swung into the lot without signaling and pulled up next to his truck. He looked up as she lurched to a stop and rolled down the window in one movement, a startled look on his handsome face.

"Hi," she said coolly. "Remember me?"

CHAPTER FOUR

ALEX RYAN CLIMBED out of her car and stalked toward Nick with murder in her eyes. Apparently he had something to answer for, which was odd, because wasn't he the one getting screwed over in this deal? Wasn't he the one who quite literally had to traverse ten miles of bad road to get home?

She came to a stop a few feet away and pointed a finger at him. "*You* had me black-balled at the lumber store."

"Cooper's Building Supply?"

"Yes."

"I didn't."

She gave him a *puh-leeze* look as her green gaze burned into him. "I'll drive to Missoula to get what I need. And you can enjoy the fact that you're putting me out, but remember this—petty revenge is bad for the soul."

"I'll remember that when I take the ten-mile detour to my ranch." He folded his arms over his chest and looked down at her. Steam was practically coming out of her ears. "And *if* I engaged in vengeful behavior, it'd be a lot more creative than having someone black-balled at Cooper's." His voice was little more than a growl, but it must have carried, because he heard the wheels of a grocery cart come to an abrupt halt behind him, then start moving again.

"People are looking," Alex said in a hissing whisper.

"Of course they're looking. Wouldn't you?" He glanced over to see Mary Watkins and her three kids staring at them as they loaded their SUV with groceries. And the cart that had stopped so abruptly behind him was being pushed by Lester Granger, who would totally enjoy spreading this tale at the co-op coffee klatch. Nick smiled tightly and raised a hand at his neighbors.

Nothing to see here, folks.

Mary waved back.

When Nick shifted his attention back to Alex, she let out a breath that seemed to come from her toes. "I need to go."

The expression she'd worn when he'd come to her ranch that first day was back. Half cautious, half defiant. Fully self-protective. What was this woman running from? Was she a criminal? An abused wife on the run? His gaze strayed to her ring finger, which was bare and showed no signs of a ring having been recently removed. Okay, probably not married, but one didn't need to be married to be abused, and she was as jumpy as he would expect an abuse victim to be. She'd asked him not to judge until he knew her circumstances. Fair enough. Of course, it'd be nice if she explained her circumstances, but he didn't see that happening anytime soon.

"I'll talk to Emmie at the building-supply store."

"I…" She swallowed, obviously not expecting the gesture. "Thank you." It was as if politeness was so deeply engrained in her that now that her anger had faded, she couldn't simply get in the car and slam the door like she so obviously wanted to.

"You're welcome," he replied. She was there, living on the property he'd wanted, and avoiding her wasn't going to change the situation. "What did you need at the building supply?"

"A hinge. I'm fostering a dog. I have to have a secure enclosure."

Fostering, not adopting. As in, she wasn't committing to anything permanent. That could work out in his favor if he didn't totally alienate the woman.

"Want me to fix it for you? I'm a contrac—"

"No." The word burst out of her mouth, and then she glanced around again as if to judge how much attention she'd garnered with this outburst. None, since Mary had driven away, and Lester was now in his truck. She and he were the only people in the parking lot. "All I want from you is the freedom to shop wherever I want."

"I didn't blackball you. Emmie asked how things were going and I told her. That's how things work in towns this size. Everyone knows everyone else's business. It's something you learn to live with." He gave a casual shrug. "Or you leave."

Her eyebrows lifted in an incredulous expression. "Are you telling me to get out of town?"

"I'm telling you that if you came here to disappear, it isn't going to work."

It took her a second to find her voice. "Why did you say that?"

He'd hit a nerve, which told him she actually was running or hiding from something. "Because it's pretty obvious that you want to disappear. Why else lock yourself behind gates?"

"Privacy."

"How is that different from disappearing?"

"None of your business." She yanked the car door open, and, without thinking, Nick put a hand on the frame to keep her from closing it again. He wanted answers, but he wasn't yet certain of the questions. When her startled gaze flashed up, he instantly dropped his hand. He hadn't meant to alarm her, but he had.

"I don't know what your deal is," he said quietly, "but I'm not the enemy."

"I know." From the way her gaze flickered after she spoke, he had a feeling that she'd surprised herself with the muttered confession.

She got into the car and reached for the door handle.

"If you need your gate fixed, I can do it."

"No."

And that was it. No.

She pulled the car door shut and started the engine. Nick stepped back, shoving his fingers into his back pockets. Fine. She could fix her own gate.

He strode toward his truck as she pulled out of the space she'd swung into moments earlier. This woman was driving him nuts.

MISTAKE.

She'd just made a big one.

What had she been thinking, stopping to yell at Nick Callahan? And she *had* yelled at him. She, who rarely raised her voice; she, who worked her way around situations instead of plowing through them.

She, who was allergic to confrontation, had just confronted.

And even though she had made a mistake in doing that, a small part of her was proud of herself for addressing the matter.

Although…apparently, her accusation wasn't true. If she was to believe him, and deep inside she did, he'd told the lumber-store woman about the situation because she'd asked, but he hadn't demanded that she be blackballed. That had been the woman's independent response to the situation.

Apparently, in Gavin, Montana, they took care of their own.

Alex loosened her fingers on the steering wheel, forced herself to take a deep cleansing breath and view the situation logically. Her original plan of living invisibly wasn't working. As near as she could tell, the more invisible one tried to be in this area, the more one stood out. She was already known as the woman who wanted to keep to herself, lock out the world, and what better way to get tongues wagging and the locals guessing as to *why* she wanted to lock out the world?

Alex pulled in another deep breath as she fought with the obvious, and fear-inducing, solution to the problem.

She'd be less noticeable if she acted like any other person new to the area. If she didn't lock her gate and shut everyone out.

But it wasn't like she could allow every person who had reason to drive to the Callahan ranch to cross her property. She might have dropped her last name and her aunt may still be the official owner of the house on paper, but Alex couldn't help but believe that she still needed to take precautions. Jason had stolen a lot of money, and it was a given that the people who'd lost money would continue the search. She'd been officially cleared of suspicion due to lack of evidence, but that didn't mean the parties involved were convinced she was innocent. And she had no idea if the guy who'd knocked her around in her apartment was one of those who believed she had a line on the money. The thought of confronting him again…

This was her fault for being so stupid. For

trusting Jason even when she'd had a sense that things weren't right. What kind of guy dated a woman for four months and never pushed beyond kissing her good-night? She'd thought he'd been being respectful, because they worked together and too much too soon could affect their working relationship, when, in truth, he'd been setting her up.

What a pigeon she'd been.

Alex's fingers once again tightened on the steering wheel as she fought to tamp down the anger that threatened to swamp her. She wasn't by nature a violent person, but the wrongness of what had happened to her stirred feelings that were hard to control. She, the queen of finding a peaceful solution, would love to do the man bodily harm.

Meanwhile, Jason was soaking up sun somewhere, sipping top-shelf bourbon and feeling smug about the flawless execution of his scheme.

You will not act the victim.

No, she would not. She'd lock her gate, keep to herself when she could but do it without drawing attention to the fact that she wanted to be left alone until she felt more secure. No more knee-jerk reactions that she had to explain away later.

In other words, she'd be friendlier—and hope the people of Gavin had short memories.

"My guess is that he's lonely," Gloria said when Rosalie casually mentioned that Will never missed a county commission meeting. Gloria had grown up with Will and taught his children in the local high school, while Rosalie had come to Gavin as a new bride who was totally unprepared for the reality of ranch life.

"Maybe so. I just don't want him intervening again on our behalf."

"Our?" Gloria murmured, giving Rosalie an opportunity to pretend she didn't hear.

Rosalie took that opportunity because she didn't want to discuss the matter further... even though she'd been the one to bring it up.

"I heard that Nick was given what for in the parking lot of Hardwick's by a good-looking blonde."

Rosalie's head snapped up from the bouquet she was arranging. "What?"

"I heard it from Mary Watkins when I went to the drugstore this morning. Mary had no idea who it was, but the woman appeared to know Nick."

"Who would Nick know that Mary doesn't?

That doesn't make sense." Nick had been gone for almost a decade, so anyone he knew in town, Mary would probably know better.

"Maybe you should ask him?"

"Or maybe I'll mind my own business."

"Suit yourself," Gloria said with a careless shrug.

Rosalie didn't bother answering, but the truth was that she was curious. Even if Nick wasn't still grieving his lost wife, he simply wasn't the kind of man who got yelled at in parking lots.

Oh, yes. She was curious.

"How are you going to find out?" Gloria inquired, perfectly following her thoughts.

"I'll ask Katie."

"Good idea." Gloria unpacked the last porcelain teacup and set it in place on the shelf. She glanced at her watch, then went to the window and turned around the ornate Welcome sign.

The Daisy Petal had a decent number of customers, but in a few weeks, after they officially announced their opening while participating in the popular June in Bloom vendor show and picnic, they were hoping to draw in people and tourists from the surrounding areas.

Rosalie placed the bouquet in the cooler with the others, then took off her apron and hung it on the iron hook near the counter. The faint sounds of laughter filtered in through the half-open windows. Vince Taylor's guests enjoying his late-afternoon wine and cheese parties. He'd opened his doors for business less than two weeks ago, but it didn't appear that the guests were pouring in, despite the time and effort he'd put into the renovation of his properties.

Rosalie had to acknowledge that he'd done an amazing job, and in the spirit of cooperation, she and Gloria had painted their house a coordinating color. But their Grand Lady didn't look nearly as grand as Vince's. Instead, she still looked slightly timeworn due to the details they were not yet able to address—wavy-glassed windows and gingerbread trim, to name two. Vince's houses, on the other hand, were pristine re-creations of the mansions in their glory years. Considering what he charged for a stay, those houses could be nothing less than pristine.

"Oh. My." Gloria turned away from the window.

"What?" Rosalie asked, her heart beating a little faster.

"Will."

Sure enough, a second later the door opened and Will McGuire walked in, stopping just inside the door, looking both strikingly handsome and openly uncomfortable. "Ladies," he said before giving the place a quick once-over.

"Can we help you with something?" Gloria asked in her professional voice.

"My grandniece is having a birthday, and I'd like to send flowers. She's thirteen, so I thought it would be a nice way to celebrate her becoming an official teen."

"How very thoughtful." Gloria gave him a teasing smile. "Not everyone welcomes the onset of the teen years."

"She's a good kid," Will said, relaxing an iota. "I thought maybe roses and daisies?"

He glanced at Rosalie, who nodded because she didn't seem able to find her tongue. Funny, but she'd been able to find it just fine when she'd given him what for a few months ago.

But, true to his word, Will had not intervened on her behalf again.

Gloria pulled out the catalog she'd created of the various bouquets she made and helped Will choose one while Rosalie busied herself rearranging items that were perfectly placed to begin with.

Really.

She rolled her eyes at herself, then gave a start when Will said, "I heard that Nick had a bit of a go-to with the new neighbor in Hardwick's parking lot."

"The new neighbor?" Rosalie and Gloria said in unison.

"So I gather from what Lester said at the co-op. He'd seen her at the real-estate office when she'd picked up the keys Juliet had left there, and he swore that was who was shaking her finger at Nick."

"I don't know anything about it," Rosalie said. She moved a few steps closer, folding her arms over her pale pink tunic, the ridiculous self-consciousness she'd felt a few minutes ago melting away now that she had a topic of conversation to latch on to. It was good to feel like herself again. "I wonder what was going on."

"No idea. You know if Lester knew that, everyone would know."

Gloria laughed and then bustled back into the kitchen area to see what vases she had available, leaving Rosalie and Will alone. *Very* much alone.

"How are things on the ranch?" she asked, determined to act normally. There was no reason she shouldn't.

"Travis and his crew have everything under control. I don't have that much to do anymore other than to fill in as needed."

"Does that bother you?"

"There's good and bad." He glanced down at the antique counter, then back up at Rosalie. "I never really apologized for overstepping my boundaries a while back. I'd like to do that now."

Rosalie's eyebrows rose. "Apology accepted, Will."

He looked as if he was about to say something else when Gloria came back with three delicate porcelain vases.

"The butterflies," Will said before she had a chance to set them down.

"Excellent choice." Gloria marked a box on the order pad.

Will gave the delivery details and paid for the flowers, then with a nod at both women headed to the door, leaving Rosalie to wonder what he'd been about to say before Gloria had unknowingly interrupted.

"Daddy, if we tie kite strings around our bellies, could we fly?" Kendra spread her arms as far as she could stretch them. "I mean a really big kite. Like this." She wiggled the ends of her fingers.

"How would you steer?"

Kendra gave him a look as the stiffening breeze blew her hair across her face, as if wondering why anyone would want to steer. Why not just let the wind take you wherever?

Nick smiled at his daughter, glad that she was embarking on a flight of fancy. Unlike Bailey, rules and norms were Kendra's security. He knew it was tied into her mom's death and maybe her age, but even before the accident had taken Kayla from them, Kendra had loved a good rule. She took after her Aunt Cassie, who loved rules and overachieving, which made her a perfect fit for her job as a school district administrator.

"Those kite men on the TV didn't steer."

Ah. The hang-glider show they'd watched the night before. Nick hated the thought of his kid sailing through the air on one of those things. "I think they did steer, kiddo. It was hard to see, but they were using their arms and legs. I don't think you can steer with a string."

"I don't think I could hang on to the kite like they did. I'd get tired and let go, so I'm tying the string on."

"They're strapped into a harness that holds them to the hang glider."

"Really?" Kendra sounded delighted by the prospect of being strapped to a pair of wings. "That would be a lot safer, huh?"

"Yes. Although the safest thing would be to keep both feet on the ground."

The wind gusted again, this time knocking Kendra back a few steps. Nick reached out to swing her up onto his shoulders.

"Hey. It's windy up here."

"Get used to it if you're going to hang glide."

Kendra knotted her hands in his hair and laughed. "I hope Bailey doesn't have bad dreams tonight."

Sobering thought, but yes, sometimes crazy weather did seem to spark the night terrors.

"You can sleep with Aunt Katie."

"No. Bailey wants me there."

End of discussion. Nick started jogging toward the house, and Kendra giggled as she held on tightly. The wind was swaying the trees and creaking limbs, and it was time to take cover and see what Katie and Bailey had been up to while he and Kendra had walked to the pasture to check the feed. The last Nick had seen, they were arranging herbs on a drying rack. His sister's fresh herb business, which she'd started shortly after moving home last year, was starting to take off, and she was now experimenting with drying and packaging.

The house smelled of sage and thyme when he and Kendra almost literally blew inside. He fought to keep the door from banging into the counter, then pushed it shut against the gale.

"You guys are crazy to be out there," Katie muttered.

Bailey was wearing a wreath of braided curly parsley on her head, and Kendra immediately went to inspect it.

"Aunt Katie made you one, too." She jumped off her stool and headed for the fridge. "They won't last long," she announced as she pulled the parsley wreath out and handed it to her sister, who carefully set it on her head.

Indeed the greenery was starting to wilt, but nothing his girls liked better than a nice crown of any sort.

"The wind wasn't so bad when we left, but I'm lucky it didn't blow Kendra away by the time we started back." Nick headed for the coffeepot. There was just enough there to fill half a cup. "How's it going?"

Katie's face lit up. "It's going well. Obviously, production will slow down in the winter when I can only grow in the greenhouses, but drying herbs will help bring in some bucks." She smiled at him. "I have a wedding to pay for."

Indeed, she did.

"Are you okay?"

Nick looked up from where he'd been studying the floor while sipping coffee. Both girls were staring at him, waiting for his answer.

"Yeah. I'm great." The girls looked down again, carefully arranging sage leaves on the small, flat pans that Katie had given them. Katie raised her eyebrows, silently saying she wasn't buying it, and he gave up.

"I ran into our new neighbor in town," he said as if starting a new conversation. He hadn't had time to talk to Katie after he'd returned home.

"Oh?" his sister responded in an overly casual tone. Neither of his daughters were paying any attention, so he continued.

"Emmie took it upon herself to chasten her when she tried to buy a hinge. Our neighbor had some views on the matter."

"Did she think you were the mastermind?" Katie asked as she continued to spread herbs.

"Yep. But we worked it out."

Katie paused, looking up from beneath her lashes. "For real?"

Nick gave his head a shake. "Probably as well as we're going to."

"Okay." Katie picked up her tray. "This one's ready. How're you guys doing?"

"We're ready, too," Bailey said. She'd arranged her leaves into a wobbly heart.

"Looks good, ladies."

A gust of wind tore over the house, and Kendra gave an exaggerated shudder. "Sure glad I'm not on a kite."

Katie gave her an odd look, and Nick laughed. "Me, too, kiddo. I don't think there'd be any steering in this wind."

ALEX SETTLED ON the sofa with a cup of tea spiked with a splash of bourbon—the same concoction she used when she was suffering from a cold—but in this case there were no sniffles. Only a desire to feel cozy. Safe. Warm.

Both gates were locked; her doors were locked. She had no reason to believe that anyone cared that she'd disappeared after getting the official "we can't pin anything on you even though you're the most convenient suspect" from the authorities. Yet she couldn't relax.

It was the lack of closure. The fact that she hadn't been cleared, but rather released because of lack of evidence, which in turn meant that someone might still think she was the key to everything. The end result was that she was turning into a paranoid basket case who jumped at every small noise.

The question she wrestled with in the aftermath of her confrontation with Nick Callahan was *could* she become friendlier? Unlock that gate and allow traffic through? Believe that she wasn't being sought after in connection with Jason's crime?

The answer might have been yes if it hadn't been for the apartment break-in. Was the timing a coincidence, or had the intruder been searching for something connected to Jason's crime? Was the reason he hadn't taken anything that he'd heard her coming? Or was it that he hadn't found what he was looking for?

She went to bed early but had a difficult time sleeping due to the wind, which had picked up and was rattling limbs against the house. She needed a tree trimmer in addition to everything else. Another drain on the bank account.

But maybe someone would catch up with Jason and wring the truth out of him. Then the cloud of suspicion surrounding her would dissipate and she could sell this property to Nick Callahan and return home. Where she would do what? It wasn't as if she could slide back into her old life. That was gone.

Would people forget? Or would she always be side-eyed as a possible embezzler? Would every major purchase she made make people wonder if she was using stolen money?

Alex punched her pillow a few times and then curled up on her side.

She wouldn't go home when this nightmare ended. She'd find a new place to live, probably on the West Coast. A brand-new life, a brand-new her.

And the brand-new her would not be overly trusting. Jason had cured her of that.

You got this, girl.

Alex smiled into her pillow. Maybe if she continued the pep talks, she'd believe herself eventually.

She was just drifting off when a high-pitched squeal brought her upright, heart thudding against her ribs as she fought to identify the horrifying sound. A split second later a house-rattling crash had her rocketing out of bed. She tripped over the slippers she'd left on the rug and went down hard, hitting her chin. She scrambled back to her feet, then froze, breathing hard as she listened, trying to make sense of what had just happened.

Wind buffeted the house, which creaked like an old wooden ship, making it difficult to hear, and the blood pounding in her ears wasn't helping matters.

Finally, she knelt and felt under her bed for the Louisville Slugger—her only form of protection—then crept forward toward the door. When she opened it, air swirled inside, making her shiver. A door or window was open. Her heart hammered to the point that she felt light-headed while silently moving into the hallway, her breath coming quick and hard as she stepped over the loose board that invariably squeaked.

A low screeching from somewhere below her gave her a small heart attack, and she flattened herself closer to the wall, as if she could disappear inside of it.

What on earth…?

Another small series of rhythmic screeches sounded as she hugged the wall and listened, while the sane part of her brain struggled to link clues together.

No assailant would burst into her house like a banshee on the attack and then simply stop.

She hoped.

Alex eased forward toward the top of the staircase and started easing her way down, gripping the baseball bat so firmly that her hand muscles were starting to cramp. A blast of wind hit her halfway down, and she crouched low to get a better look at her living room. At first, she had a hard time wrapping her brain around the dark, bushy mass quivering next to the front door, and then she recognized it for what it was. The leafy end of a gigantic branch protruding through her front window.

Alex closed her eyes and sank down onto the stairs, leaning her head against the banister spindles as tears of relief damped her lashes.

No assailant. Just another big problem to address.

She blinked against the tears, but a few slipped down her cheeks before she was able to control them.

What now?

What freaking now?

CHAPTER FIVE

"ANY DAMAGE?" NICK asked as he filled two coffee cups with life-giving brew. Katie shook her head as she pulled her hooded sweatshirt off over her head. He'd offered to check for damage to the greenhouse when they'd both staggered out of their bedrooms at daybreak after the massive windstorm had abated, but Katie had insisted on going.

"A near miss. The wind brought down an elm branch, but it landed short of the greenhouse by a couple feet. I think we might need to take that tree down. It's old and brittle." She hung the sweatshirt over the back of a chair and then took a long, hard look at him. "You look awful. Did Bailey have another round of night terrors? If so, I slept through it."

Nick had a hard time believing anyone could sleep through one of Bailey's episodes, even with a bedroom at the opposite end of the house. He yawned. "No. Wind terror. Both of them."

Katie took the cup he set in front of her. "Those trees do make scary sounds when they bend. I hate the one that scratches on the side of the house."

"That was the biggest culprit," Nick agreed. He'd had a time trying to convince Bailey that it wasn't something big and mean trying to claw its way into the house through the wall. "We spent a couple hours in the rocking chair." After his girls fell asleep, he managed to struggle to his feet and put them both in Kendra's bed, where they were still snuggled together.

"There are limbs everywhere. I wish the great-great-grandfolk had planted another type of tree. Cottonwoods are shallow rooted and elms break. We're lucky those old cottonwoods are still standing."

"How're the goats?"

"I let them out. They're happily exploring the mayhem."

Nick rubbed a hand over his face and yawned again.

"Maybe you can slip a nap in later today."

He shook his head, giving her a bleary look. "I gave up napping when Kendra was born."

Katie laughed. "That said, you might try. We're going to plant seeds today, so the house should be quiet."

"I'll keep that in mind." Even though there was no way he was going to waste time napping. Nick drained his cup and got to his feet as his phone rang. He didn't recognize the number, which meant a robocall, a wrong number or someone who'd picked up one of his cards at Cooper's Building Supply. He answered in case it was a potential job. Windstorms did tend to bring in work.

"Nick Callahan."

"Hello." There was an intake of breath and then, "This is Alex Ryan."

Nick frowned first at the phone, then at Katie, who mouthed, "Who is it?" He held up a finger before saying, "Yeah. Alex. What do you need?" Katie's eyebrows shot up at the mention of their neighbor's name.

"I…uh…" She cleared her throat as her voice wavered. "I need a contractor."

"When?"

"Soon."

There was a definite wobble in her voice. Something had happened, and it had to be dire if she'd called him after yesterday's performance.

"I know I have no right to call after yesterday, but you're the only person I know in the area."

"Wind damage?"

"There's a branch sticking through my window, and the porch...the porch is ruined."

He let out a silent sigh, meeting Katie's gaze.

"I'll watch the girls," she said as if he'd asked the question out loud.

"Do you have coffee?" he said into the phone.

"I...I can have coffee ready."

"I'll be right over."

"The lock."

"Give me the combination," he said reasonably. "Or meet me at your back gate." Which he could unlock in about three seconds by undoing the wires of the fence to which it was connected. Besides that, bicycle locks were more of a statement than a deterrent, even when used with bicycles.

"The combination is 6-10-92."

Which was probably her birthday. "Got it. I'll be there in twenty minutes. Maybe sooner."

He hung up the phone and gave his head a shake as if to clear it. It didn't work. "Our neighbor needs a contractor. Are you sure about the girls?"

"We already made plans for planting."

"They'll probably be asleep for hours after being awake for most of the night."

"I've got stuff to do in the house, too."

"Then I guess I'm off to see Ms. Ryan." He drained his cup and rinsed it, then started toward the door.

"Hey, Nick?"

He glanced back at Katie.

"Maybe you can use this situation to negotiate for right-of-way through the property?"

He grabbed his ball cap off a hook and slipped it onto his head. "Yeah. My thoughts exactly."

"You know what that means."

"Be tactful..."

"I think you have an advantage this time."

"Agreed." Now all he had to do was not blow it.

Fifteen minutes later, Nick pulled into the Dunlop ranch and parked next to Alex's car, which appeared to have suffered no harm despite being surrounded by small broken branches. He turned off the ignition, palming the keys as he studied the damage. Like many of the older ranches in the area, the house and outbuildings of the Dunlop were surrounded by elms and cottonwoods—trees that gave shade but, as they aged, fell victim to windstorms.

One particularly large limb had crushed the porch and broken the front window, its leafy fingers extending into the interior of the house. He hoped Alex had already called her insurance company and submitted photos, because this was going to be a beast to clear, and he wanted to get started. He needed to order the window and would probably have to drive to Dillon to get it. It was unlikely that Emmie could get one there on short notice, and he had a feeling that Alex wasn't going to want to sleep with cardboard duct-taped over a gaping hole in her house.

He got out of the truck just as she appeared from behind the house, dressed in a flannel shirt and jeans, her hair twisted up into a bun that looked like it was seconds away from allowing gravity to take control. Yet somehow, despite the flannel and denim and slept-in hairdo, she managed to look elegant as she picked her way around and over branches and limbs. He could easily picture her overseeing some kind of ritzy charity function, and maybe she had at one time. Maybe she would again. In his gut he knew that, who-ever Alex Ryan was or had been, she didn't belong in rural Montana.

Once clear of the branches, she strode to-ward him like a woman on a mission, her chin up, her jaw set. She stopped a little farther away from him than necessary. Far enough that he clearly got the message not to get too close, but near enough that he could see the effect of sleep deprivation in the shadows beneath her green eyes. She must have had a hellacious night.

She moistened her lips and he tried not to stare, but she did have a really nice mouth. "I appreciate you coming after yesterday." She shifted her weight and her cheeks flushed a little before she added, "And the day before."

He regarded her for a long moment, debat-ing about how involved he wanted to get. If it would get him access, then he wanted to get very involved. But even if he hadn't had an agenda, there was something about the woman that stirred things inside him, made him want to help her if he could. She had se-crets, and even though he was a live-and-let-live, mind-your-own-business guy, he wanted to know what they were. He wanted to know what had brought her to this rural corner of

Montana, made her desperate enough to buy a property out from under him—a property that did not seem to suit her in the least.

"Maybe we can start over."

"You'd be willing to do that?" She seemed surprised, as if such occurrences were rare in her life. Or maybe unheard of.

"I'd be willing to look for common ground."

Her lips parted, then closed again. She gave a small nod and said, "Very well."

He wondered what she'd been about to say, then forced his mind to the matter before him. One big mother of a branch. "I'll take a look. See what we're up against."

She took a step back. "Thank you." Spoken in a prim, polite way, a way meant to keep a distance between them, even if she looked like a person who needed a hug.

Fortunately for her, he wasn't the hugging type, so no danger there.

He'd just started toward the damaged porch when the phone rang in his back pocket. He pulled it out, glanced at the screen, then said, "Hello."

"Hey, sorry to bug you," Katie said, "but have you seen Bailey's elephant?"

He stopped walking and put a hand on his forehead, closing his eyes as he tried to remember where he'd last seen his youngest daughter's security buddy. "The unicorn won't do?"

Alex shot him a curious look, and only then did he realize how his perfectly logical response must have sounded to someone who didn't know his daughter.

"Nope," Katie said. "She has the unicorn but wants the elephant, too."

"A double-buddy day? Well, she did have a bad night." No terrors, but that wind-monster-clawing-the-house thing had really bothered her. She'd hugged the unicorn all night long, but the elephant… Nick frowned. "She doesn't think the house-clawing monster got it, does she?"

"Bingo."

He had a sudden flash. "Try my sock drawer. I think she put it to bed there yesterday."

"Just a sec…" He could hear Katie navigating her way through the house and chanced a look at Alex, who looked away guiltily when their gazes connected. She'd been staring and he'd caught her. But he really couldn't blame her for staring, given the conversation. "Yes! Ellie is here. Thanks, Nick."

"No problem. Call if you need anything else located."

"Everything going all right?" Translation—was he going to be able to negotiate for access?

"Yeah. I think it is," he said. "Talk to you later."

He pocketed the phone and met Alex's gaze blandly. "Shall we?"

"Yes." This time her response didn't sound prim and proper and restrained. Instead it sounded curious and a touch hesitant. "Do you have kids?"

"I do."

"Ah. Good."

The exaggerated relief in her voice made him want to smile. "What would you have said if I'd said no?"

"I'm not sure." She pushed her hands into her front pockets. "I do need this limb removed and the window replaced, so... I'd have kept my distance and kept my Slugger at the ready."

"Your slugger?"

"I played softball at school. I have my bat with me."

"Huh."

"What does that mean?"

He stopped at the front gate, looking her over. "I guess that means that I took you as more of a dancer than a softball player."

She frowned at him. "Is that an insult?"

He considered for a moment, then shook his head. "I don't think so." Although, again, he never would have pegged her for a softball player.

A smile teased the corners of her mouth, fascinating him, then she remembered herself and the smile faded. "There's a lot to do," she stated, gesturing at the branch and the crushed porch.

"Yeah." He tipped back his ball cap. "I can get the debris cleared and the window ordered, but I won't get it in time to install today."

"Can you come back tomorrow?"

"Can you live with cardboard taped over the hole?"

As he'd suspected, she did not appear thrilled at the prospect. But she squared her shoulders and said, "I'll manage."

But would she sleep? Probably not.

He thought about pointing out that break-ins and crime in general were rare in the area, but Alex Ryan wasn't hiding from local hoodlums. No. Something else had her spooked. Something from her past.

"Before I get started, why don't I take a look at your broken gate?"

"Uh…yes. Sure."

She led the way over and around branches, then through a side gate in the rickety picket fence. That gate listed badly, but it had two hinges. The gate at the rear of the weed-choked yard hung by one.

Nick crossed the yard and lifted the sagging gate with one hand. The remaining hinge broke free, and Alex gave a groan. He turned in time to see her shoulders sag, but she lifted them as soon as his gaze connected with hers.

"The post is rotted."

"How do we fix that?" she asked.

"We have to replace the post." He rubbed a hand over the back of his neck as he studied the rest of the fence. He didn't dare touch it, or it would fall down. "Wanda will never approve this."

Her mouth opened as though she was surprised he knew that Wanda would make a home inspection before allowing one of her dogs into a foster home, then seemed to recall that Gavin was a small town.

"I…"

Nick waited a couple of seconds, watching her as she inspected the fence and then gave a slow nod.

"I hadn't really looked at it before."

"If you want, I can fix the fence, too."

She shot him a wary look, obviously waiting for him to drop the ultimatum—*I'll fix the fence if you allow me access through your property*. It was the perfect moment, but Nick kept his mouth shut.

She frowned, her light brown eyebrows drawing closer together as she studied him. "How long would it take and how much do you think it would cost?"

"I can do it in two days—one day to tear out the old fence, another to build the new one once I get the materials."

"I see. And the cost?"

He told her his hourly rate. "Plus materials."

She gave a nod. "Very well. Can you take care of ordering the materials? I don't seem to have a lot of luck at the lumber store."

He accepted the zing with good grace. "That's part of the job."

She studied him for a moment, her expression holding an edge of caution, as if she was still waiting for him to spring the deal on her.

He did not…and he couldn't explain to himself why he didn't.

You're playing the long game.

Of course. The long game.

If she came to trust him, it would be better for everyone.

And you may lose this opportunity if she doesn't come to trust you.

Yes. He might. But he was going to take the risk. Go for the bigger reward, which was not only access but perhaps first option on the house if she decided to sell again.

"When can you start?"

"What kind of fence do you want?"

"One that's dog proof."

"I'll price out some options and go over them when I bring the window tomorrow. In the meantime, I have cardboard to tape over the open space."

She nodded as if she'd come to terms with a night behind cardboard, but he didn't believe she had.

"If you want a place to stay until we get the window in, there's room at the ranch. The manager's house is—"

"Oh, no," she said hurriedly. "I'm fine. My gates are locked. No issues."

Right. "Then I guess I'll measure the window and clear enough debris away to put the cardboard in place."

"I'll help."

He almost said "Are you sure?" but he'd already insulted her by not pegging her as a softball player, so he kept his mouth shut. "Got some gloves?"

"I think I might."

"Great. I'll meet you in the front once you find them."

TRUE TO FORM, Aunt Juliet hadn't completely moved out of the house when she'd left. She'd crammed boxes of odds and ends into closets and the pantry and the half basement. Alex was fairly certain she'd spotted a pair of gardening gloves in a box somewhere. Judging from the condition of the gardens, it had been a while since the gloves had seen any use, but they would see use today. The sooner Nick got the debris cleared away from the window, the sooner he could commence fixing things. And maybe he could get a start on the fence and then Alex could bring Gus, her soon-to-be-fostered golden retriever mix, home with her.

She needed the companionship, and last night she would have given just about anything to have had the dog with her after the branch had come crashing in through the window.

And tonight was the same—she'd give just about anything not to be alone in her house with only cardboard and tape standing between her and the outside world, but she couldn't bring herself to accept Nick Callahan's offer to stay on his ranch. She'd barely allowed him to finish making the offer.

Why?

Part of it was logic. Glass wasn't much better than cardboard and tape if someone wanted to enter a house. Both gave way easily, so she really had no more reason to stay at his ranch tonight than she did any other night. The level of risk was approximately the same.

And part of it was just her nature. She'd never liked to be beholden to anyone, or to pin her hopes on anyone having her back, with the exception of her few close female friends, who were now scattered around the country, building careers, having families. Living full lives. Her parents had taught her through their actions that she could depend only on herself—heaven knew she couldn't depend on them. She'd made an exception and allowed herself to depend on Jason, and then he'd screwed her over and taught her that she couldn't trust her own instincts.

That isn't exactly true.

Her small voice was correct.

Every now and again, she'd had a vague feeling that something was off, that Jason was there in some ways, not in others. But she couldn't identify exactly what the problem was, and he somehow knew the exact moment to turn on the charm and quell her doubts. Eventually she'd assured herself that she was thinking too much. Looking for trouble where there was none.

Big mistake, that.

Thumps and bangs came from the front of the house as Alex continued her search for the gloves, finally unearthing them from a plastic container stored in the bedroom closet. She brought the gloves into the light and grimaced. Stiff floral canvas with orange leather palms. Very festive.

She pulled them on as she trotted down the stairs, flexing her hands to take the stiffness out of the leather. She heard the rattle of a chain as she hit the last step, and by the time she'd gone out the back door and come around the house, Nick had his truck backed up to the front gate and had attached one end of the chain to the limb and the other to the trailer hitch of his truck.

"Better stand back," he said as she came to a stop.

Alex obligingly stepped back to the side of the house, where she had cover if something broke and went flying.

Nick got into the truck and slowly moved forward. The chain tightened, popped once, then the branch moved across what was left of her porch with a low screech that had Alex putting her hands over her ears. Nick dragged it through the gate and to the far side of the wide driveway before stopping and backing up a few inches, allowing the chain to go slack.

Alex surveyed the damage while Nick dealt with the end of the chain. The front of her house was in rough shape. The branch had torn the porch roof free of the house, and the floor was now tilted at an odd angle. This had money written all over it.

She had money, but she didn't want to spend it on something like this.

It isn't like you have a lot of choice.

True.

Nick got out of the truck and strode toward the wreck of a porch, a man on a mission. Since his attention was on the house, Alex allowed herself a moment to study him for the first time from a bit of a distance, as opposed to being toe to toe. He was something. Lean muscled, broad shouldered and, frankly, gorgeous.

Abruptly she yanked her thoughts back to the straight and narrow. The guy was married. He had kids, for Pete's sake. When his wife had called with some kind of unicorn emergency that involved house monsters, a small part of her had protested the fact that he was not available. Another part cheered because, well, problem solved. He was attractive, but she wasn't in a position to be attracted—in fact she couldn't think of a worse time to be attracted to someone, after having been gut-punched in her last relationship.

So, yay. Nick Callahan was married and had kids.

That didn't diminish the fact that he looked hot while he was undoing the chain from the branch and gathering it back up, but it did help Alex keep her head where it was supposed to be—worried about her present and her past, not lusting after the neighbor.

He turned toward her, and she lifted her chin in an innocent way—perhaps a little too innocently, judging from the way his eyes narrowed ever so slightly. "Why don't you hand me the glass and debris inside the house, and I'll clear away the stuff on this side."

"Sounds good."

She was about to head toward the back door again when she heard him say, "Nice gloves, by the way."

She shot him a wry look over her shoulder, then continued on her way, surprised that he'd teased her. Surprised, and warmed, and of the mind that perhaps she needed to be careful around this man.

"Let me get this straight," Katie said as she sprayed stain remover on Bailey's pale blue sweatshirt. "You had the perfect opportunity to exert some leverage yesterday, get us easy access, and you chose not to."

"That pretty much sums it up," Nick agreed. But that didn't mean he wasn't going to broach the matter—he simply wasn't ready to broach it yet, because the next no would be a definitive one.

Katie regarded him for a long moment, then

bunched up the shirt and tossed it into the open washer. "And your ultimate goal is..."

Nick lifted the coffee cup to his lips. "Friendly relations," he said before he sipped. "She doesn't belong here. She's not comfortable, and I think it's totally possible she might sell once she figures that out."

"Then *we* could buy."

"Preferably before the place goes on the market."

Katie gave a considering nod. "Good plan. If she decides to sell."

"Yeah." Nick sipped again. "I don't know why she's here, but I have a strong feeling that it's not because she's living the dream."

"Huh." Katie twisted dials and the machine made a series of clicking noises as sensors went on. He missed the old-school agitator washer he'd left behind in California. Easy to run, easy to fix. This thing required a technician.

"I need coffee," she said as soon as she was done. "You didn't take it all, right?"

"Like I would."

She made a sputtering noise that had him smiling. It was good to be back home. Good to have his girls close to family.

"By the way, Grandma called and very

casually asked whether you'd had any recent issues with our new neighbor."

"That was to be expected, what with both Mary Watkins and Lester witnessing the event. What did you tell her?"

"That it was a misunderstanding. I told her how Emmie had gone all protect-o and the neighbor thought you were behind it." Katie shrugged. "She said she could totally see that happening."

"Pretty much because it did," he said as he sat in his usual spot at the kitchen table. "By the way, can you watch the girls while I repair the window and tear out the fence tomorrow?" The glass was stored flat in the bed of his truck, wrapped in cardboard and a blanket, and the pricing figures for various dog-proof fences were printed and lying on the front seat.

They'd agreed yesterday that he would put in the window first, then tackle the yard, so that she could get her dog as soon as possible. After that, he'd go to work on the porch.

A shadow crossed Katie's face. "Grandma and I are driving to Dillon tomorrow for a doctor appointment. A last-minute cancellation came up, so she took the appointment."

"Guess I'll take them with me. Kendra's pretty good with a claw hammer."

"And Bailey?"

"I'll find her a light one." The last time she'd gotten hold of his heavy framing hammer, she'd raised it too high and almost conked herself in the head. He wasn't going to let that happen again.

"Maybe Gloria can babysit them at the shop?" Katie suggested.

"No. That's fine." He'd keep the girls busy by letting them "help" him.

Katie cocked her head. "Do you think she's going to mind? The neighbor?"

"Alex?" He wondered at the need to say her name. To make her a person instead of just "the neighbor." Something he might have to think about at some point. He'd caught her watching him the day before and assumed she was trying to decide whether or not to trust him. Her cheeks had flushed a guilty pink when their gazes connected, so apparently, in Alex's world, people didn't stare. "My guess is no, because I'm the only game in town as far as she's concerned." He truly doubted she wanted to find another contractor and give him the combination to the gate lock.

"If you're sure…"

"This is how kids learn. We'll make it work."

"You're such a dad," Katie said.

Yes. He was. Parenting was the scariest journey he'd ever embarked on, especially now that he was going it alone, but he wouldn't trade it for anything.

The next morning Nick loaded his girls in the truck and headed for the Dunlop ranch. Everyone was ready to go to work. He'd found a light tack hammer for Bailey, as well as a box of carpet tacks, which should keep her busy "building," while Kendra was excited to pull nails. He'd have to pull them most of the way out first, but she could finish them off and put the used nails in a small pail.

Emmie had agreed to waive the delivery fee for the fencing and porch materials once they were chosen, maybe to make up for almost making Alex cry. She had, of course, been terrifically interested in how it happened that Alex had left the building-supply place angry and close to tears and then Nick had showed up to buy fencing for her place less than six hours later.

"We met at the grocery store," he'd explained.

"Must have been some meeting," Emmie

said as she rang up the cost of the hinges and screws he'd need no matter what kind of fence Alex wanted.

All Nick did was smile and shake his head. Emmie was a close-enough friend to know that when he didn't feel like talking, he wasn't going to.

"Someday you'll have to tell me the story," she called after him.

"Nothing to tell."

"Ha."

Nick pulled the truck to a stop near the wire gate with the bicycle lock looped around it.

"Why are we stopping?" Kendra asked from the back seat.

"I have to open the gate."

"No bumpy road?"

"Not today."

Nick left the bicycle lock hanging over the gate brace after he drove through and closed it again. He'd lock up when he left, even though the only people he'd be locking out were himself and his family. If it made Alex feel safer, then so be it.

Safe from what?

He told himself it couldn't be that bad, or she would have taken up his offer to stay on the ranch. Maybe she was someone famous, trying to keep the paparazzi at bay...except that Emmie, who'd been addicted to pop culture for as long as he'd known her, would have recognized her. So that left woman on the run. Or a criminal.

Somehow criminal didn't seem to fit. If it had, his daughters wouldn't be there with him.

Alex was picking up branches as he drove into the place. She stood up straight at the sound of his truck, a branch in each flowery orange hand. The girls were going to love her gloves.

"Good morning," she called as he opened his door. The first friendly greeting he'd gotten from her.

"Morning," he replied.

Today her hair was loose, falling almost to her waist in damp waves, giving her a softer look. He imagined that once it dried, she'd contain it again, but he had to admit to liking it loose.

"I brought some help," he said as he opened the rear door of the truck, acting as if it was perfectly normal to bring one's kids to a work site. He folded back the cushioned arms on Bailey's car seat while Kendra undid her own buckles and reached for the door handle. She dropped to the ground as Nick lifted Bailey out of the truck.

"These are my daughters, Bailey and Kendra."

Alex's face relaxed into the first genuine smile he'd ever seen from her, and Nick felt the impact. Alex Ryan was a natural beauty, but when she smiled, it seemed to light her from the inside out. Bailey seemed to be having the same reaction. She leaned her head against his leg as she stared at Alex, who gave a small nod.

"Hello, Bailey and Kendra. I'm Alex."

"Hello," Kendra said solemnly, while Bailey hugged herself more tightly against Nick's leg. Kendra glanced up at him as she held her utility belt against her pink striped shirt. "I need help with my tool belt."

"Sure." He knelt down and tied a bow while Kendra held the tool belt in place. Once he was done, she smoothed her tool belt. "I'll get my hammer," she said in an important voice, heading back to the truck without glancing at Alex. "Do you want me to get yours, Bailey?"

Bailey nodded, still staring at Alex, and Nick called, "Please do that."

When he finally glanced back at Alex, he found her studying him with an expression he couldn't read.

"Quite a crew," she said.

Bailey let go of Nick's leg and took a few steps forward. "You have princess hair," she said.

Indeed, Alex's golden-blond hair did appear princessy as it fell over her shoulders and down her back. Stick a crown on her head and she'd look positively medieval.

"I try," Alex said, running her fingers down the dampish waves. Nick found his gaze following the movement and instantly brought it back to her face.

"Usually my sister or grandmother babysit, but they weren't available. I hope you don't mind."

"No. Not at all."

She appeared sincere, and he noticed that she seemed as fascinated with his daughters as Bailey seemed fascinated with her. She had to be wondering about where the girls' mother was, so he would explain rather than have her guessing or depending on gossip, which she wouldn't get because she was an outsider.

"Hey, Bailey, would you help Kendra find

your hammer?" It must have slipped into a crevice, because he could hear Kendra digging around in the back seat.

Bailey instantly ran around the truck as if glad to have an excuse to escape, and Nick met Alex's gaze. "I lost my wife two years ago."

"I'm sorry." The words were automatic, but heartfelt.

"Yeah. Single car rollover on a foggy night." He cleared his throat. "Anyway, as a single dad, there are times when things come up, so I try to make it clear from the beginning that the job will get done on time, but, like I said, things happen."

"Like today."

"Exactly. I wouldn't normally take the girls on a job."

"I don't mind."

He managed a smile, and he was fairly certain it looked genuine, but the truth was that, even two years in, it took something out of him when he explained his situation. It was like breaking open a wound yet another time. Granted, the healing came faster with each passing day, but he still had a ways to go.

"I appreciate that." He tore his gaze away from hers and glanced toward the backyard.

"Emmie will deliver the fencing material, so the main gate needs to be open. In the meantime, I'll install the glass, then my crew and I will tear down the back fence. I'll be able to get a start on the new one as soon as Emmie delivers."

"Great. I'm excited to get my new dog."

"Yeah. I imagine its lonely here."

"I'm looking forward to the company. It's been a while since I've had a pet."

"City living?" Even though he knew better, he pushed for another clue.

"Exactly." She rubbed her hands down the sides of her jeans, and the girls slammed the door on the far side of the truck, giggling to each other. Nick clearly heard Bailey say "Wapunzel," her name for the fairy-tale heroine. Alex must have heard it, too, because her cheeks went a little pink. "Quick question—do you mind if I pay in cash?"

Gee, could he handle putting cold, hard cash into his pocket instead of waiting for a check to clear?

He kept all hints of irony out of his voice as he said, "Not at all." He'd pretty much expected the mystery woman to pay in cash, anyway.

"Excellent. I'll…see you later." The girls

came around the truck, Bailey dragging her tool belt with one hand and holding the tack hammer in the other. "It was nice meeting you, Bailey and Kendra." She smiled at his daughters, then turned and headed back to the house.

"Isn't she going to help?" Bailey asked, sounding disappointed.

"Not today, sweetie." He bent down to fasten her tool belt around her waist. "But if we're going to get done in time for an ice cream in town, we'd better get started."

OF COURSE NICK CALLAHAN's daughters were adorable. And of course he was a widower, instead of a firmly off-limits married guy.

He's still off-limits. Daughters. Stable life. All that stuff you don't have at the present moment.

Alex took comfort in that thought as she watched through the kitchen window as little Bailey enthusiastically assaulted a large nail sticking out of a fence post with her tack hammer, angelic features screwed up into an expression of extreme concentration. Meanwhile, Kendra, the older daughter, was dutifully prying nails out of pickets that Nick had laid out for her. He'd started each nail and then she proudly finished it off. He'd told Alex before starting that he was deducting two hours off his rate because having his daughters there slowed him down. She almost told him to forget it, then reminded herself that he was correct. A deal was a deal. She was paying for the time he put in on the fence, and yes, having his daughters there slowed him down.

But bringing his daughters to work, and offering to adjust his time, firmly shifted him into good-guy territory.

Was that good? Or bad?

Alex pushed off the counter and turned to face the cluttered kitchen. The glove search convinced her that she needed to deal with Juliet's junk ASAP, so she'd hauled stacks of boxes that had been tucked away in various nooks and crannies of the house into the dining room, where she could sort through the junk. Ninety percent of it would go to the trash or donation, but she needed to sort, just in case there was stuff she could use in her new life.

She almost jumped out of her skin when the truck carrying the fencing rolled to a stop in front of the house. She'd always as-

sumed she was a shake-it-off kind of girl—
that she could shake off the effects of being
knocked down by a stranger in her own home
the same way she'd shaken off the effect of
her parents not showing up on visiting weekends at her boarding school.

Not the same critter. Not even close.

You'll get better with time.

She hoped.

Alex let out a breath and willed her taut
muscles to relax before opening the next
box to reveal a treasure trove of crafting
materials—feathers, beads, felt and ribbon.
Fun stuff. She might have even used some of
this stuff back in the day when she'd visited.
Perhaps she'd call the local school district
and see if they took donations of art supplies.

*Or maybe you can try your hand at
crafting...something.*

She'd always loved creating, but never
found the time to embrace a full-fledged
hobby. She lifted a string of beads which
glittered in the warm sunlight.

Maybe she would embrace a hobby. She
had time on her hands. Alex set the beads
back in the box, closed it and moved on to
the next.

Nick would deal with the fencing, and she would deal with this, the odds and ends of her aunt's life. And while she did it, maybe she'd make some sense of the odds and ends of her own life.

CHAPTER SIX

AFTER NICK AND his girls drove away, Alex poured a glass of wine and went outside to inspect the work. The old fencing lay in neat piles, ready for Nick to haul away when he had less help.

Alex had purposely refrained from interacting with the little girls while they'd been there, but she had watched them, and when she'd gone out to the screened back porch to drop a load of junk, she'd seen Bailey watching her. Or rather her hair, which she'd plaited into a loose braid after it'd dried.

Princess hair.

She should probably cut her princess hair. She'd taken to wearing it up at work a few years back, thus keeping it off her neck during the warmer months, and had simply let it grow. And grow.

Yes. A haircut.

She looked down at her beat-up nails. Maybe a mani, too?

Not yet, because she didn't feel like being snubbed in a salon, and she also didn't feel like driving to Dillon, which was almost an hour away.

So here she would stay, sorting junk in her new house and watching the guy who was helping her put things back together through the window when she got antsy.

After a frozen dinner and another bracing glass of wine, Alex dialed her mother, hoping that this time, instead of hearing how people were talking, she'd hear that they were no longer talking. That something else had caught their attention.

That was a long shot, because Cécile always thought people were watching her, talking about her, admiring her, envying her. And currently she assumed they were anticipating her downfall after her daughter was sent to prison for a crime she didn't commit. Cécile, however, did have news.

"You'll never guess who I ran into."

"Who?" she asked dutifully.

"Lawrence."

A frisson of surprise caused Alex to sit up straighter. "Lawrence Stoddard?" Jason's younger brother?

"Yes. The authorities put him through the

wringer, too. However, he has chosen to stay put. He even began a new job."

Alex ignored the barb. She'd always liked Lawrence, a free spirit who kept his distance from his workaholic brother, probably because Jason lectured him about the consequences of his live-for-today attitude. She'd met him only a handful of times after she and Jason started dating, but the same thing had happened every time—big brother had taken little brother to task. Little brother had put up with it, but Alex had sensed that he couldn't wait to end his duty visit and carry on with his happy existence.

"He wanted me to pass a message along to you."

"He did?" Alex went still, having no idea what to expect.

"Yes," her mother said with a sniff. "He said to tell you that Jason fooled everyone and not to feel bad about being duped."

"So he thinks I'm innocent?" That was important to her—that someone in the know believed in her.

"He does. I asked him where he thought his brother was hiding out."

Alex rolled her eyes. Of course she had. "Did he tell you?"

"He said he doesn't know. I believe him."

Alex pinched the bridge of her nose. Her mother astounded her at times.

Cécile cleared her throat. "And how are things there?"

If they'd had a normal mother-daughter relationship, she'd have told her about the windstorm and the broken porch, and the neighbor whom she'd hired to help her out. But all that was stuff that Cécile would use as ammunition in her quest to get Alex to return home so that people wouldn't talk.

"They're good. I'm settling in and enjoying the change of scenery. Montana is beautiful."

"I hear the winters are intense."

"I think we've seen a few intense winters in Virginia over the past several years."

I'm not coming home.

The thought had barely formed when her mother said, "How long do you think you'll be staying?"

Well, they were on the same wavelength in that regard. "Until I decide what to do and where to do it."

"Have you been in contact with Juliet?"

Her mother seemed to think that her sister was encouraging Alex to do the wrong thing to spite her, just as Jason had assumed that Lawrence was living the free and easy life to thumb his nose at him.

She'd never before realized how similar Jason and her mother were in their life views. Did that mean that Cécile might commit a felonious act? She almost laughed.

"Is something funny?"

"No. Juliet's hard to pin down, so it might be a while until I hear from her. And in the meantime, I'm clearing her junk out of the house and enjoying time to just be in my head."

A silence fell and became increasingly strained as it stretched on. "I'll call in a few days, Mom."

"Yes. Have a good evening." A second later the phone went dead, and Alex dropped the device onto the cushions beside her and drew her knees to her chest, wrapping her arms around them.

She would have a good evening. It might be a touch lonely, but with each passing day, returning home felt less and less like something she wanted to do. Nick promised to get the fence done tomorrow, and Wanda was scheduled to make her official home visit the day after. Alex was not yet ready to put herself out there and attempt to become part of this tightly knit community, so she was looking forward to having a dog for company.

She was looking forward to not being so very alone.

ALEX HAD TO admit to feeling a twinge of disappointment when Nick showed up sans crew the next morning. She'd enjoyed the energy the girls had brought to her quiet house, enjoyed watching them interact with each other and their father.

Nick went to work on the fence while Alex cleared out the kitchen cupboards. The keep pile was small. Everything else was sorted into boxes earmarked for donation or destruction.

When she finished sorting, she'd wash the interior of the cupboards, then sand the wood in preparation for painting. She had no idea what color she would paint the kitchen, but she had to do something to cover the grease spots on the ceiling and the worn paint everywhere else. After talking to her mother, she felt more determined than ever to stay in this house—at least until she figured out her next move—and that meant brightening up this depressing room, where she spent a great deal of her time.

Funny how the kitchen hadn't seemed one bit depressing when she and Juliet had baked cookies there fifteen years ago, but her aunt had a way of commandeering a space so that the only thing you saw was her. That was the one characteristic Juliet and Cécile shared. Other than that…nothing. The sisters were polar opposites in all regards, and Alex didn't take after either of them.

Physically she took after her long-departed blond-haired, green-eyed father, who'd dutifully sent support checks each month and presents for all the prescribed holidays and, other than that, ignored his only daughter. Perhaps the three boys he'd had with his second wife had something to do with that. Alex had convinced herself long ago that it didn't matter, but when she'd glanced out the window yesterday afternoon and watched as Nick Callahan stopped working to take a long look at the butterfly his oldest daughter was carefully holding in cupped hands, her heart had twisted. Neither of her parents had ever taken that kind of care with her.

Her five-year-old self had been deeply jealous.

Alex shook her head and went back to sorting.

It was getting close to lunchtime when Nick came into the kitchen and stopped dead when he saw the lines of donation and destruction boxes. "Are you getting rid of all of this?"

Alex glanced down at the clothing, rags, battered plastic cookware and mismatched dishes. "What would you do with it?"

Nick gave a small laugh. "Point taken."

"When my aunt moved out, it appears that she only took the essentials."

"Your aunt?"

The air froze in Alex's lungs as she realized what she'd just said. There was something about this guy—quite possibly the butterfly incident—that had lulled her into a sense of security, and she'd forgotten herself. He seemed so trustworthy and dependable.

As had Jason.

After a few silent seconds, Nick said, "That explains a few things."

It did, but she didn't owe him any further explanation. Alex pushed her hand through her hair, stunned at how one simple sentence could have such potential impact. So much for being Alex Ryan, stranger to these parts.

"Who or what are you hiding from, Alex?"

Her gaze flashed up as her heart almost stopped. "What makes you think—"

He gave her a weary look. "It's pretty obvious that you're hiding from something. What I need to know is will it affect me and my family?"

It took her a second to understand what he was asking—would danger follow her?

"I'm not in witness protection or anything. It isn't like a mobster is going to show up and take everyone out."

Nick gave a nod. He seemed to do a lot of that—nod and wait until Alex felt the need to fill the silence. Well, this time she wasn't filling anything. She crossed her arms over her chest and stared him down.

"Who are you afraid is going to show up?"

"No one who will have any effect on you whatsoever."

"Ex-husband? Boyfriend? Boss?"

Damn her fair skin and the telltale blush that warmed her cheeks.

"I'm escaping a stressful situation."

"Work? Family?"

She gave a short laugh. "Yes." A half-truth, but she'd go with it.

Nick cocked his head waiting for more, but

he wasn't getting any more. She would take control of this situation, instead of backing up and deflecting, as she always had with her mother. It was easy to simply acquiesce, let her mother have her way, and, frankly, she'd done the same with Jason when she'd had concerns. But Nick Callahan had no hold over her whatsoever, so it was time for her to take charge. To stop backing up.

"Do you think a locked gate will keep your family out?"

"I think a locked gate will give me time to mentally prepare if they do show up."

He gave her a dubious look, and she had to admit the whole thing sounded fishy. "Isn't your aunt, the person you bought the house from, part of the family?"

"My aunt is estranged from my mother, but she and I have always gotten along. We're the renegades, you see."

Nick raised an eyebrow, and she could see his point. She didn't appear one bit renegade-ish. Well, there were varying levels of renegade-ism, and in her family, she met the qualifications.

"When I decided that I wanted to disappear, I contacted her to see about buying this place."

"That you'd never seen."

"No. I spent a summer here."

"Did you?"

"Yes." She'd been there, two miles from where he lived, for two whole months.

"And you still outbid me for it?"

"It was in better shape back then."

"I don't think so. This property has been falling apart since Dunlop's first wife died. I assume your aunt is Juliet, Dunlop's second wife."

There was a note in his voice that conveyed very effectively the fact that Nick didn't care much for her aunt. Well, Juliet had that effect on people. Alex simply tilted her head and kept her mouth shut. He apparently took that as a yes.

"You're going to wish you'd found a better place to disappear than this money pit."

"I'll fix things as I can afford to."

Nick walked to the arched dining room entryway and took a long, hard look. She had a feeling he didn't miss a thing as his gaze swept over the room. What exactly was he seeing beyond cracked plaster and water-stained ceilings?

Structural damage?

She hoped not.

Or was he setting her up, making her think there were major issues, so that he could buy the place cheap?

Remember when you weren't so suspicious of everyone and their motives?

Her inner self took offense at the thought and fired back, *"Yes. And look what happened."*

Trusting had brought some major consequences.

"Sounds like you have quite a family," he said as he scanned the ceiling with its rusty stains. It was obvious from his tone that he wasn't anywhere near convinced that she was here because of family issues.

Alex closed her eyes. If she didn't do something now, her contractor would quite possibly wonder about her out loud at whatever social gatherings they had in this corner of Montana. Or people would ask questions and he would mention his theories and suspicions. She didn't need that. She mentally squared her shoulders and decided to not exactly trust, but to explain in a way that might just shut him up.

"Some serious issues developed at work, which created a great deal of stress in my life and then I was assaulted in my home. I no longer felt safe, so I moved into my mother's house. However, my mother and I see eye to eye on nothing. I wanted to get away and I have. I don't want traffic traveling through my property, because it makes me nervous to think about people driving to my place in the dead of night. Thus the locked gate. It seems I'm suffering from post-attack PTSD, and this is my way of dealing with it." She had the satisfaction of seeing color rise from his collar at her blunt statements.

"I—"

"Was curious as to my story and now you know." She took a second for that to sink in, then said, "I'd appreciate it if you keep it to yourself." Which was why she'd cut loose with the truest version of the story she could handle someone in her new life knowing.

"I will."

She believed him.

But her downfall in life was always linked to believing people—her dad would take her on a father-daughter vacation, her mother would find time to attend parent-teacher conferences, her boss was setting things up so that she could buy into the business.

She'd played the chump more times than she cared to think about by believing the best of everyone, and maybe she was playing the chump again.

It was a depressing thought.

But as she stared up into Nick Callahan's dark eyes, she felt herself...believing.

She stiffened her spine. No. She wasn't going to believe. She was going to take care of herself. She'd screwed up and had to talk her way out of it. Nick Callahan may or may not spread her story—time would tell—but she wasn't going to lull herself into believing he was a good guy just because she wanted life to be easy.

She told him stuff because it seemed the best thing to do, but she needed time to process. Now. "I think you should go."

She needed to have the place to herself so that she could get a grip. Regain control.

"Do you want me to come back?"

She gave him a silent nod. She wanted him to come back.

Less than a minute later, he was in his truck, driving toward her back gate with its pathetic bicycle lock.

Alex squeezed her forehead with one hand. Hiding out was so much harder than she'd anticipated. And she wondered if she needed to be hiding at all. Lawrence Stoddard, who was more tightly connected to Jason than she was, had gotten a job, stayed in the community. She could have done the same.

But she would bet dollars to doughnuts that Lawrence hadn't suffered a break-in and an assault. That he hadn't found that someone had broken into the hiding place where she kept her good jewelry and safety-deposit box key—the only thing that had disappeared during the robbery, if she hadn't lost it earlier. She couldn't recall the last time she'd seen the key. Only that it was supposed to have been there and wasn't. Not that it mattered. The authorities had her box opened and were disappointed to find that there was no record of anyone recently accessing it, and that it contained nothing except for the documents she'd stored there for safekeeping. No hoard of cash or bearer bonds or whatever it was they'd hoped to discover.

And while she might have been vindicated, the trauma of being suspected followed by the break-in had stabbed deeply. Her mother's insistence that she just get over it and start looking for a new job hadn't helped. Running in an attempt to find a less stressful life elsewhere had been a simple response to a complex situation. Had it been a mistake?

Alex paced through the house, pausing to stare out her new front window at the neatly stacked weathered lumber that had once been her porch.

No.

She really didn't think so. Not yet, anyway.

YET ANOTHER DELAY.

But Rosalie refused to show her disappointment when, just prior to the county commission special meeting, the chairperson caught up with her in the hall and pulled her aside to say that the ecologist's report had been submitted too late for the commission to review it. Therefore, the only thing on the amended special agenda was the request for an expansion of the lumberyard parking lot.

"Are you saying it'll take another two weeks to get the answer?"

"I'm afraid so, Rosalie."

She reminded herself that showing her feelings in public wouldn't change the situation, so instead she gave the chairperson a grim smile. "If you don't have time to review the report before the next meeting, you will be hearing from my attorney."

"Now, Rosalie—"

Her name died on his lips as he took in the

expression that had caused her grandchildren to confess instantly to their transgressions on countless occasions.

"I am serious. I know, and you know, why the commission is dragging its feet. Well, the point has been made, and I believe I have made my point. I am not selling my house to *anyone*, and while he may want to punish me for that, the fact that you're allowing him to do it through you…well, that is a breach of public trust."

"Rosalie, I don't know what you're talking about."

She smiled at him. "In a pig's eye," she said in her clearest voice before turning away and marching into the meeting room to get her usual seat near the back door. She settled in, placing her purse on the floor, and only then did she notice that someone was missing. Will McGuire was not in his usual seat.

She hoped nothing was wrong. He hadn't missed one meeting since March, when Rosalie had first started to attend—not even the special agenda meetings, such as this. Some commissioners had made jokes about their permanent audience members a few meetings back, and Will's name had been mentioned.

Hmm.

Probably nothing.

Rosalie pulled out her notebook. There would be no formal okay on their bridge, but she would still take notes about the parking lot expansion, be an informed citizen… and wonder what had kept Will from the meeting. She was still wondering when she got home but could think of no logical reason why it was weighing on her so heavily… except that his presence had become something of a given and the room had seemed oddly empty without him.

Tomorrow she'd walk past the co-op and see if his truck was there at the usual coffee hours.

And if it isn't?

We'll cross that bridge when we come to it.

"WHAT'S UP?"

Katie's casual-sounding question wasn't one bit casual. Nick was well aware from the looks she'd been sending his way that it was prompted by that sibling radar both sisters had. After he'd lost Kayla, Katie had visited a lot, driving up from San Francisco to spend time with him and the girls. And when the one-year mark had ticked by and his life had settled back into a numb routine and he could make it through the day looking normal, she knew—absolutely knew—that he wasn't anywhere close to being normal. And when she'd asked and he'd insisted he was fine, she always let him know that she was there if he needed to talk.

So what was he supposed to say now? That he was conflicted about a woman that should be little more than a blip on his mental radar?

"Just thinking about the neighbor." Honesty was the best policy. It just didn't have to be total honesty.

"Alex?" she asked, in the same way he had when she'd referred to Alex as "the neighbor." "In a good way, or bad way?"

"Both."

Katie gave a half laugh. "Explain."

"Good in that she wants me to come back. Finish the job I started."

"Bad in that…"

He turned toward his sister, wiping his hands on a dish towel. "Bad in that there's something going on with her, and when I pushed her on it, she told me to leave. I'd say I've lost some ground on the access front." It'd been a stupid move, pushing her, but he'd been concerned. The woman brought out his protective instincts. And now he knew that, yes, she was running, and that Juliet Dunlop was her aunt, which explained why his deal to buy the Dunlop ranch went south, but he hadn't told Katie any of it. He'd promised Alex, and he still needed to make sense of everything.

"Maybe you shouldn't have pushed. Or maybe you should have hammered this deal out when you first had the advantage."

"You think?" he asked in an ironic tone.

"Why did you push?"

"I don't know. It was like—"

"You saw a problem and needed to fix it."

"That isn't how I am."

She made a face at him. "You are so self-aware, Nick. You really put the rest of us to shame."

Nick started slowly spinning the dish towel in a threatening way, as he'd done dozens of times as a kid, when he and Cass and Katie had engaged in dish towel snapping fights instead of washing and drying the dishes.

"Do you really want to go there?" Katie said with a gleam in her eye. Indeed, she had been the quickest of the three of them, able to snap a towel at an exposed leg or arm, then dance out of range before her victim could retaliate.

Nick let the towel go limp. "No. That would make me a poor role model."

Katie laughed. "You are a great role model. Just…don't butt into the neighbor's affairs in the future."

NICK HAD A feeling that Alex was a morning person. Both times that he'd arrived early to talk about that day's work, the coffeepot had been nearly empty, indicating that she'd been up for a while. Today he'd put his theory to the test, since the sun was just climbing over the top of the trees when he got into his truck with a big thermos of coffee and his lunch cooler.

Sure enough, Alex was in the backyard, pushing an ancient manual mower over the weeds, and, judging from the amount of territory she'd already covered, he was correct about that morning thing.

She stopped pushing as he got out of the truck and headed toward him, walking briskly, her expression businesslike. There would be no secrets shared today—and he wasn't going to push for any. He had another agenda.

"You're early." She pulled the orange flowered gloves off her hands.

"I thought we could talk before I started work."

She tilted her head, her expression carefully neutral as she waited, but he'd seen how her body had stiffened at the mention of a talk.

"I want to apologize for putting my nose into your business yesterday."

"Accepted," she said in a conversation-ending tone, but Nick wasn't done.

"It's not easy being new to a tightly knit community, especially when you have other…concerns, let's say." He'd known that this wasn't going to be an easy subject to broach, and judging from the way Alex was mentally retreating, he needed to get to the point now. "Your house needs a lot of work. You need to have someone you can trust doing that work. And you need someone you can trust to help you ease into the community. Right now you're the neurotic lady with the locked gates."

Her eyes narrowed. "Are you suggesting that someone is you?"

"Yes. I am."

"Why would you offer?"

"Because I want something."

She let out a surprised laugh. "Let me take

a guess. You want me to trust you enough to allow you to drive through my property."

"That's part of it."

"And in return you'll…?"

He leaned a shoulder against the elm tree that had lost its limb, could feel the rough bark through his T-shirt. "I'll give you a cut rate on the house repairs. All of them. Squelch any rumors I hear. Pretty much let it be known that you're A-OK."

"In return you get to use my road," she reiterated.

"The ecologist's report has been turned in to the county commission, and if all goes well, construction will start on the new bridge in a matter of weeks. I don't want to pay for the crew to go the long way day after day. It hits my pocketbook hard and it shortens the workday."

She tilted her head back and closed her eyes. She didn't want to agree to this.

"You can lock the gate in the evening, after the bridge crew goes home. They don't need to have the combination."

Her eyes popped open. "Then get up bright and early to open it again?"

Good point. "How about I'll be in charge of opening it until construction is done?"

The wind lifted long blond strands that had escaped her ponytail and blew them over her cheeks. She brushed them back. "It's been a rough couple of months, Mr. Callahan."

"I know what rough months feel like."

"Yes." She glanced down for a few seconds. "My rough doesn't compare to yours."

He was about to mouth some platitude, his usual distracting technique to avoid talking about his loss, when Alex met his gaze and said matter-of-factly, "A lot of money disappeared from the place where I worked. Along with my boss. There are people who think I'm involved."

It was on the tip of his tongue to ask "Are you?" He swallowed the words.

"I was dating my boss when it happened."

"Ah."

She met his gaze dead on. "He played me."

Nick's gut said she was being truthful, but that might be because he wanted to believe her. "And you were cleared?" As opposed to being on the run, which would explain a whole lot.

"They couldn't find any evidence that I'd been involved, but somehow, when the guy you've dated exclusively for over four months takes off with a large chunk of the company, people have a hard time believing that his girlfriend, who worked with him, didn't know. And then that ski-masked man showed up in my apartment. I don't know if it's related, but the timing suggests it was."

Nick drew in a long breath, then exhaled. He understood now why she was jumpy. Guilty or innocent, she had reason to hide herself away. "You know that anyone with a pair of bolt cutters can get past either of your locks."

Her throat moved as she swallowed. "Thus the dog. I pick him up tomorrow."

He shifted his weight, folding his arms over his chest. "I need an answer, Alex. So I can make plans. If I work on your place, I'll be here while the gate's open. You won't be alone. The gate will be locked every night. I'll handle that."

"I…" Alex let out a soft sigh, pressing her lips together as she frowned down at the ground. "What percent will you take off my repairs, and how involved are the repairs you're talking about?"

"A big percentage, and how involved do you want to get?" They'd work it out on paper if she agreed to the deal.

"We'll negotiate as we go."

"Fair enough." He unfolded his arms.

"I can cancel at any time."

He nodded in agreement. "I know this isn't easy."

"The gate *has* to be locked at night. That's my...difficult...time."

He hated the thought of her—of anyone, really—having difficulties getting through the night. He knew what it was like to lie awake, haunted by thoughts, wishes, regrets. Alex could add fear to the list. He wished he hadn't mentioned that bit about bolt cutters.

"I'll see to it."

Alex stood a little straighter, bringing her gloved hands together. Neither of them moved from where they stood.

Finally, she said, "Should we shake hands or something?"

Nick's lips twitched. "I think we're okay."

She took a small backward step. "Great. I need to get back to my mowing before it gets too hot."

"I need to get to work myself." He smiled, wishing that they both felt good about this deal. "Thank you, Alex." *I won't let anything happen to you.*

She gave a quick nod, then turned and headed back to the old mower that probably needed to be gone over. He'd see to that some other time.

Right now he had a porch to build, and later in the day he was making a run to Cooper's Building Supply. And while he was gone, he'd lock the gate for Alex's peace of mind.

CHAPTER SEVEN

ALEX'S STOMACH REMAINED in a cold, hard knot as she finished manhandling the cranky old mower over the weeds that pretended to be a back lawn. This was the first step in making the cozy backyard retreat she'd always dreamed of—one where her dog could sleep in the grass and she could relax and read—but she wasn't able to keep her mind on the matter at hand. Instead, she replayed the conversation with Nick Callahan in her head, going over the deal she'd made. It wasn't so much allowing people to drive through her place—she could live with the gate being unlocked during the day, while Nick was working on the house—but rather the fact that she'd shared more of her situation, which all of her instincts told her to hold close.

You had to tell him something.

True. And by giving him a skeletal overview, she'd set it up so that she controlled the narrative. He'd already figured that she had an issue, that she was hiding out, so what could she do but to explain the situation in the briefest way possible? Hopefully, that would be enough for him to drop the matter, fix her house and then leave her be. Stonewalling would have kept him guessing, maybe even doing a little checking of his own to make certain that she was a safe person to be around, as in not hiding from the mob or some such thing.

Maybe that was her silver lining. She wasn't hiding from the mob. She was putting distance between herself and legit investigators, who still thought she knew something, even though they had no evidence, and from whoever had broken into her house. That person had not been a legit investigator. If he had been, he'd gone rogue.

Whether the guy was rogue or not, she was hopefully two thousand miles away from him, in a place where he wouldn't come looking. Maybe he'd been a common thief, there for her jewelry and small electronics. Maybe he'd figured out where she hid her stuff, because professional thieves knew that kind of thing.

But Nick did have a point about blending

with the community. She'd messed that up. If she'd just come in and acted, well, normal, then the locals would have…what?

Forgotten about her?

Probably. But she hadn't, and the fact that Nick had offered to squelch rumors meant that she'd botched matters but good in that regard.

Okay…so this is your rebuilding phase.

Right. And after a month or two of rebuilding her local reputation, as well as her house—if no investigators or thieves showed up—she'd decide what she was going to do with her future. And in the meantime, she'd wait. Assess. Do her best to enjoy life instead of jumping at shadows. Decide if this place, which was so different from her former home, was where she wanted to put down roots.

ROSALIE WAS RELIEVED to see Will's truck parked outside the co-op when she took her morning walk, and she was also ashamed of herself for stalking him instead of simply calling his ranch to make certain everything was okay, like a concerned former neighbor might do.

The problem was that she didn't feel like

a casually concerned former neighbor, and she was too old to kid herself as to why that might be.

She was attracted to Will McGuire, and she was scared to death that he might feel the same.

It wouldn't do. Not now. Not when she was building something she'd dreamed of for years. That was where her energy needed to go—into her dream.

She'd had a happy fifty-year relationship. Fifty years. She wouldn't change a thing about it. Even though she'd never loved living on the ranch. Carl had, and he would have been miserable elsewhere. He'd been happy, so she'd been happy.

Did that make her codependent?

Not really, because his happiness was not the only satisfaction in her life related to the ranch. She'd raised her son and three grandchildren there, and they'd thrived. Even Katie, who'd been her cooking and crafting buddy because she hadn't been a natural cowboy like the rest of the family, had benefited from the ranch. To the point that she was back on the ranch, elbow-deep in herbs and loving life.

The ranch had been good.

But that part of her life was over, and she wasn't about to go back to worrying about calving and cows, rain on hay or blight in grain. Instead, she'd worry about deliveries being made on time and customer satisfaction. She'd knit and sew and quilt in her spare time, and make crafts with her great-granddaughters.

She wouldn't worry about whether the entire cattle herd was about to come down with foot rot.

Her former life was Will's current life, and she wasn't about to go back. So while she might find Will attractive, she wasn't going to do anything about it.

The co-op door opened and several men she knew emerged.

"Hi, Rosalie," Lester Granger called.

She smiled and lifted a hand in greeting. Will was the next guy out, and she also nodded to him, glad that she'd had a pep talk with herself. He headed her way, a slight hitch to his gait brought on by the day-to-day rigors of the lifestyle he'd chosen.

"You missed the county commission special meeting," she said by way of greeting. "I had a disappointment there."

"I heard."

She nodded a little too fast but told herself she was doing a decent job of acting casual, as a former neighbor would.

"I told them I expected an answer next meeting or else."

"Let's hope it's the answer you want."

Her expression sobered. "If not, I will seek advice from my attorney."

"The good-old-boy network can be a hard thing to work around."

"What do you call what goes on in there?" she asked as she pointed at the co-op building with her chin.

Will smiled, his teeth white against his tanned skin, and Rosalie felt something shift inside her. Will smiled so rarely, and when he did, it transformed his face. His whole being, really.

"I'd offer you a ride to your house, but I think I know what the answer would be," he said.

"I like to walk."

"And to stand on your own two feet."

He was referring to the things she'd told him right here at the co-op when she'd explained rather forcefully that if she wanted assistance, she would ask for it. "That, too."

He smiled again and then touched his hat.

"I have an appointment, but it's good seeing you, Rosalie."

"You, too, Will."

She bit her lip as he headed to his truck, then turned and continued toward her house, walking a bit more briskly than usual, needing to expend the energy that seemed to have pooled inside her during her conversation with Will.

It had been good to talk to him in a casual and neighborly way, because that was the relationship she wanted to have with the man. Casual and neighborly.

Because at this point in her life, she was staying on paved streets.

"EVERYTHING CAME IN," Emmie said when Nick walked into the office of Cooper's Building Supply. "Even the newels that they didn't think they had. Lucas has the odds and ends on a pallet out back. The newels are in bay two."

"Great." He nodded a greeting at the other woman standing at the counter, Jenna Hayes, who did Emmie's books. Her twin sister, Reggie, had been brokering the real-estate deal between him and Juliet Dunlop before

Alex came into the picture—another reason Emmie might have picked on Alex.

"How's it going, Nick?" She adjusted her glasses as she gave him a smile. The glasses were the only way to tell the Murray twins apart when they wore the same haircut.

"Can't complain. Brady will be back just in time to do the heavy lifting on the ranch, so I can continue taking jobs on the side." He read over the invoice Emmie printed out and slid across the counter, then signed his name. Emmie tore off the bottom copy and handed it to him.

"Your new neighbor is settling in okay, then?" Jenna asked with just a little too much concern.

"She's doing fine," Nick said.

"Reggie thinks the whole deal was a little screwy. First one thing was happening— that would be you buying the house," she explained helpfully, "and then *wham bam*. You're out, and this gate-locking chick is in."

Nick let out a breath. Part of his deal with Alex was that he would tamp down rumors. He looked first at Jenna, then at Emmie. "This is confidential, okay?"

Both women nodded.

"My new neighbor was mugged before she

moved here and is still suffering from the trauma. Thus the locked gate and not wanting anyone to drive through her property. She's nervous, okay? But she's loosening up."

Jenna tilted her head, a sympathetic expression on her face. "Well," she said softly. "That explains a lot. But it doesn't explain the screwy real-estate deal."

"I can't explain that, either." Or rather, he wouldn't. "But here's the thing. I can live with it."

"Reggie is still out her commission."

"That bites," he agreed. "But I think that's more on Juliet Dunlop than on this new buyer."

Jenna nodded, but she wasn't agreeing with him. Her brain was working, and that was never a good thing if that brain happened to be working against you. Jenna was the kind who took calculus for fun. He knew—he'd seen her do it.

"I'll head out and help Lucas load," Nick said, patting the counter. Because he knew better than to protest too much. He just hoped that Jenna and Reggie would be able to let the lost commission go. It was part of being a real-estate agent. But losing dollars hurt no matter what, and Alex was an easy target to blame.

ALEX WHEELED HER car through the gates of the Rescue Society and parked next to the office, thankful that Nick had finished the fence and that she could finally pick up Gus, her foster dog. With the gates open and traffic ready to drive through, she was going to appreciate the added sense of security a dog would bring.

She had one of Juliet's old blankets spread on the back seat to protect the leather from canine toenails and a new harness and leash sitting on the seat beside her. A ripple of excitement went through her as she got out of the car, leash in hand.

This was it. Companionship. Protection. Affection. No more nights alone wondering whether the creaking was something to worry about or just the house doing old house stuff.

Alex headed into the office and was met by a trio of tabby cats sitting side by side on the desk where she'd filled out her application form several days ago.

"Hello?"

"Just one minute," Wanda called from the back, setting off a new round of barking.

The cats blinked at Alex simultaneously,

then one lifted a paw and began licking it in the most casual way.

"I'm here to get a dog," Alex explained to the cats, who blinked at her again.

All three cats gave a start at the sound of a kennel opening, followed by toenails on concrete. "Roger! Roger, no."

After a brief scuffle, Alex heard the kennel shut again, and a few seconds later Wanda appeared leading the gentle giant that was to be Alex's new dog. She immediately knelt, and the golden retriever mix ambled up to lean his head against her arm. A blood-curdling howl from the rear of the building made her back snap straight. She looked at Wanda, who rolled her eyes.

Another howl sounded, followed by the sound of nails desperately digging at concrete.

"Roger, calm down," Wanda called in a weary voice. She was answered by a howl that sounded like a cry of pain.

"What is that?" Alex got back to her feet, shooting an alarmed look toward the kennel area on the opposite side of the cinder-block wall.

"That is Roger." Wanda gave a glance

over her shoulder as the digging continued. "Roger is Gus's best friend."

"And I'm going to separate them?"

"Sweetie, it beats the alternative."

"You mean keeping them together?" A heartrending howl reverberated through the room.

"Yes."

No explanation. Just yes.

"Can I see him?"

Wanda shook her head. "Roger has issues."

Yes. He was losing his best friend.

"What kind of issues?"

"Well, for one thing, he has separation anxiety. For another, he's an escape artist."

"Did he and Gus come in together?"

"Oh, heavens no. But they bonded when Gus first came in. Gus was in a state of depression after losing his owner, and Roger demanded that they share a kennel." Wanda frowned at Alex's disbelieving expression. "Roger has been here for almost a year. I pretty much understand everything he says."

"That makes sense." Even if it sounded a little out there.

Gus moved closer to her and sat, leaning his weight against her leg in a comforting way. Then he glanced up at her with sad brown eyes. He didn't want to leave his friend behind any more than Roger wanted to be left.

"Maybe I could foster Roger, too." As another heartrending cry echoed through the building, she knew she had to do something.

Wanda gave her a look that clearly said she didn't think Alex would be able to deal with Roger, which in turn made her all the more determined. For the past several weeks, she'd focused on nothing but herself. Her needs. Her fears. It wasn't healthy.

"I'm afraid he'll get away and go back to roaming the country," Wanda said grimly.

"Do you think he'd leave Gus?"

The older woman's lips pressed together. "I don't know."

"Could we give it a try?" It occurred to her that she was working hard to bring trouble into her life, but this was a different kind of trouble. Positive trouble, if there was such a thing.

"Do you have a photo of the fence?" Wanda asked in a resigned voice.

Alex dug her phone out of her pocket and brought up photos of the fence that Wanda had inspected personally the day before.

"Nick built a barrier into the ground to

keep a dog from digging out," she added helpfully.

Wanda glanced up. "Did he add something to keep the dog from climbing the fence?"

"Roger climbs?"

"He does."

Alex wavered, thinking that maybe it was best if she headed home with the perfect, trouble-free dog who was already looking at her as if she was some sort of a hero, when another cry came from the back kennel and all but crawled up her spine. Wanda stiffened, too.

"Please let me try. A week. If he gets out... well, he won't," Alex promised recklessly.

"Maybe you should see him first," Wanda said. "I'm not trying to keep Roger from having a home. I'm trying to reduce the stress on Gus. Leaving his buddy here is different from having his buddy leave the new home they share."

"Maybe there won't be any stress on Gus. Maybe Roger will become part of my family."

"Very well," Wanda said on a sigh. "Follow me."

Roger turned out to be a cartoon of a dog. A scruffy little terrier mix with bat-like ears that lifted in the most comical way when Gus lumbered back into the kennel area. He started yipping, turning circles and doing little barrel rolls.

Alex couldn't help laughing.

"It's not so funny when he does those things just out of arm's reach when you're trying to catch him," Wanda warned.

Gus's tail hit Alex's leg with a slow *whump, whump* as he went to the kennel fence and pressed his nose against the chain link.

Alex looked at Wanda. "Do I need to fill out another form?"

"Yes. For my files." She let out a long breath. "I really hope this works out, but Roger should go to an experienced dog handler."

"There doesn't seem to be any of them lining up to offer him a home."

"Good point." Wanda opened the kennel and Roger shot out like a scruffy rocket, scrambling around Gus as the big dog gave him a few nudges with his head. "I'll have to lend you a collar and leash."

"I'll get them back to you next week."

Without Roger wearing them, she hoped.

"Do you want a cat?" Wanda asked absently as she pulled a notebook out from

under one of the triplet tabbies, who in return gave her a glare.

"Maybe next visit?"

Wanda lifted an eyebrow. "If you have any
trouble with Roger, any trouble at all, call."

"I will," Alex promised, crossing the fingers on the hand that held Gus's leash. If
she had any trouble with Roger, she would
deal, unless it was some major issue, like him
climbing a fence and disappearing.

GUS RODE HOME in the back seat of the car,
staring out the window in a dignified way.
Roger spent the drive ricocheting between
front seat and back, scrambling over the console to check on Gus, then scrambling back
into the front to ride shotgun and watch the
oh-so-interesting scenery pass by. He barely
looked at Alex.

Trust issues. She understood. She had a
few herself.

Her big hope was that he wouldn't feel
the need to escape her yard and leave Gus
behind. Gus, she hoped, would be his anchor. Anchors were good. She wished she
had one. Maybe this house was her anchor.
This wreck of a house that could be a home.

If she didn't keep it, she would sell to Nick

Callahan, which was what he wanted. He wanted access to his ranch, but more than that, he wanted friendly relations so that if and when she sold, he would be in the running. Or so she deduced.

And she was certain she was right.

Alex might have been overly trusting of Jason, but recent events had cured her of making that mistake again. Not that she'd been particularly naive concerning Jason; he'd groomed her, eased her into trusting him more than she should. She couldn't say that she'd fallen in love with him, but she'd liked him. A lot.

And then he'd absconded with the company funds and left her, his guilty-looking girlfriend, to deal with the fallout.

Roger perched himself on the console, balancing as she rounded a corner, then, assured that all was well in the back seat, turned to the front, staring straight ahead, his warm little body only three or four inches from her arm.

An overture? A test?

She didn't know, so she murmured, "Good boy, Roger," before slowing for the turn into the driveway. When she got out to unlock the gate, she was careful not to let Roger have a means of escape, but he showed no interest in leaving Gus.

Excellent. She hoped the attitude stuck. She did not want to confess to Wanda that she'd lost her charge after being so adamant that she wouldn't. Yes, she was a dog rookie in many regards, but she really wanted the situation with the little terrier to work out.

Once home, she led Roger into the house, then returned to the car for Gus, who nudged her with his nose before lumbering out of the vehicle. He looked up at her with those trusting brown eyes, then ambled beside her through the front gate and up the porch steps. Roger's head appeared at the window, disappeared, appeared again. The dog had springs in his feet.

"You two are quite the pair," she said. "Let me show you your bed and your dish." The singular would have to become plural, since she had a bonus dog.

She'd bought a bed for Gus and a big ceramic dog dish at the local general store, but now she had to improvise for Roger. One of Juliet's ramekins with the mushrooms on the side and an old pillowcase stuffed with rags would do until she had a chance to visit Gavin again.

"What do you think, boys?"

One of her boys thought it was prime time for a nap. Gus flopped onto the floor next to his new bed rather than in it, thus bringing a frown to Alex's face, while Roger commenced exploring. Alex watched as Roger snuffled his way into the dining room; when he disappeared from view, she went to the sink to fill the kettle. The energy of her house had shifted. Life was no longer all about her and her fears and anxieties. And by fostering dogs, she'd locked herself into a future where she had partners to consider when making choices. Partners who wouldn't sell her out or do her wrong. Roger might not acknowledge her, but he wouldn't do her wrong.

She was sure of it.

As NICK LEFT his truck and headed for Alex's back door to discuss the most pressing house issues, he was welcomed by a duet of deep rumbling barks and high-pitched yips. Either Alex's new dog had a dual personality, or she had two dogs.

He raised his hand to knock as one of the dogs started scratching furiously at the floor on the other side of the door. Then, before his hand connected with wood, the door swung open and Alex held back a small dog with her foot as she quickly ushered him inside. Once the door was closed behind him, a stately golden retriever gave him the once-over before ambling up for a pet, but it was the smaller dog that stood stiffly to the side that caught his attention.

"Roger?"

Alex shot him a surprised look. "You know him?"

He crouched low and held out a hand. Roger looked at him suspiciously. "Well, you know how it is in a small town. Everyone knows everyone."

"Right," she said dryly.

Nick stood up again and the big golden-brown dog thumped his tail on the floor. "You're fostering two dogs."

A wry smile curved Alex's lips, and there was something about seeing her smile as if she was in on a joke that made Nick feel like a barrier was starting to come down. "I hadn't planned on getting two. Wanda didn't want to let me have two, but here we are. Roger adopted Gus, and he threw a fit at being left behind."

"So you took him."

"I did." She settled a hand on Gus's head. "How do you know Roger?"

"His owner lived in the house next to the one my grandmother bought. The guy moved and left him behind."

"That's so cold."

"Roger kept looking for his owner. He traveled between the house and the office where the guy worked. He refused to let anyone near him. Dog on a mission."

"I hope he'll stay with me because of Gus, and I hope that he'll warm up to me eventually. He's slow to trust."

"That happens when you get burned."

"Yes."

The heavily ironic note in her voice reminded him of why she was slow to trust. The guy she'd dated had stolen from the company and, as near as he could figure, left her holding the bag.

"I'll put these guys into my very secure backyard so that you can work."

"Before I forget, my grandmother is driving through to the ranch today. Red SUV." Until she was familiar with who drove what, he'd fill her in on the comings and goings of his family and, hopefully soon, the bridge crew. "And... I told Emmie at the building supply that you had a mugging incident in your past and that was why the gate was locked."

Alex gave him a cautious look followed by a works-for-me shrug. "That's not far from the truth."

"I won't say anything else, but it seemed best to throw something out there for people to chew on. I just thought you should know."

"Thank you." She appeared to mean it.

Alex opened the back door and Gus lumbered out. Roger gave Nick one last suspicious look, then trotted after his big friend. He instantly spotted a black-and-white bird on the opposite side of the yard and charged after it. The bird took to the air and Roger skidded to a stop, staring after it as if to say, "Next time will be different, Mr. Magpie."

Alex shook her head, and when Nick smiled at her, she gave a comical grimace in return.

"I've probably gotten myself into a situation, but how could I leave the little guy behind?"

"Apparently you couldn't."

She was different today. Less guarded, more open. Because of the dogs? Or maybe because of their talk yesterday? Whichever, he liked this new side of Alex.

He tamped the thought down before asking, "Are you okay about the gate?" He'd already opened it so that his grandmother could drive through. She and Katie were working on some summer wreaths and welcome signs using ranching odds and ends.

"I am. It seems I have bad nights even when the gate is safely locked, so…" She gave an eloquent shrug.

"I know about those nights," he said. She'd told him something of her life; he'd tell her something of his. "My youngest daughter has trouble sleeping sometimes." He couldn't bring himself to say that she had night terrors, because he still felt it was somehow his fault. "I spend a lot of time up late at night after she wakes me. Thinking too much."

"What do you think about?"

"Parenting." He said the word lightly, but his thoughts on the matter were anything but. He wasn't about to confess that he worried about messing up, and filling voids. That he worried about filling the roles of two parents. Katie and Rosalie helped fill the mother role now that he'd moved home, but he still worried. Wondered. Prayed that his girls felt secure and loved and that he'd be there when they needed him.

"Big responsibility."

"Yes." Nick swallowed, not certain where to go from there conversationally. Seconds ticked by and then he said, "I'll get started on the porch. Before I leave this afternoon, we can talk about the house and make a priority list."

"Need help?"

He shot her a surprised look. "I'm used to working alone."

"Just thought I'd offer, in case you needed someone to hold an end or something." She spoke stiffly, and Nick let out a silent sigh. She'd made an overture and he'd accidentally squelched it.

"You know, if I do need help, I'll give a shout."

She gave a businesslike nod. "I have some sorting to do upstairs. So just...yell."

"Will do."

Nick let himself out the front door, carefully stepping onto the tilting porch floor that he'd bolt to the house again after jacking it into a level position. He felt oddly tense. Because he was seeing Alex differently? Because of the uncomfortable silence that had brought back memories of awkward teen encounters with the opposite sex?

Both?

Yes.

Nick put his head down and strode to the truck to get his tools. He'd handle this the way that he handled all stressful situations—by losing himself in his work. And he would not be calling Alex to help him.

CHAPTER EIGHT

ALEX HAD TWO dogs in her backyard and a man she couldn't stop thinking about working on her porch. As she dragged the last of the storage boxes to the middle of the floor, she ticked off the reasons she really should stop thinking about him. She was in a tenuous position. Nick was a single father. He stayed awake at night worrying about parenting, which suggested that he wouldn't want to do anything that had the potential to disrupt his daughters' security. Like, say, getting involved with the woman next door.

Get involved. Get real.

It was, of course, highly unlikely that her next beau would set her up to take the blame for a major embezzlement; however, she still didn't fully trust her gut, even if the guy pounding around downstairs appeared to be the picture of integrity and dependability.

Alex pulled the lid off the box, determined not to think about Nick Callahan for at least a minute or two, and moved aside the tissue that covered the contents.

Dear heavens...

Alex picked an intricately pieced quilt top out of the box and unfolded it. The work was amazing in detail. Postage-stamp-sized squares formed a pixelated picture of what appeared to be flowers. Alex got to her feet, and after laying the quilt top carefully on the floor she'd spent a good hour scrubbing the day before, she backed across the room. The riotous floral bouquet came into focus. Alex realized her mouth had fallen open and closed it again.

Alex went back to the box and pulled out two more quilt tops—a mountain scene and a sunrise over rolling hills, the latter only partially finished.

Juliet had *a lot* of talent, but she also flitted from interest to interest, throwing herself into her passions with laser focus, only to lose interest and move on to the next best thing. Her marriages had been similar, except that she had a penchant for choosing men who had money to share.

At the bottom of the storage container was a flat cardboard box, which held several pieces of intricate lace rolled over cardboard tubing. Another of Juliet's talents? Or had she simply purchased these pieces and stored them away? Alex unrolled one piece and made a *tsk* noise with her tongue when she spotted the stain on one edge. She lightly fingered the rusty area, wondering if there was a professional cleaning service in the area that specialized in delicate jobs.

Carefully she rolled the lace back over the tube and began folding the floral quilt top. Perhaps she could hire someone to finish the quilts so that she could display them or actually use them to cover beds. The colorful pieced tops were energizing, and it struck Alex that perhaps this was what she needed to dispel the aura of neglect and decay that seemed to permeate her old house. Maybe she needed color in addition to repairs.

Alex set the tissue on top of the quilt tops, then closed the lid on the container. She'd never really used color before, having grown up with off-white walls, polished wood, neutral colors. Her mother's idea of a pop of color was a few pale rose-colored accents here and there. The house was beautiful with its subdued color scheme, and Alex had, without giving the matter much thought, chosen neutral and muted colors herself when she decorated. And when she dressed. Even the flannel shirt she wore was a muted plaid.

Sitting back on her heels, Alex considered the room, wondering why Juliet, who obviously adored color, hadn't gone a little wild herself. The interior of the house was painted almost the same color as the interior of her mother's house.

Maybe her husband hadn't liked the idea of painting the rooms bright colors. Or perhaps Juliet liked to use the neutral walls as a backdrop for colorful artwork and accents. Alex recalled a number of bright paintings adorning the walls. Yes. That was probably it. The next time she talked to Juliet, she'd ask her.

After stowing the box away, Alex went to the bathroom to run a bucket of soapy water. The floors were a mess, with built-up dirt in the cracks between floorboards—the kind of dirt that required a scrub brush rather than a mop.

Before tackling the floor in the last upstairs bedroom, Alex went to the window overlooking the backyard to check on her dogs and to make certain that Roger was still there.

He was. Lying on his back in the grass, all four feet in the air as Gus took lazy fake bites at his tummy, poking him with his nose as he closed his teeth on air. Yes, Roger was still there, and Alex was glad she'd brought him home. His owner had broken his commitment to the little dog, and now Roger needed stability.

And you're not going to break your commitment?

Different commitment. She'd agreed to foster dogs, not adopt.

Like Roger and Gus will understand that.

Alex pushed her hair back from her forehead as she stepped away from the window. If she stayed, she'd adopt. The question was *would* she stay. Only time could answer that one.

Alex got onto her knees and dunked the scrub brush into the bucket and then started scrubbing away, the brush making a rhythmic scratching sound as it moved over the floorboards.

Working her way backward from the far corner to the door, Alex scrubbed, dragging the bucket along with her. She was halfway across the room when a yell from outside the house startled her into dropping the brush. Dirty water splashed onto her shirt, but she barely registered the yuck factor as

Nick once again yelled her name, his voice strained.

Alex raced down the stairs, taking them two at a time. When she reached the living room, she could see Nick straining his body against a steel bar, struggling to pry… something…upward.

As soon as he saw her through the glass of the newly installed window, he called out, "Go out through the back door."

Out the back door she went, startling the dogs, thus giving her time to get through the side gate and close it again before either of them considered following her.

When she got to the front of her house, she instantly saw the problem. Nick had been supporting the porch base with jacks, and somehow one of them had slipped. He was now single-handedly holding up one corner of the porch with the steel bar, one end of which was levered into the dirt under the porch.

"Can you get the jack back under that corner?" he asked through gritted teeth.

Alex knew nothing about jacks, but she grabbed the implement and set it upright like the one holding up the other corner.

"See if you can shove it under that joist,

but if I say to get clear, then get out of the way quickly."

"Got it." This was no time for performance anxiety. This was a do-or-die situation. Alex bit her lip as she struggled to get the jack back in place. Nick let out a low groan as he shoved on the bar, prying the edge of the porch up just high enough for her to get the job done.

Gently, he lowered the bar. The porch settled onto the jacks and he let out a long breath, dropping the bar with a heavy thud and planting his hands on his thighs as he fought to catch his breath.

"When I said just yell, this isn't what I meant. How did this happen?"

"I thought I could snug the porch up closer to the house with the bar, but the jack shifted, and next thing I know, I'm holding up the corner. If I dropped it, then I'd be rebuilding the whole thing from scratch."

"I think I'll help you for a while," she said. He started to respond, then apparently thought better of it when she gave him a look. "I'm tired of working inside."

She could scrub floors anytime. Right now she wanted to be outside with her contractor and make certain he didn't get himself into trouble again.

"You'll need your gloves."

"I'll go get them, but you have to promise not to knock the porch down while I'm gone."

The corners of his mouth twitched, but he didn't smile.

As soon as Alex disappeared around the house, Nick blew out an audible breath and then studied the porch that had almost done itself in due to its own weight and a poor decision on his part. He rubbed the shoulder that had put most of the work into keeping the thing from destroying itself. He'd taken a chance. Gambled. Lost.

Almost lost.

Thanks to Alex not freaking out or asking questions. She'd done as he'd asked…and now he had a helper.

Was she afraid that he'd stupidly get himself in trouble again? Or did she want some human contact?

Nick reached down into the cooler he'd stashed under the old elm tree that had caused the damage he was now repairing and pulled out his water bottle. He took a

long drink as noises came from the back-
yard. The house door opening and closing.
The scramble of canine toenails on the steps.
Then "Roger, no. Good boy. Stay back."

The side gate opened and then banged
shut, and Nick put his bottle back in the
cooler. Alex came around the house, orange
flowery gloves on her hands and a sheepish
look on her face. "That's one fast little dog."

"But I see that you're alone."

She smiled, and he felt the impact, the
warming sensation deep in his gut, the sense
of a tenuous connection. He liked Alex without all those barriers up. And maybe he liked
the idea of working with her today.

"What's the plan?" She came to a stop a
few feet away from him, bringing her hands
together in a let's-get-it-done gesture. He
pointed at the porch.

"We're going to bolt the porch back to
the house, then replace the newels and start
building the roof. I don't think I can match
the roofing exactly, but I can come close."

"I'm good with that."

He looked back at her. "The proper thing
to do would be to reroof the entire house. It
leaks."

"I know. My first night here, when I was

wondering what I'd gotten myself into, it was raining, and after I got into bed, there it was—a nice, slow drip. Drip. Drip."

"Just enough to keep you awake?"

"Trust me. I wasn't going to sleep." She followed him as he went to the porch and picked up his drill. "Did you know that when you sleep in a strange place, there's a part of your mind that doesn't relax? It's hyper-vigilant."

"I didn't know that, but it explains why I can never sleep in motels."

"Yeah. Me, either." Alex put her hands on her hips. "What do you want me to do?"

His gaze slid from the earnest expression in her eyes to the soft curve of her lips, and a thought that had no business in his head struck him hard and fast, like a thunderbolt.

"I…"

She titled her head, her expression openly curious, making him feel like a jerk. This was not a woman who trusted easily, yet here she was trusting him, and he was thinking about kissing her.

Except that she was looking back at him in a way that set his nerves humming, making him wonder just what she was thinking about.

Oh, man.

"To begin with, why don't you just hang with me, hand me stuff when I ask for it. Then after the porch is bolted on—"

"You'll come up with something to keep me busy?"

His smile broke through on that one. "I need to assess your skill level."

"Novice."

"Then we'll start by handing tools. How are you on a ladder?"

"Fearless."

"You sound certain."

"I used a ladder more than once to climb to the top of the caretaker's house, jump to the roof of my dorm and climb in through a window."

"College?"

"Boarding school. Upper elementary. It was common practice when we wanted to swim after dark or some such thing. I was not a big rule breaker, but sneaking out at night was pretty much the norm."

"You went to boarding school?"

She gave a casual shrug, but her carefree attitude became a touch more self-conscious, as if she'd suddenly become aware of the cultural gap between them.

"I went to public school," he said, crouching down to take a look at the job ahead of him. "Kindergarten through high school."

"Then college."

"Cal Poly."

"Impressive."

"I'll just bet your college was equally impressive," he said. She didn't answer, but when he glanced over his shoulder at her, she was half smiling, her expression once again relaxed.

"Do you need a tool yet?"

"Almost." He eased his way under the porch.

"You know that this makes me nervous after what just happened."

"Well, since there isn't a big lunkhead levering the corner of the porch up off the jack, everything is fine."

"If you say so." There was a touch of amusement in her voice.

"I do." He crawled out from under the porch. "I won't need much tool handing for this job, but when we start putting in newels and building the roof, I will."

To his surprise, she held out a hand, so he took it as he got to his feet. And the crazy thing was that he could feel the warmth of her palm through those silly gloves.

She cocked her head at him. "I'll stand back and supervise during this phase of operations. You know…make sure you don't accidentally bring everything down on top of you."

He tucked his thumbs into his front pockets, looking down at her. "It's going to take me a while to live that down, isn't it?"

"Maybe a little." She smiled, making a dimple show near the corner of her mouth, and Nick felt another gut punch of attraction.

This could turn out to be one interesting project.

"THE NEIGHBOR ADOPTED little Roger?" Katie said as she put the finishing touches on a salad. "I have to meet this woman."

Nick looked up from where he was cutting onions to fry for the top of the hamburgers. "He was kind of an add-on to the dog she intended to foster."

"A poochie plus one?" Katie asked. She went to the fridge and moved items around to make room for the salad until dinnertime.

"That sums it up."

"Well, I'm glad Roger found a home. Remember how many times animal control came by Grandma's house trying to nab him?"

"Yes. Roger was that poor guy's white whale."

Nick laughed. The dogcatcher had taken not being able to catch Roger personally after weeks of near misses. The terrier had spent the night in the bushes near the empty house next to Rosalie's after she and Gloria had first moved in. They'd taken to feeding him, but he was a crafty little canine and would eat only after the animal-control man went off shift. By morning, he was long gone, roaming the streets of town, looking for the jerk who'd abandoned him.

"I'm glad Wanda got him first, so that he went to the no-kill rescue instead of to the pound."

Wanda didn't work by the clock, so she was able to trap him after hours with a nice, juicy chunk of meat set in a small portable enclosure.

"He's pretty attached to the golden retriever, so yeah. Happy ending. Unless Alex leaves the area."

"Then what?"

Yes. Then what? "She's fostering the dogs rather than adopting."

"Ah. Well, easy fix. She leaves, we adopt."

He gave his sister the eye. Katie had long been a rescuer of anything with four legs— or two. She'd nursed her fair share of injured birds back to health.

"And it begins."

Katie laughed. "I promised Brady that I wouldn't overload the place with orphaned animals, so I give money to the rescue society when I can. But—" she wrinkled her nose at him "—this is a special case. Right?"

"Probably."

And he didn't like the idea of Alex leaving before he got to know her. For the first time since meeting Kayla, he was looking at another woman with interest and curiosity. He wasn't certain how to handle the situation, but he figured he'd work his way through it. The only given was that his daughters would not be affected by anything he did in his adult non-daddy life. That part of it he'd have to figure out as he went along.

"So when can I meet her? The new neighbor."

He frowned at his sister. "I'm not in charge

of that." He finished the onions and slid a pan onto the stove, pouring in oil to warm.

"You like her, don't you?"

"She's okay." No sense getting all enthusiastic about his response—not when his bloodhound of a sister was homing in on the scent.

"Okay?" Katie said on an amused note. "You sound like a teenage boy who's been asked about his crush."

Nick gave her a look. "I'm getting to know her. She's getting to know me, but it's strictly a working relationship."

"Ah." Katie said the word a little too lightly.

"No *ah*," he muttered. He gave his sister a look. "I don't need you butting into my business."

Katie laughed, unfazed by his stern answer. "Yeah. Just like you didn't have a hand in trying to get me and Brady together."

"That's different."

"How?" she asked on an incredulous note.

"I knew Brady was staying, no matter what he said he was going to do. As to Alex… I'm pretty sure that she's going to leave."

"And we'll buy the property."

"Yeah." But somehow, while owning the

property was important, it didn't seem as important as it'd been less than a week ago.

Katie pulled out a drawer and dug through it, pulling out a pair of salad tongs.

"I heard from Cassie while you were gone," she said in the conversational voice she used when dropping a bombshell.

"Finally." Their sister was a school district administrator in a small Wisconsin town, and, ever the overachiever, had the bad habit of immersing herself in her work. It wasn't unusual for weeks to pass with no contact. "Has she been hospitalized for exhaustion?"

"Probably close to it. She's determined to solve every problem in her district single-handedly, and the fact that it's summer isn't slowing her down one bit. But she plans to visit before the new school year starts."

"I will believe it when I see it." Because despite Cassie's good intentions, it seemed that something always came up and her visits got pushed back until they were no longer on her calendar.

"I think Grandma chewed on her for missing Christmas with the family this past year, so she's going to make it home this time."

"Once again, I'll believe it when I see it."

Katie gave a small shrug. "She'll make it home for Christmas no matter what."

"I'll give you that one." Cassie wouldn't miss a visit from their dad, who'd emigrated to Australia five years ago after marrying a fellow veterinarian who had a practice there. They all missed him, but he was so happy with his new wife and new life, that seeing him only once a year seemed a reasonable tradeoff. Unlike Cassie, he wrote the occasional newsy email, so in that regard, they heard from their dad on the other side of the world more often than they heard from their sister who lived on the same continent.

"Hey," Katie said softly. "You know Cassie isn't purposely distancing herself."

"I know, but I also think she hasn't figured out what's important in life." Or how fragile life is.

"Not our call."

Nick smiled a little as he stirred the onions which were beginning to sizzle. "I'll give you that one, too." But he wished his sister would realize that crises were going to keep coming in her chosen profession, so she may as well take her vacation days when she was supposed to.

"By the way," Katie asked, expertly shifting the subject. "Are you serious about adopting the dogs if the new neighbor moves?"

"I am." If it came to that, he'd give Roger and Gus a home.

Katie beamed. "Good."

"ALEX, NO ONE IS looking for you. Come home."

Alex pushed her hand up into her hair and put pressure on her head as she fought to keep her tone neutral. It was not unusual for her and her mother to go for months at a time with no contact, and now she could count on a call every couple of days. And it wasn't because her mom was concerned about her. Or, if she was, it wasn't the top reason on her list for making contact.

"I have two dogs, Mom."

There was a deathly silence followed by "Please tell me you are pet sitting."

"Not pet sitting. I wanted companionship."

"Then join a club. Oh, yes, that's right, you can't join a club because someone might learn your name."

Just what she needed. Her mother belittling her situation. But as always, the situation was all about Cécile.

"Lawrence—"

"Attends to matters in his way, which isn't

my way." She did not need to hear again about how Jason's little brother was successfully weathering the storm surrounding his brother and the missing money. "Tell people that I took a job on the West Coast. No one would fault me for moving for a job."

"If you hadn't disappeared the second they dropped the investigation."

Her mother was like a pit bull. Once she clamped down on something, she was not letting go.

"Nobody cares, Mom."

"You haven't been to my sorority meetings."

"Like those women have perfect lives, perfect relatives."

"None of their relatives are possible felons."

"Thanks for the vote of confidence." Alex was rarely snarky with her mother, but something had shifted. Suddenly, the little girl in her no longer cared about pleasing her mother. The little girl wondered why her mother wasn't more concerned about supporting her in her time of need.

"Alexandra." The chill in her mother's voice used to bring her to her knees, but Alex was done with that.

"Mom." She echoed her mother's tone and could easily visualize her mother blinking, as she did when she didn't get the response she anticipated. "I have to go. Goodbye."

And then she hung up the phone and turned it off.

It was the first time she could remember ending a call instead of waiting for her mother to decide she'd spoken long enough. Her heart was beating faster than usual, because, as always, she felt as if she'd just completed an exhausting fencing duel after speaking with her mother. She was about to get up and walk off the tension when Roger crossed the room and threw himself down close to her feet. Then his little chin worked its way onto her sneaker.

Alex froze at the contact, half-afraid that the dog would retreat again if she moved. But Roger had staked out his territory, and after a few seconds, Alex allowed herself to relax back into the cushions. It was amazing how comforting that little furry chin felt as it pressed down on the top of her shoe.

Gus ambled in from the kitchen, where he liked to nap in front of the fridge, apparently realizing that he was missing a bonding opportunity. He padded across the room, laid his chin on Alex's thigh long enough to get a pet and an ear scratch, then flopped down next to Roger, his big body pressing up against her leg.

That clinched it. She wasn't going to be moving for a while. For the first time in forever, with one dog holding down her shoe, and the other pressed against her leg, she felt content to just sit and be.

NICK FOUND HIMSELF whistling as he undid the useless bike lock from Alex's back gate. He could give Alex another couple of uninterrupted days before he had things to take care of on the ranch. Brady would return in two weeks, and then, with the exception of the really busy times—fence building, branding, et cetera—he'd be free to put his time into building.

He'd already received a few inquiries, directed to him by Emmie at the building supply, and it looked as though the summer months would be full after he completed Alex's projects. The summer may well be full if all he focused on was Alex's projects, but he didn't yet know the extent of her renovation plans. He got the idea that all she wanted to do was to shore up the old house so that rain didn't seep through the roofing and the plumbing didn't leak. If so, fine.

She was in the backyard with the dogs when he drove in, and as he approached the side gate, he saw that she was playing a game with Roger. The little terrier had his teeth clamped around an old bicycle inner tube, and Alex was tugging at him as he growled and jumped his butt backward. Gus watched, a canine smile on his face.

"Morning," she called as she gave one last tug, then released the tube. Roger proudly trotted across the yard, dragging black rubber behind him, and hid his treasure behind a lilac bush.

"Looks like you and Roger have made friends."

She smoothed the hair away from her face with one hand. "Yes. He took pity on me last night after I talked to my mom on the phone."

"Bad news?"

"Oh, no," she said lightly. "Just a normal mother call. Fraught with stress. You know. The usual."

Actually he didn't, because his family didn't work that way. Yes, they had their fraught moments, but it wasn't the usual. "Everything okay?"

"She wants me to come home. I don't want to go." She motioned with her head toward the house. "I have coffee, if you'd like a cup before we go over the plans for the house."

"Coffee sounds great," Nick said, ignoring the fact that he had brought his largest thermos to get him through the day. Sometimes coffee was more than coffee.

Alex smiled at him and led the way to the back door. Roger jumped to his feet, as if afraid of missing something—or perhaps he was already afraid of Alex leaving him. He trotted to the door and Alex held it open, waiting for him to go inside before entering the house herself. Gus seemed content to lay in the grass, but Alex left the door open so that she could see him through the old-fashioned wood-framed screen door.

Nick waited until she'd poured coffee into handmade ceramic mugs before saying, "Let's start with your renovation budget. How much do you want to spend?"

"Let me answer that with a question. What are the essentials that need taken care of and how much will they cost?" Roger had settled under the table, close to Alex's feet, and was keeping a close eye on Nick, as if expecting him to snag Alex away from him at any second.

"We can patch the roof instead of reroofing. The plumbing is going to be your biggest expense."

"Let's start with that—patching the roof and fixing the plumbing. I'll need a written estimate."

"Of course."

A brief silence fell between them, then Alex said, "My aunt Juliet didn't have much of a reputation in these parts, did she?"

Nick sucked in a breath. He could be tactful, or truthful. Not both. "Juliet took old Dunlop to the cleaners, then left him when he needed her."

"That's par for the course," she said on a sigh.

"Will she do the same to you?"

"Maybe, but she's helped me out thus far, so I'm hoping for the best." When Nick didn't answer, she said, "My aunt always had a soft spot for me." Her mouth tightened ever so slightly. "Because I'm not my mother."

"Your family dynamic sounds interesting."

"No. It's boringly normal in my parents' social circle."

"Are you rich?"

"No."

"Well, your talk of social circles and elementary boarding school got me thinking."

"My *parents* are wealthy."

Nick could see the barriers clicking into place at the mention of her parents. She once again brushed strands of golden hair away from her face, and one corner of her mouth tightened ruefully before she added, "And I have a trust fund."

"I see." She was edging toward defensiveness.

"It's not a lot of money. More like a monthly trickle. If I want to live like a college student, then I'll survive without a job unless the cost of living jumps. That's how I'm living now, but frankly—I hate not working."

"I understand that feeling." He was a bit lost himself without work; however, the idea of having money just "trickle in"? That was something he couldn't imagine.

Alex squared her shoulders, seeming to sense the direction of his thoughts. "Other than the trust, which came from my late grandparents, the only help I've gotten from family was when my mother allowed me to move into her house after my place was broken into. My idea, not hers. It was a—" she swallowed "—tense time."

"You don't get along?"

"I'm a bit of a disappointment."

An awkward silence followed her words, and Nick drained his coffee cup. "Let's take a look at the plumbing and any other small jobs that won't eat up your available budget."

Alex set aside her untouched cup of coffee. "Yes," she said a little too briskly. "Let's." She got to her feet and Roger scrambled out from under the table, ready for action. She started for the dining room without waiting to see if he was going to follow.

"Alex…"

She stopped and turned, giving him a curious look, as if wondering why he'd re-engaged when they could have both quietly went to their separate corners.

"I was out of line asking if you were wealthy." He got to his feet and crossed the room to where she stood. Her chin lifted when he came to a stop.

"No. It was a valid question. And I didn't mean to give an impression that I need sympathy when I answered."

He had a feeling that sympathy was the last thing Alex Ryan wanted. "None given," he replied with a half-smile as he reached out and touched her shoulder in a reassuring gesture. He didn't know what possessed him to touch her, but for one brief second her muscles relaxed beneath his palm before snapping taut again. He dropped his hand and Alex's lips parted. She looked almost... regretful...as his hand fell back to his side.

She moistened her lips. "As to disappointing my parents, that's simply a matter of record. I didn't go to law school or embark on a flashy career that would impress people. I didn't marry a billionaire. Or even date one. Instead, I dated a guy who turned out to be a criminal, and my career in accounting and finance was pretty boring. But you know what?" She tilted her chin at him. "I was happy until the big surprise happened."

"The big surprise," he repeated with a lift of one eyebrow.

"Trust me—it was a *very* big surprise." She smiled then, a tenuous curving of her soft lips, and maybe it was that odd mixture of vulnerability and determination to stand on her own that got to him. Or maybe he just liked her. Whatever it was, he leaned his shoulder against the wall and folded his arms over his chest so he wouldn't reach for her again.

She opened her mouth as if to speak, closed it again and frowned at the floor. When she looked up again, she said, "I'm in one strange place, Nick."

It was the first time she'd used his name, and he liked the intimate way it came off her tongue.

"From what you tell me, I have to agree."

"I'm a little touchy about my parents. And I spend too much time overthinking."

"Maybe you need friends. You know…like the nice Callahan family who live nearby. I hear they're fun to hang with."

Alex's smile widened, making Nick's breath hitch. She was gorgeous when she smiled. "Maybe. I'll give the matter some thought."

Nick could accept that. It was a small inroad, which made him realize he wanted more. More time with Alex, more information about her.

"Hey," she said softly.

"Yeah?"

"You can bring your girls here anytime you want while you're working. I enjoy having them here."

He smiled back at her. "I'll keep that in mind. Thank you." He pushed off the wall and tucked his thumbs into his front pockets as he gestured toward the downstairs bathroom with his chin. "Let's see what we need to do to this place."

"Yeah." She started down the hall ahead of him.

Chances were that when Alex left, this house would be his, so he was essentially being paid to do his own work. But that thought no longer sat as well as it once had.

Deep down, he was fairly certain that he didn't want this woman to leave.

CHAPTER NINE

ALEX HAD SAID he could bring the girls with him, and the next morning, Nick did just that. Katie had gone to town the night before to help Rosalie make more doodads for the June in Bloom vendor show and promised to pick up Kendra and Bailey from Alex's on her way back to the ranch during the early afternoon.

The girls would have loved to have helped with the crafting, but Nick thought that Katie and Gloria and Rosalie could get more done without his girls underfoot. This show was important to them. They'd had a soft opening of their store a few months prior, but the formal announcement would come at June in Bloom, followed by a grand opening at the store, and that, in turn, would tick off Vince Taylor. He wanted Rosalie and Gloria's business to fail so that he could snap up their house, which sat between the two Grand Ladies he'd recently opened as swanky bed-and-breakfast inns.

Nick understood that having a house between his two was inconvenient, but if Vince had chosen to work with Rosalie and Gloria, instead of trying to intimidate them into selling, everyone could have benefited. That wasn't Vince's way. Nope. In Vince's mind, his way was the only way. And if he couldn't get his way, then he did crappy things like pulling in favors to slow down the permitting for the replacement bridge.

"Daddy, shouldn't you lock the gate?" Kendra asked when he drove through without stopping.

"We'll lock it on our way home, kiddo."

"My turn," Bailey announced.

"You did it last time."

"Uh-uh."

"Yes," Kendra said adamantly. "You did."

Bailey let out a defiant *humph* as Nick glanced at her in the rearview mirror. Kendra took after him—her blond hair was already showing signs of going dark, as his had done, but Bailey was going to be a blonde-blonde, like her mother. And she had Kayla's stubborn chin and short nose. He missed his wife, and he had no business thinking about

Alex so much when his primary job in in life was parenting his girls.

But he was.

After they pulled up to the house, Nick laid down a few rules. "You have books and crayons and your music. I want you to stay in the yard. If Ms. Ryan lets you play with the dogs, cool. If she says no, then that means…"

"No," the girls answered in unison.

"I want to play with the dogs," Bailey whispered to Kendra.

"You can unless the lady says no," Kendra replied in a no-nonsense way.

"The Wapunzel lady."

"*R*apunzel," Kendra corrected.

"That's the one," Nick agreed. "Okay. Best behavior. Dad has to get some work done and I don't want to worry about you getting hurt by falling stuff."

"We'll be good," Kendra promised. Bailey nodded her agreement as she unbuckled her seat.

Once again, he was greeted by the low woofs and sharp yips as he climbed the rebuilt porch stairs, and Bailey, who loved dogs, grinned up at him. He scooped her up in his arms at the last minute, so that the dogs didn't flatten her when they went into the house. Kendra was more adept at staying out of the way and keeping her footing. Lizzie Belle the goat had taught her a thing or two about playful stealth animal attacks.

Alex ordered the dogs back, then smiled at the girls. "You brought your crew again."

"Yes. They have things to keep them busy while I work." He didn't say *we*, because after their last conversation, he wasn't sure if Alex still felt like spending time with him.

"Great." Alex smiled at them, and Bailey cocked her head as she studied Alex's hair, which was clipped to the back of her head. Then she ran her fingers through her own fine locks as if wondering if she could copy the hairdo. "Can we play with the dogs?" she asked.

Alex met Nick's gaze. "I can't think of anything the dogs would like more."

"Great." He set Bailey down, keeping one hand on her shoulder. "Maybe they could play in the backyard."

"Great idea."

As soon as Bailey's feet hit the floor, Roger's ears went up, giving him a comical bat look, and both girls laughed. Then, sensing an appreciative audience, he circled the girls at high speed before flopping down onto his belly with his paws spread in front of him in an invitation to play.

"He likes kids," Alex said in a low voice.

"Apparently," Nick agreed.

Bailey laughed, and Roger ran another circle while Gus sat down and offered a big paw to Kendra, who giggled as she shook his hand.

"Hey, girls," Nick said. "Why don't you see if you can get these guys out the back door?"

"Okay," they chimed together.

"Come on, Woger," Bailey said as she headed through the dining room to the kitchen. Roger trotted beside her while Gus walked next to Kendra.

"R-r-*R*oger," Kendra said as she followed her sister.

"R-r-r-*W*oger," Bailey repeated.

Nick tipped back his hat as he watched his girls head out the back door, little Roger dancing beside Bailey, giving her his best canine smile.

"Big change in that dog," he commented when he turned back to Alex, catching her midstare. From the way her cheeks went pink, he suspected that she hadn't been studying him in a casual way, which in turn piqued his curiosity. Why the blush? What had she been thinking?

He let the moment pass, jerking his head toward the hallways leading to the bathroom and saying, "I guess I'll get to it."

"Yes…do you need any help?"

He gave her a long look. "I might."

"I'm pretty good at handing tools," she said in a serious tone, but he saw a flicker of amusement in her eyes. Whatever embarrassment she'd felt at being caught studying him in that thoughtful way had dissipated, but he still felt the crackle of awareness between them. The big question was what to do about it?

Don't mess up—that's what you do about it.

Alex had issues, he had daughters, so he had to move slowly; allow her time to get to know him as he got to know her. It was the only logical way to proceed, and Nick prided himself on being a logical man.

WHY?

The question kept circling through Alex's head as she watched Nick assess the extent of the necessary repairs. Why this man? And more than that, why this man at this particular time, when her life was in turmoil?

You wouldn't be anywhere near this man if your life wasn't in turmoil. You'd be in Virginia.

True.

Alex followed Nick as he checked the plumbing in the kitchen and bathrooms, then crawled under the house to see what kind of shape the pipes were in. After that, he made his way into the attic to determine the extent of the water damage there, then climbed up on the roof.

It was interesting to watch how attuned Nick was to his daughters. Despite the fact that he was all over the house, if things became too silent out in the yard, he'd excuse himself to check on the girls and assure himself that all was well.

"I've heard that silence is more telling than loud noises," Alex commented the second time it happened.

Nick smiled. "Yes. Definitely." He turned his attention to the pink postage-stamp tiles covering the walls above the old pink tub in the downstairs bathroom. "I have bad news."

Alex's heart skipped. "How bad?"

"Wall repair bad." He put a hand on the tiles and applied gentle pressure. Sure enough, the wall gave a little. "My guess is that they didn't use water resistant wall board behind it. Judging from the color and style of tub, this tile was probably put in during the late fifties or early sixties. Dampness seeped in and disintegrated the wall. All that's holding it up is the tile."

"Cool," Alex said on a breath.

The corners of Nick's eyes crinkled at her wry statement and once again her heart skipped—but not for the same reason as before. And darned if he didn't look as if he knew exactly what was going on inside of her—that he was aware of the hum of attraction which made her nerves more reactive than usual and her breathing a touch more shallow.

Maybe because he felt it, too?

It was possible, judging from the way his gaze held hers, and the thought made her cheeks go warm.

Again, why?

Alex let out a long breath.

"Is something wrong?"

Oh, no. Just having a moment here...

She forced a smile. "I was just thinking about my budget."

He nodded in a way that told her that he was going to let her get away with her white lie, but that he suspected she wasn't being totally forthright. "I think this is something you have to address. They make fiberglass tub surrounds, which would save time and money, but I'll still have to replace the walls behind it with cement board, which is water resistant."

"I agree. This has to be done."

"You want to tear out a wall today?"

"Could we?" she asked brightly, and Nick laughed, causing a pleasant warmth to tumble through her.

"Yeah. We could. We should bring in the big trash can from beside the house and lay a cover over the tub to protect the enamel... unless you want to replace it?"

"Are you kidding? I love a good pink tub."

"You and my oldest daughter. We tried to raise them color neutral, but Kendra loves pink."

We.

Alex's heart squeezed. The "we" had become "I" a few years ago and she felt for him.

"I'll get the tarp and catspaw from my truck. Would you mind getting the trash can?"

"Meet you back here," Alex said, suddenly glad to get out of the small space they'd been sharing. She needed a moment to regroup, catch her breath.

The smart thing to do would be to leave Nick to do his work alone, and that way avoid the tug of attraction that seemed to be growing with each passing moment, but Alex didn't do the smart thing. Instead, she hauled the trash can into the hallway next to the bathroom and waited there while Nick covered the tub with the tarp. And when he asked if she was ready for some demolition, she simply said yes.

There was something cathartic about demolishing a wall, knocking that first big hole into the crumbling wallboard and old tile and then prying off pieces and breaking them up to fit into the trash can.

"So," Nick asked as he ripped a hunk of wallboard off the framing, "what else do you like besides pink bathtubs?"

Alex took the debris from him and pushed it into the trash can. Not long ago the question would have had her giving a trite answer and then changing the subject, but today, after knocking a hole in the wall with him, she answered honestly. "I like having things organized."

He laughed. "Is that like a hobby of yours."

She smiled back, trying to remember another time in her life she'd felt so comfortable, yet so on edge. She couldn't recall a single one. "It makes me feel like I'm in control." She tore off a hanging chunk of tile and dropped it in the can as she tried to think of something she liked that wasn't totally boring. "I like dogs."

"Obviously."

"I like shopping, but I don't do it very often."

"Maybe that's why you like it."

"Could be." She tipped the trash can so Nick could shove in another piece of wallboard.

She thought of the boxes of crafting supplies in the upstairs closet, next to the container with the quilt tops and old lace. "I really like doing crafts and handwork, but haven't had the time to indulge."

"I suggest that you hang with my grandmother, then. She's good at that stuff."

"Maybe I will," she said noncommittally. But she didn't see it happening.

They emptied the trash can twice into the bed of Nick's truck, then dragged it back for a third go.

"This looks so sad," Alex said as she surveyed the framing that showed through the gaping hole over the tub.

"It'll look better soon," Nick assured her, bringing one hand up to rest on the door jamb. "I do good work."

"I bet you do," she said softly. She met his gaze, and what was supposed to be a brief glance turned into something more as their eyes met and held. It took her a moment to remember to breathe as the intensity of the moment grew.

And grew.

How was this happening? One moment they were discussing pink tubs and shopping and now…oh dear heavens. She was going to kiss him. Or he was going to kiss her.

Nick made the first move, leaning toward her, and instead of stepping back as a sane woman would do, she lifted her chin to meet the kiss. Doing anything else would have been impossible.

Nick's lips met hers lightly, his mouth warm and firm and perfect. Alex's hand slipped up around his neck, but all she did was savor the warmth of his skin rather than pull him closer. The pressure of his lips increased, and Alex's knees started to give a little as the kiss deepened.

When Nick lifted his head, she had to fight to keep a small murmur of protest from escaping her lips. She gazed up at him, and he returned her stare, looking a touch shell-shocked.

"I hadn't planned to do that," he said huskily.

"But you did."

"Yes."

"Um…" Alex stepped back, putting up her palms in a no-big-deal gesture as she put space between them. "No need for alarm. Just two healthy adults—" she hesitated "—being healthy."

Nick laughed, showing white teeth as his cheeks creased. "That's one way to put it."

Alex should have felt more alarmed than she did, but it was now patently obvious that she wasn't the only one treading on unfamiliar ground. "I don't know what to do here, Nick."

Honesty felt amazing. She didn't know what to do and she said it aloud instead of pretending she was in control.

"Me, either."

"The last guy who kissed me set me up to take the blame for a crime."

He moved closer, once again setting his hands on her shoulders. "I won't do that. I promise."

She bit her lip, but a smile broke through. "I can honestly say that I believe you."

"Daddy! Where are you?"

The screen door slammed behind Bailey as she came into the kitchen and Nick took a slow step back, dropping his hands. "Don't disappear on me," he said in a low voice.

"Do you think I will?"

"I don't know," he said as Bailey called his name again.

Neither did she.

"We're here, kiddo," he called to his daughter.

"There you are." Bailey came down the short hallway and hooked an arm around Nick's leg before peering into the bathroom.

The little girl's expression was so horrified that Alex pressed her hand to her mouth to stifle a laugh. Talk about a seesaw of emotions over the course of the last two minutes.

"You made a bad mess," Bailey said in an awed tone.

"We'll clean it up tomorrow," Nick promised as he ran a hand over Bailey's blond head. "Do you guys want lunch?"

"Kendra's making a place for us to have a picnic." Bailey looked up at Alex. "Do you got paper plates?"

"I do," she said. "I even know where they are." She gave Nick a quick look, then headed to the kitchen to pull a package of plates out of a cupboard.

"Thanks," Nick said as Bailey left the house a few minutes later with plates and plastic forks.

He looked down at her, a serious expression on his handsome face. "Are we in an okay place?" he asked softly.

"Yes," she replied. "I think we are."

It was a half-truth. *They* were okay, but she wasn't certain if she was okay. Kissing the neighbor had not been in her game plan, which meant she was going to have to asses and come up with a new plan.

KENDRA AND BAILEY played with the dogs, read books and colored while Alex and Nick finished up the bathroom demolition and then started removing kitchen cabinets so that Alex could sand and paint them the following day while Nick attacked the old plumbing. Nick's sister Katie drove in midafternoon, and Alex thought she did a pretty good job of not jumping a mile at the sound of an engine—but her heartrate did step up at the thought of meeting another Callahan.

She's a neighbor. No need to be nervous.

She was also the sister of the guy Alex had kissed a few hours ago.

"Is that my sister?" Nick called from the bathroom.

"It is," Alex said before opening the front door to meet her new neighbor. She started down the porch steps as a dark-haired woman climbed out of a red pickup truck.

"You must be Alex," she said as she approached the gate. "I'm Katie. Nick's long-suffering sister."

"Nice to meet you." The resemblance between Nick and his sister was striking. Nick's eyes were darker, and the angles of Katie's face were softer, but Alex had no trouble pegging them as brother and sister.

"Thank you for adopting Roger."

Alex lifted her eyebrows at the unexpected and heartfelt pronouncement. "You're welcome?"

Katie beamed at her. "The little guy is legend, you know. But no one else would take him on."

"I'm glad I did." She also felt as if she'd

passed some kind of test when Nick's sister gave her an approving nod.

The front door opened, and Kendra poked her head out. "It *is* Aunt Katie," she called over her shoulder, as if settling an argument. "Get your stuff, Bailey."

After the gathering of scattered kid accoutrements and shooting down a suggestion that "Woger" go home with them, Katie and the girls took off for the Callahan ranch, leaving Alex and Nick very much alone.

"And here we are," Nick said as his sister drove away.

"Yep. You and me." Thanks to the kiss that morning, Alex had no idea what to expect now that there were no little girls on the premises. It wasn't a dinner invitation.

"I think," Nick said after gathering his tools together, "that you should consider coming to the ranch for dinner tonight."

Alex lifted her eyebrows. The truth was that she wouldn't mind company for the evening, but did she want to get more deeply involved with the Callahan family? "I couldn't put anyone out like that."

He her an ironic look.

"What?" Alex demanded.

"I kind of knew you were going to say that.

As it happens, dinner is yet another slow-cooker meal. The ranch would collapse if that thing went on the fritz while Brady, my cooking brother-in-law-to-be, is away at school." That sexy mouth tilted up at the corners. "You won't be putting anyone out."

She held his gaze, unable to tear hers away. "You kind of make it hard to say no."

"But you're free to."

"No?" she said, her gaze still locked with his. Could he see how surprisingly difficult it was for her to utter that simple word? She loved having the dogs, but she'd had no idea until she'd moved to Montana how much she appreciated human company.

"Do you mean that?"

She shook her head and he smiled, making her heart race a little faster. Chemistry was an amazing thing—something one didn't go looking for. Something that just… happened. So why did it happen with this guy with whom she had so little in common? He was a single dad, whose first obligation was to his daughters. She was a woman with secrets she didn't want to share. Not a great combination.

"I want to be back before dark."

"I'll drive you back and check the house."

It was on the tip of her tongue to say "No. I'll handle it." Instead, she said, "Yes. I'll come to dinner. Thank you."

KENDRA AND BAILEY were delighted to have company for dinner. They instantly launched into plans to use Grandma's pretty plates.

"Good idea," Katie said. "And while your dad shows Alex around, maybe we could pick flowers and make bouquets so that the table is really pretty."

"Yeah!" the girls said in unison.

But after putting on her mismatched shoes, Bailey said, "I want to go on the walk with Daddy and Alex."

"Works for me, Bill."

Alex glanced up at Nick and he explained, "Bill Bailey—"

"Won't you please come home." She smiled. "One of my roommates took banjo lessons and she sang that song a lot. She also did a nice rendition of 'Oh! Susanna.'"

"There aren't any songs with my name," Kendra informed Alex.

"Maybe you could write one."

Kendra bit her lip as the idea sank in. "I

don't know how to write a song, but maybe when I'm older."

"Maybe," Alex said.

Katie nodded her agreement, then said, "I'm going out to the garden to see about early flowers. We should have dianthus and carnations and who knows what else."

"I'll help," Kendra said.

Bailey looked torn. She took hold of Nick's hand as he started for the back door, then shook her head. "I'll help with flowers."

"Pick the prettiest ones," Nick said, his hand bumping against Alex's as he stopped at the door.

"I will. I'll get the purple ones!"

Alex laughed as Bailey raced after her aunt and sister. "You must be constantly entertained."

He smiled down at her. "It's the best kind of entertainment."

He opened the door, and Alex stepped out onto the porch where the breeze lifted the tendrils of hair around her face.

"Ready for the tour?"

"Totally."

Nick took her through Katie's greenhouse, where she grew the herbs, and showed her the first buildings his great-great-grandfather had built, which were made of squared-off logs with white chinking in between. They toured the barn, where a little goat seemed to appear out of nowhere.

"That is Lizzie Belle," Nick said as the animal blinked up at Alex with a curious gold gaze. "Somewhere in the vicinity is Wendell, her goat partner-in-crime."

"She's adorable."

"Until you find her standing on your truck," Nick said dryly. "Just ask Brady. Lillie Belle likes his truck best of all." As if to prove the point, Lizzie Belle scampered up a stack of hay bales, then back down again.

"When will I meet Brady?" A bold statement to Alex's ears, because it implied that she was going to be involved enough with this family to meet everyone.

"He'll be home in a matter of weeks. He's at welding school and taking a side course in horse shoeing. He's always been good with horses, and shoeing will give him a sideline career."

"It's good to do something you love."

"Did you?"

She shot him a look, telling herself there was no need for the barriers that started shifting into position. "It was a job that I was good at. Lots of people work in jobs they don't love but are good at. That's why we live for weekends and vacations."

Nick laughed. "Right you are."

"I bet you like your job."

"I'm lucky. When Brady gets back, he'll handle a lot of the ranching with Katie's help, and I can work contracting jobs, thus bringing in some income to help support the ranch." When she frowned at him, he explained, "Ranching is an occupation that can be hit or miss, depending on markets. It's good to have outside work for security."

"Ah," Alex said, skirting the large puddle in the middle of the driveway, the little goat coming up to peer curiously into the water before doing an adorable jumping buck and then retreating behind Nick.

"I have to bring in a load of gravel and fill that," Nick said, nodding at the puddle. "It's been getting bigger with each storm this spring."

"It's practically a lake. Maybe you should build a dock instea—"

Before the last word was out of her mouth, something knocked the back of her knees in the perfect spot to cause them to buckle. Nick made a grab as Alex pitched forward with a startled cry, but he was too late. The next thing she knew, she was on her belly in the puddle, sputtering against the mud and water that had hit her square in the face. Nick was instantly beside her, a strong hand under her arm as he helped her to her feet.

"I am so sorry." He reached out to wipe a dab of mud off Alex's face with his thumb.

"I don't think it was your fault," Alex replied, shooting a look at Lizzie Belle, who blinked at her, then scampered off, tossing her head.

"Sometimes she gets playful with guests. She means well," Nick said. Alex made a face at him, then looked down at her muddy front. At least her jeans were still relatively dry. Nick's jeans were totally dry, with the exception of some splash marks. Only his boots were muddy, from when he'd come to her rescue.

"I'll lend you one of my shirts." He took her wet hand in his and led her into the house, where he released her fingers and pointed down the hall.

"The bathroom is that way. I'll see what I have that might come close to fitting you."

"It doesn't have to fit," she said as he took off in the opposite direction. Like anything he wore would come close to fitting her.

She pulled several paper towels off the roll on the counter, then went into the bathroom. One look in the mirror and she wished she'd taken more towels. And thank goodness she'd pinned her hair up, or it would be as muddy as the front of her shirt was. She grimaced as she pulled the shirt away from her body, then sucked in a breath and pulled it over her head. Where to put it? She was still holding the shirt a few seconds later when a knock came on the door. "I found something."

She cracked the door and reached her arm out. Nick pushed a soft sweatshirt into her hand.

"Thank you. Do you have a plastic bag?"

"I'll get one."

Alex closed the door and set the gray sweatshirt on the edge of the bathtub and sacrificed a few of the paper towels to set the wet, muddy shirt on, then used the rest to clean the grime off her face and neck. At least it was only mud. It could have been so much worse if the little goat had pulled her trick in the cow pasture Nick had toured her through.

"Plastic bag," Nick said from the other side of the door.

Alex opened the door and took the bag, dropping her shirt and dirty paper towels inside.

"Dinner smells great, by the way," she said as she came out of the small room, pulling the door shut behind her.

"We can wash your shirt, you know."

"That's okay. The shirt will help me make a full load," she said facetiously. Actually, if she put all of her clothes in the washer at once, she'd barely have a full load. She'd brought only the basics to the wilds of Montana— jeans, T-shirts, cozy flannel shirts. Clothing she thought would make her invisible.

"You sure? It'd be clean before dinner is over."

"Are you pressuring me into having my laundry done?"

He smiled, but the expression in his eyes was serious as he said, "No pressure. I promise." He was not referring to laundry.

"Good," she whispered back.

For a long moment they stood, connected

by silence, then he reached for her, his hands warm against her waist, and lowered his head until his lips were within a breath of hers. Alex closed the distance, sliding a hand around the back of his neck, his skin warm beneath her palm as she met his lips in a long, satisfying kiss.

Satisfying and at the same time unsettling.

"Daddy!"

Alex and Nick jerked apart, Nick stumbling over his own feet as he put space between them.

"Oh, *there* you are," Kendra said as she came into the room, carrying a bouquet of freshly picked flowers, obviously intended for the empty vase sitting on the counter.

"Yes. Here I am," Nick agreed, sounding like a guy who was not used to hiding his actions.

Kendra gave him an odd look, and Alex pressed her lips together to keep from smiling. An astute little girl who knew that her dad was acting funny. "Lizzie Belle is all muddy."

"Imagine that," Nick said seriously. "Maybe she fell in a puddle."

Kendra appeared not to have heard him.

"Hey…isn't that your sweatshirt?" she asked, pointing at Alex.

"*I* fell in the mud, and I probably splashed Lizzie Belle." She held up the plastic bag. "My shirt's in here. Your dad lent me his shirt to wear home."

Kendra regarded them both suspiciously, as if wondering if they were putting her on. "Girls shouldn't wear boy clothes."

"I see," Alex said seriously.

Kendra looked at both of them again, then moved to the counter and stuck the flowers in the vase. "Aunt Katie and Bailey are bringing more, then we'll fix them to look pretty."

"They already look pretty," Nick said.

Kendra beamed at him. "I'll go help Bailey bring her flowers."

Once she was gone, Nick gave Alex a look. "I'll, uh, work on that girl-clothes, boy-clothes thing."

"I think it's the age," Alex said, half remembering something from her basic psychology classes.

"Or her penchant for rule following."

"I had that same penchant."

"Yeah?" he asked softly. "When did you outgrow it?"

Alex pretended to consider. "I think it was about two months ago."

Nick smiled down at her. "Better late than never, I guess."

CHAPTER TEN

GETTING KNOCKED INTO a mud puddle by a renegade nanny goat shouldn't have been the catalyst for forging a closer bond with Nick Callahan, but that was exactly what had happened—on her end, anyway. Maybe it was the genuine concern he'd shown as he'd picked her up out of the puddle and made certain she was okay. Perhaps it was the offer to do her laundry.

Or the kiss.

Their first kiss had been experimental. They'd both wondered, and considering the time they were spending together, it may have been inevitable.

But the second kiss was different—it had been an offer of comfort and closeness, which Alex had accepted and now half-regretted. Nick and his family were working their way into her heart, bypassing her defenses, rendering her emotionally vulnerable.

She wasn't ready to risk emotional vulnerability, but she didn't want to be totally alone, and she definitely wanted her house fixed.

In other words, she was in something of a bind, and the only remedy was to tactfully set some boundaries for the good of everyone involved, because it wasn't as if she was going to be spending less time with the Callahan family. She'd volunteered to help bake cupcakes for Nick and Katie's grandmother's booth at a big event in the Gavin City Park.

Alex had somehow mentioned that one of her few creative talents was piping frosting, something her mother's cook had taught her on summer break when she was thirteen and battling boredom, and the next thing she knew, she was part of the volunteer baking crew.

She hadn't mentioned the cook or a break from boarding school. Nick had probably already filled his family in on the fact that she had an independent income, but in case he hadn't, she saw no reason to highlight her privileged upbringing. Despite alarm bells going off as she became more involved with the Callahan family, she didn't want to set herself apart as a person whose background had nothing in common with theirs.

Maybe that was yet another warning sign.

But she'd promised to make and pipe frosting onto cupcakes, and she would follow through. Ryan-Evanses were big on following through. In her mother's case, it was due to noblesse oblige. In Alex's case, it was because she didn't like to break promises.

Bailey and Kendra toured Alex through the house, showing her all the stuff "Dad did." He'd put in French doors and built decks outside of each bedroom and had totally remodeled the kitchen before Bailey was born, but the girls still seemed aware of everything he'd put his hand to in the ranch house. Nick enjoyed hero status with his daughters. It was well deserved. He was a good guy, and part of her wondered why she had to meet this good guy when her life was so unsettled.

After admiring several dozen stuffed animals that resided in the corner of Kendra's bedroom, Nick announced that it was time to take Alex home.

"Can we come, too?" Kendra asked hopefully. She tightened her grip on Alex's hand, making Alex's heart melt. Kendra came off as a stoic little girl upon first introduction, but she'd been all smiles as she toured Alex through the house.

"Our seats are already in the truck," Bailey added. "And we'd go to bed really fast when we get back."

"It's bath night," Katie reminded the girls.

"We can take a bath in the morning," Kendra said.

Alex knelt down between the two girls, still hanging on to Kendra's hand as she put herself at eye level. "How about you guys take your bath and go to bed on time, and when I come over to help with the cupcakes, I'll teach you how to make a frosting flower."

Little Bailey's mouth dropped open. "You can teach us that?"

Alex gave a solemn nod. "I can and I will."

"Can we eat the flower?" Bailey asked, shooting a look up at her dad.

"You can eat the flower," he agreed. "And you can make one for me to eat, too. But I want a big one."

Kendra laughed and let go of Alex's hand. "Okay." She smiled at Alex, then threw her arms around her, giving her a quick hug. Bailey did the same from the other side, and Alex went still before she put an arm around each girl and returned the hug. She'd never been the recipient of a spontaneous child hug and was stunned at how it turned her heart to jelly.

"Okay, guys," Nick said, putting a hand under Alex's elbow and helping her to her feet. "You'll see Alex soon. Now scoot off to the bath so that I can get her home before dark."

Nick kept his hand at her elbow as she said goodbye to Katie and the girls, his grip warm and reassuring, and wildly distracting.

Could she afford to lean on this man for reassurance and warmth?

The best answer she could come up with was "to a degree." She wanted to stay close to the Callahan clan, but she wasn't ready for deep emotional attachments, which meant that before the night ended, Alex needed to draw a boundary.

THE SUN WAS just setting when Nick pulled up to Alex's house, where Roger's head appeared as a flash of white at the front window, then disappeared again as Nick turned off the ignition.

"Well, he's still there," Alex said dryly.

She'd left the dogs in the house to make certain that Roger didn't escape the backyard while she was gone, although, to Roger's credit, the little dog showed no sign of wanting to leave. Nick just hoped that he hadn't destroyed a pillow or something. Alex had had enough animal adventures for one evening.

"Appears so," Nick agreed as Roger's head appeared and disappeared again. "But if he'd had opposable thumbs, it would be a different story."

The head appeared again, only this time less of it showed before he disappeared again.

"Maybe I should set a chair there, so that he doesn't have to jump so high."

"Jumping is good exercise." Nick gave her a quick sideways look, which she met with a sideways look of her own. It was becoming more and more obvious—to Nick, anyway—that they shared a wavelength, a connection that had seemingly come out of nowhere, and it was more than just a physical attraction. More than two healthy adults being healthy. He wondered if Alex shared his assessment of the situation.

She smiled at him as she reached for the door handle. "You don't have to check the house. I very much doubt anyone is there with Roger and Gus on guard."

"I'd feel better."

"Would you?" she asked simply.

He shrugged. "I get protective."

"As long as you don't get controlling, we'll do okay."

He wanted to ask what they would do okay with, but there was time for that. Right now, he was content to let this fledgling relationship grow in fits and starts. There was really no hurry.

Alex opened her door and Nick did the same. Together they walked up the front walk to the rebuilt porch, which looked great, even if he did say so himself. For one brief moment he flashed on the first time he'd taken Kayla home, and how they'd kissed on a porch very much like this.

That part of his life was gone in a physical sense, but he would always love his Kayla.

Two years after losing her, he was a different guy with different emotional needs, although he hadn't yet pinned down what those needs were. Again, no hurry. Things that developed organically were so much more stable than those that were forced.

Alex shifted her weight, then tilted her head toward the door. "Do you have time to come in for a bit?"

Judging from her tone, she had something she needed to say, and he didn't think it was that she needed to be kissed again. "I do."

The dogs greeted Alex joyously, then turned their attention to Nick, giving him a somewhat less exuberant greeting. "They like you better," he said as he rubbed Gus's ears.

"Well, I do feed them." Roger gave a particularly springy leap as she spoke and ended up in her arms. Alex almost went over backward as she automatically clutched the little terrier to her chest. "That's a first," she said as she caught her balance. Nick was glad she wasn't knocked flat for the second time that evening.

"I believe you have been accepted."

"I guess so." Alex held the little dog closer, running a hand over the wiry hair on his head.

She sank down onto the sofa, still holding the dog. "Thanks for an exciting evening," she said. "I'll get your shirt back to you as soon as I do laundry."

"No hurry," he said.

"What are we going to do about this?" Alex asked. He raised his eyebrows in a silent question, and she lifted her hand from Roger's head to point first at him, then at herself.

Nick crossed the room and sat down on

the sofa next to her, their shoulders not quite touching. "I don't think there's an easy answer here, Alex. I never saw this coming." He'd had only one super-serious relationship in his life, and it had ended in marriage.

"I'm not ready for...more," she said as she hugged Roger to her like a canine shield.

"I understand. You have unknowns in your life." Some of which he was certain he didn't yet know about.

"I feel like I'm on a runaway train at times. So many things over which I have little control."

He brought a hand up to lightly trace the curve of her cheek with the back of his fingers. "I told you earlier, no pressure. I meant it."

Alex pressed her lips together, then nodded. "I won't make promises I can't keep. I won't get involved in something I can't see through."

Nick's stomach tightened. "Is this goodbye?"

She gave him a startled look. "I need my contractor."

"And that's all?"

Alex's throat moved as she swallowed. "No."

The simple word brought a rush of relief.

She wasn't done, but she did need space. When she met his gaze over the top of Roger's head, she looked as if she was willing him to understand and to agree to the terms she hadn't yet laid out.

"No more kissing?" he guessed, figuring he may as well address the silent question hanging between them.

"It does tend to fog my judgment," she said on a note of wry humor that both surprised and charmed him. "And... I don't see to be saying no in the moment very well."

He smiled a little. Neither of them was very good at that. "Well, if you want to be kissed, you only need to ask."

She smiled back, but it faded as she hugged Roger a little closer. "Thank you for understanding."

"Yeah." He reached out to lightly touch her upper arm. "I'll get going if you're sure about the house."

She stroked a hand over Roger's head. "I'm sure."

"Okay, then." He got to his feet and nodded at the door a couple of feet away from him. "I'll see myself out."

She stood up. "I'll see you tomorrow."

"Yeah." Nick let himself out into the warm

early-evening air and crossed the porch. The deadbolt clicked into place behind him before he reached the steps. Alex was locking him out in more ways than one. On the one hand, he was glad she was physically safe. On the other, he wished that she was willing to take a cautious step forward with him.

She needs space. So do you.

The unfortunate thing was that he didn't want space.

GLORIA OFFERED TO go to the county commission meeting with Rosalie to learn the final determination of the board concerning bridge construction now that they'd had time to go over the ecologist's report, but Rosalie had politely waved the offer aside, just as she'd waved aside Nick and Katie's offer to drive in.

"If they do not approve the permitting, then the three of us will tackle it together," she'd said. But right now, she saw no need for her grandchildren to make the drive to town.

Will was in his seat when she made her way into the meeting room, and her heart lifted at the sight of him. She was getting used to that happening. No, she didn't want to get involved with a man who ranched for a living, but she liked Will, and after the meeting, no matter what happened, she would talk to him. Maybe accept that ride home he always offered.

He turned his head as she took her seat, then, to her surprise, rose from his own and made his way back to sit beside her.

There was no reason on earth that her heart rate should have doubled, but it did, and as Will settled beside her, she felt both alarm at her reaction and a deep sense of everything suddenly being all right.

That made no sense. She simply hadn't had enough contact with the man to have such a reaction, but there it was.

"I have a feeling this is going to work out just fine," Will murmured while keeping his eyes on the board members taking their seats.

"Did you put in a fix?" Rosalie asked.

"Maybe."

Her back automatically stiffened, and Will turned his head to smile at her. "No. I don't work that way. But Travis did meet with the chairperson of the council on another matter and made it clear that the bridge benefits our ranch as well as yours."

"Only when you deliver hay." They some-

times bought extra hay from the McGuire
ranch.

"Still a benefit."

Rosalie bit her lip, then rose to her feet for
the Pledge of Allegiance. Once seated again,
she clasped her hands together and waited
while the commission dealt with minutes
and warrants and the like. Finally, the matter of the bridge came up and again her heart
pounded a little faster, although it didn't get
nearly the workout it had gotten when Will
changed seats.

"After careful consideration of the evidence, we're granting all permitting for the
reconstruction of the bridge leading to the
Callahan ranch and adjoining properties."

Will smiled at Rosalie, who couldn't help
smiling back. "Finally," she murmured.

"Congratulations. I just wish Vince Taylor were here."

"Word will get back shortly."

"No doubt," Will agreed.

The remaining agenda items were dealt
with in short order, and the chairperson made
a quip about wishing that all the meetings
would go so smoothly, then lowered his gavel
and adjourned the meeting.

Will and Rosalie joined the small crowd

exiting the room. Once they were outside, Will turned to Rosalie and said, "Does this mean no more commission meetings for you?"

"It might. I'm pretty busy with the shop right now."

"Then…will you let me buy you a cup of coffee and a piece of pie?"

"Yes."

Will's silver eyebrows lifted at the simple yet adamant response. "Maybe I should have asked before."

Rosalie laughed. She was so very relieved about the bridge that everything seemed just that much rosier. Will drove to the Cold Creek Restaurant on the edge of town, a place where you could eat either casual or fancy depending on your mood. Tuesday seemed to be primarily causal.

Will held Rosalie's chair, then took his own seat, turning over both coffee cups. When the server arrived, he rattled off the list of pies and they both chose apple.

"Coffee and apple pie," the server said with a smile. "You guys are easy."

"He doesn't know you," Will said in an aside.

Rosalie flattened her mouth, but she

wanted to smile. Relief that the bridge ordeal was over. That was it.

"Rosalie," Will said after the coffee cups were filled, "I know I butted into your business a few months ago, but…do you have something else against me?"

Rosalie's mouth fell open. "I… No." Will lifted one eyebrow and she glanced down briefly. "You are a rancher."

"So are you," he said in a perplexed tone.

Slowly Rosalie shook her head. "I'm not. My grandchildren are ranchers. I run a gift shop. It's what I always wanted to do." She turned her cup. "I'm a town girl, Will. I always have been. I don't want to get involved with another rancher."

"But…"

"I loved Carl with all my heart. I was a ranch wife because I loved Carl, but that part of my life is done."

"That's some plain speaking, Rosalie."

"It is," she agreed, lifting her cup to take a sip. It felt good to say it aloud instead of dodging the man.

"Do you think there's a danger of us getting involved?"

"Yes." Her heart hit her ribs, but she was too old to pussyfoot around like this. She found Will attractive, and she believed he felt the same about her. If not, then she was reading this situation all wrong. If so, she'd apologize and go home.

Will's eyebrows drew together in a thoughtful frown, broken only by a quick nod at the server when she set a piece of pie in front of each of them.

"Well, what do you say we do not assume that we can't work out some kind of a compromise in this situation?"

"What kind of compromise?" Rosalie asked as she cut into the buttery crust.

"I understand your position and now I'd like you to understand mine. I've been alone for almost five years now. I've grieved. I've come to accept my loss. I have a lot to fill my time. I wasn't looking for you, Rosalie, but somehow you just showed up on my radar about a year ago, and I thought to myself, 'I like that woman.'"

"That's very flattering, Will." And a touch terrifying.

He reached across the table and lightly touched her free hand. "How about we just agree to be friends? Maybe we can see a movie or go to dinner? Do…things. You don't have to set foot on the ranch."

Rosalie gave him a wry look. "I don't mind setting foot on your ranch, Will. I just don't want to *live* miles from town."

"Fine. Then you don't have to live on my ranch."

Rosalie rolled her eyes, but inside she felt a warm glow of anticipation. Friends. She could do that. She'd been truthful and so had he. Maybe they didn't have to be lonely.

"And I know that you have Nick and everything, but I'm a pretty good carpenter. If you need any work done on that old mansion of yours, I'd be happy to help."

"Would you?"

Will made the first cut into his pie. "I don't say things I don't mean."

Rosalie gave a satisfied nod. "Neither do I, Will."

He met her gaze, the intensity of his brilliant blue eyes making her catch her breath. "Then I think we'll do all right together."

Rosalie nodded and focused on her pie. Suddenly life had gotten just that much more interesting.

ALEX WOKE EARLY the next morning, just as the sun was topping the mountains to the east and spilling sunlight into her bedroom.

She pushed her hair out of her eyes as she propped up on one elbow and yawned, surprised that she felt so rested. When she'd gone to bed, she'd assumed she'd lie awake, thinking about Nick and the boundary she'd drawn between them, but instead she'd fallen into a deep sleep and now felt remarkably ready to face the day.

It had helped that Nick had been so understanding when she'd asked for space. But that understanding had also nudged him even further into good-guy territory. He was the kind of guy she wished she'd met instead of Jason. It stunk that the timing wasn't right, but it wasn't. End of story.

Alex pushed the covers back and swung her legs over the edge of the bed, her feet skimming over Gus's warm body. Roger was curled up at the foot of her bed, and he crawled across the lumpy covers to nudge her arm up and over him.

"Okay, guys. What say we have breakfast, then take a walk to open the gate?"

Even though Nick had promised to take care of the gate, she liked the walk. It gave Roger a chance to explore and Gus seemed to enjoy padding along beside her. She munched on a granola bar as she walked, enjoying the breeze that lifted the hair from her forehead. She'd loosely braided her hair but hadn't pinned it up in case the girls came with Nick that day. Bailey liked her hair down, even if it was in a braid, so down it would be.

When she reached the gate, she swung the heavy cable padlock around to her side and started the combination, then stopped as she realized that the lock should have been on her side to begin with, since it had been locked from her side the previous day.

That was when she noticed the fresh tire tracks. She was not a master tracker, but it was easy to see where the vehicle had stopped, and there was a footprint in the dirt where someone had obviously tried to open her gate.

A chill went through her.

It's nothing. Somebody on a wrong road. Or someone trying to get to Callahan Ranch, who didn't realize there was a lock on the gate.

You hope.

She swept her gaze over the surrounding area, turning in a slow circle. The vehicle that had made the tracks was long gone, but that didn't mean there wasn't someone there.

Except that her dogs seemed to think everything was okay.

Gus poked his nose at a gopher hole near the gatepost, his tail slowly wagging, and Roger darted over from where he'd been sniffing in the ditch to see what his big friend had found. He started digging with both front paws, throwing dirt at Gus, who winced as it hit his nose.

Definitely no problem in the area as far as her bodyguards were concerned, but Alex still took a moment to study the road on her side of the gate. There were no large footprints as near as she could tell.

She shook her head as dirt from Roger's frantic digging hit her shoes, then undid the lock and resolutely swung the gate open.

False alarm. Just someone who'd driven down the wrong road.

But her perfect morning wasn't quite as perfect-feeling as it'd been before she'd walked to the gate.

NICK'S DAUGHTERS CAME to work with him that morning, spilling out of the truck and racing to where Alex stood on the porch with a mug of coffee.

"Hi, Alex," Kendra called as she stopped

to open the gate. "We brought stuff to do at your table."

"Excellent," Alex said.

Nick smiled self-consciously as he followed Kendra through the front gate, and Alex had to admit to feeling a little self-conscious herself after yesterday. Although, truth be told, she'd feel a lot more self-conscious if she hadn't spent the last hour convincing herself that the gate incident was random. It was, but there was still that small speck of doubt that kept her from totally relaxing. By the time Nick left that afternoon, she was certain she'd have more of a grip on the situation, but for now it was nice to have him there.

"I brought help," Nick said, as if that wasn't patently obvious.

"You know I like your crew very much." And she was glad he'd brought them; he got time with his daughters, and their presence practically guaranteed an environment in which there would be no long looks, or accidental touches.

The girls' colorful tote bags were filled with books and art projects and a tablet with videos and games. They spread everything out on the table, and then Kendra spent the day shadowing Nick and Alex while Bailey divided her time between following her sister and playing with Roger and Gus.

"My grandma did that," Kendra announced after leaving her dad banging on pipes in the cellar to touch base with Alex, who was sanding a cabinet door down to wood. "She wore a paper mask."

Alex stopped sanding. "I should wear a mask. You're right. And so should you."

"I'll bring some tomorrow," Kendra said importantly.

"That's a good idea." Alex stopped sanding and set the sanding block on the kitchen counter. "I'll stop until I get the mask." She wanted to be a good role model, and she didn't want Kendra and Bailey breathing in sawdust. She should have thought of it earlier.

"I didn't think to buy dust masks for sanding," she said to Nick later in the day after he'd shown her where he was going to have to put holes in the kitchen wall. She'd barely seen him as he chased down pipes and decided how he was going to tackle the plumbing issues, but she'd been aware of him—both in her house and in her head.

How was she not supposed to think about

him when he was banging around, and when all she had to do was close her eyes to recall what it was like to kiss him?

When she wished things were different so that she could kiss him again?

"I should have thought of that, too," he said, fixing his amazing dark gaze on her. He might have taken a step back, but she sensed that he wanted to kiss her as much as she wanted to kiss him.

"Kendra is bringing me a paper mask tomorrow. I hope that won't short you."

He laughed, and she tried not to appreciate the way his cheeks creased. Total fail.

"I buy them by the gross," he said.

One corner of her mouth lifted. "You can add one onto the bill."

"Twenty-five cents for a dust mask. I'll make a note."

"Hey…"

He lifted his eyebrows at her overly casual opening. "Hey, what?"

"Were you expecting anyone at your ranch last night?"

"No."

Drat. Another comforting theory shot. She tried for a casual shrug. "I just noticed tracks on the opposite side of the gate, and the padlock had been moved so that it hung down that side of the gate."

"Huh." Nick shook his head. "It's possible that someone wanted to just drop by our place, I guess. They might have checked the padlock to make sure it was locked and not just fake-closed."

"Yes. That's probably it."

Nick reached out to touch her arm as she started toward the sink to rinse the glass she was holding, and she stopped in her tracks. He instantly dropped his hand back to his side, seeming to remember that he'd agreed not to touch her. "You know that this is a safe area in which to live, right?"

"I do." She was more concerned about people who weren't from the area.

"Unless you have reason to believe that someone you knew from before you moved here is stalking you, I'd say that having someone drive to the gate was a total fluke."

It was a nice bit of mind reading, and, after he spoke, Nick watched her face while she formulated her response.

Alex honestly had no reason to believe anyone from her old life was stalking her. Everything had been quiet on that front. Her mother had recently assured her via text that no one had been asking about her, and her mother had a large network of "friends" who'd be happy to report questions being asked about her daughter.

"What are the chances of someone following me here?" she asked, speaking more to herself than to Nick.

"Slim, I hope."

"Yeah." She let out a breath and glanced down at his sturdy leather work boots. There was something about Nick Callahan that made her feel safe. Made her feel like she could confide in him. "I've had a lot of bad things happen in a short period of time."

He tucked a long strand of hair behind her ear. "And maybe you're still dealing with PTSD?"

"Maybe," she allowed.

"You know the invitation to stay at the ranch if you feel overwhelmed stands."

She worked up a smile. "Thank you. I'll remember that."

"And if you get nervous, call me or Katie. Anytime at all."

"Darn it, Nick," she said on a breath, meeting his dark gaze.

"What?" He looked genuinely perplexed.

"You're making it hard to keep a distance."

He waggled his eyebrows, and Alex fought a smile as the girls came in through the screen door, letting it bang shut behind them.

"You can smile," he murmured to her in a low voice. "I won't look." True to his word, he turned to his daughters. "Gather your things, girls. We're heading home."

"If they're coming back tomorrow, they can leave what they don't need," Alex said. "That way they can save a step."

"You're catching on to this parent thing fast." Nick knelt down to tie the shoe Bailey held out to him, oblivious to the fact that he'd made her heart jump with the casual statement.

She was catching on, and she loved interacting with his little girls. In another place and time she would have been all about interacting with him.

But maybe…

Not yet.

THE NEXT MORNING Alex walked to the gate again, heart pounding harder as she approached, but today there were no new tracks and the lock was hanging on her side of the gate. When she got back, Nick had already arrived and the girls were waiting for her in the kitchen.

"I brought the masks," Kendra said, pointing to the stack of dust masks on the table.

"Excellent. I'm so glad you remembered." Alex picked up a mask and put it on. Kendra did the same, but Bailey announced that masks made her nose feel funny and that she and Roger would help her daddy.

The day passed pleasantly as Alex and Kendra sanded and Bailey played. The house, which had been so lonely and depressing when she'd first moved in, was a whirl of activity with dogs and little girls and a ridiculously attractive man knocking holes in her walls to access pipes. Holes Nick assured her would be properly patched when he was finished with the pipe work.

After the pipe work, he planned to climb up onto the roof and patch as much as he could. He warned her that the patches might be ugly, since they would involve a different shade of roofing and a lot of tar, which in turn had her thinking about investing in a brand-new roof. She'd truly have to live like a college kid if she decided to do that, but patches could take her only so far.

Words to live by, she decided as she wrote out a check for Nick's first week of work.

She felt like she was slapping patches on her life instead of dealing with the real issue, but it was hard to deal with the real issue when she wasn't certain what exactly she could do to fix things. She'd run to a safe place but still didn't feel safe. She may or may not be conjuring things up in her head. The fact that a set of tire tracks made her jumpy spoke volumes. She had a ways to go before she was ready to ease back into normal life.

When she presented Nick with his wages after he'd buckled the girls into their seats, he gave her a surprised look. "A check."

"Do you prefer cash?"

"No. I'm good with a check."

He thought she was avoiding bank accounts. Well, she had been.

"I'm not going to live like a fugitive when I did nothing wrong."

He had no way of knowing that when he looked at her with his gaze edged with protectiveness, it was all she could do to keep from moving closer, sliding her arms around him and leaning into him.

And she was going to make sure he didn't

know that, because he looked as if he was equally close to reaching for her. It was as if the air was vibrating between them.

"You've been through a lot. Anyone would lose their bearings." Nick's voice was gentle, but the look he gave her made her breath catch in her throat.

Breathe.

She folded her arms over her chest, taking a half step back. "I'm fine. The tire tracks unnerved me, but I understand why I'm unnerved, and that helps me deal with matters."

"Daddy, can we go?" Bailey asked. "I think my unicorn is lonely at home." She'd brought only her elephant that day.

"Just one more second," he called.

He looked as if he was about to say something that Alex didn't think she was ready to hear. So she changed the subject. "As to your payment, I can get cash next time if you prefer."

"I don't work under the table, so no need for cash." He patted the pocket where he'd stashed the check. "It's good, right?"

She let out a choked laugh. "If not, I have yet another issue to work through."

"Am I one of those issues?" There was a note in his voice, a quiet intensity to the mildly spoken question, which made it difficult to answer.

"Maybe."

Yes.

"This is new territory for me, too."

"I get that," she said softly. New territory was always the most exciting...and sometimes the most dangerous.

CHAPTER ELEVEN

Nick was working on the roof of the Dunlop house when Rosalie drove through on her way to the ranch to make practice cupcakes. He waved from the roof, and she pulled over to have a word.

"Kind of dangerous working up there when no one else is around."

"Actually I was just scoping things out. I have some small projects in the house that I'll finish while Alex is gone." He headed toward the ladder, and Rosalie automatically put a hand on a side rail to steady it as he climbed down. "It was nice of you to ask her over."

"She volunteered. According to Katie she has some experience piping frosting and offered to help." She gave him a sideways look as they started walking back to her SUV, which she'd left running. She had a feeling from a few things Katie had said that Nick was interested in the new neighbor in more than a neighborly way, and Rosalie was looking forward to meeting the woman who seemed to be bringing Nick back to the land of the living. She'd love to see him dating again, but it had to be a woman who was worthy of Nick and the girls.

Nick opened the SUV door, and she slid into the seat. "I assume that both of my girls will be covered in frosting when I get home?"

"They might be a little sticky," Rosalie agreed. "But I'll try to keep them from turning blue this time." There'd been a slight mishap with a concentrated food dye packet while making Christmas cookies.

"Good. Saves me having to squire around a couple Smurfs."

When Rosalie arrived on the ranch fifteen minutes later, the girls came racing out of the house to meet her.

"Aunt Katie said we're going to fweeze the cupcakes for later," Bailey said. "That we don't get to eat any of them."

"You'll get cupcakes," Rosalie said as she went around to the back of her SUV and opened the hatch. "Kendra, would you please carry this box for me?" She handed her oldest granddaughter the container of miniature cupcake pans. "And Bailey, I need you to carry this bag."

"What's in it?" Bailey asked as she took the handles of the tote.

"The pretty cupcake wrappers and a few other things."

Bailey beamed at her, then hugged the bag to her chest as she followed her sister up the walkway to the house where Rosalie had spent almost all of her adult life. Yes, she loved the house, had great memories, but she didn't belong there anymore.

And Will understands that.

She was still marveling over the fact that Will hadn't thrown down his napkin and walked out of the restaurant when she'd told him she didn't want anything to do with ranching. Not that he'd do anything so dramatic, but she'd expected questions, not acceptance.

"Is there anything else, Grandma?" Katie asked as Rosalie followed the girls through the door.

"No, I believe I have everything."

"In that case, let me introduce Alex Ryan, who is in for a treat today, baking with the Callahan crew."

"It's nice to meet you," Alex said, coming around the counter to shake Rosalie's hand. She was blonde and beautiful and just a touch nervous. Rosalie sensed that she was also practiced at hiding her nerves.

"Likewise. I have to thank you for allowing us to use your road. I know it's inconvenient with it running between the house and the barn, so we truly owe you a debt of gratitude."

"I'm glad to do it."

She sounded sincere, so Rosalie took her at her word. Personally, she could fully understand not wanting a stranger to drive through one's property. What she couldn't understand was why Alex had bought the place.

"By the way, Grandma. Nick made me promise not to turn the girls blue." Katie pulled bowls out from a cabinet as she spoke.

"This once," Rosalie said in a resigned voice. She glanced at Alex and got a conspiratorial smile in return. Another point in the plus column.

"I like turning blue," Bailey said.

"I'm sure you do, sweetie, but not today," Rosalie murmured. "It distresses your father."

"What would you like me to do?" Alex asked.

Rosalie glanced up. "I don't know if Katie filled you in on the master plan—"

"You'd better go over it again, Grandma, in case I got it wrong."

"Good idea. My business partner, Gloria, and I had a soft opening of our gift and garden store a little more than a month ago. We're going to announce the business in a big way at the June in Bloom event."

"It's a big vendor show and community celebration," Katie added. "Everyone comes, so it'll be a great way to spread the word about The Daisy Petal."

"There's also a lot of competition for attention, so Gloria and I are giving away mini cupcakes and having drawings for prize packages that we'll assemble a day or two before the event. Today we're making the cupcakes." She glanced down at Kendra and Bailey, who were wearing the aprons she'd made them for Christmas. "We will freeze most of them, but not all of them, because helpers need cupcakes."

The girls smiled their approval, and then Rosalie shifted her attention back to Alex. "I hear that you have a knack for making buttercream frosting."

"Actually, it's one of my few domestic skills. My mother's…friend…taught me one summer vacation."

"Excellent. I have recipes here, and I suggest we start a sort of assembly line..."

By the end of the afternoon, they'd turned out a whopping twenty dozen mini cupcakes. Alex, it turned out, not only made an excellent buttercream, but she was talented with a piping bag, too. She showed the girls how to make simple daisies, then demonstrated the more elaborate flowers in her arsenal. The girls were amazed at what she could do with a piping bag, and, frankly, so was Rosalie.

The longer they worked, the more Alex relaxed, and by the end of the day, she was laughing and sipping wine with Katie while Rosalie and the girls indulged in some fruit punch, their bright yellow hands looking very cute on the dark blue glasses from which they were drinking.

"So Grandma," Katie said after the last of the cupcakes were in freezer containers. "You haven't said a word about Vince Taylor. Is he behaving himself? Are his guests keeping you awake at night?"

Rosalie assumed from the fact that Katie made no move to fill in their guest that Alex knew all about the brouhaha between herself and her neighbor.

"He has been behaving himself," she said.

"He hasn't shown his face since we got the approval to start bridge construction."

"He's probably irked that whichever commissioner he had in his pocket failed to do his or her job."

"And I don't think he's getting as many guests as he'd hoped. There've been a few, but not the number that he bragged he was going to be getting on a weekly basis, and I don't think he's hosted an actual corporate retreat."

"That was supposed to be his main draw."

Rosalie took her glass to the sink, then took her glasses off the top of her head and settled them back on her nose. "He needs to practice patience and perhaps rethink his advertising." She looked out the window, then said, "It's getting late. I should go now before the deer come out."

"We'll help you carry stuff to the car," Kendra said, once again claiming the cupcake box. Bailey took the tote and the girls headed for the door.

Rosalie followed, stopping long enough to say to Alex, "Thank you so much for all your help."

"I'm glad to have something to do."

"Well, if you find yourself at loose ends,

feel free to join us when we make the gift baskets next week."

Alex's eyes lit up. "I'd love to."

The words were heartfelt, telling Rosalie that rural life wasn't exactly what Alex had expected it to be. That it was lonely at times and that one needed to get involved in community—any kind of community, be it a town gathering or a group of friends.

"Katie will give you the details when we firm it up. We would love to have you. Oh—bring those quilt tops and the lace you told us about. We'd love to see them and maybe give you some ideas about what you can do with them."

"Excellent. Thank you."

Rosalie nodded and then headed toward the car, where her great-granddaughters were waiting. She liked Alex Ryan and not only because of her piping skills. If Nick was interested in the woman, then he had Rosalie's blessing. She knew how hard it was to move on after losing a spouse, but she also knew that moving on was part of the process.

Part of living one's life.

DURING HER AFTERNOON at the Callahan ranch, for the first time since arriving, Alex was able to forget the circumstances that had brought her to Montana and simply enjoy her day.

It was an empowering feeling, to say the least. She couldn't say that she had friends yet, but she was moving in that direction. She was starting to build the new life she so desired. A new life where she wasn't afraid all the time.

What are your new friends going to think when they find out about your past?

Nick had accepted it.

Okay. There's that...

Nick was in his truck when she drove up, and she had the feeling that he'd been waiting for her to get home so she wouldn't be nervous going into the house alone.

"Did Roger and Gus behave?"

"They did," Nick said with a crooked half smile. "If you don't count the part where Gus ate my lunch."

"He didn't!" Alex said on a gasp.

"You had frozen pizza. I'll pay you back later."

"No need. Trust me on that."

"I locked the front gate," he said as he put his truck into gear.

"Thanks. I had fun with your sister and your grandmother."

"Did the girls get into the food coloring?"

"A little."

He rolled his eyes in an exaggerated way, and Alex smiled. Was this how normal families acted? Not taking things like dyed hands all that seriously? Actually enjoying one another's company? Watching each other's backs?

"See you tomorrow," he said in a low voice that made her think about how close she was to breaking her own rules, sliding a hand around the back of his neck and pulling his mouth to hers. From the way he was regarding her, she didn't think Nick would put up much of a struggle.

"Yeah. See you."

The dogs greeted Alex at the door, Gus with his slow-wagging tail and canine grin and Roger with a series of hops and clever circles, both of them happy to have their foster mom back with them, where she belonged. She needed to call Wanda tomorrow to make certain that if someone was interested in adopting Gus or Roger, she had first dibs on giving them their forever home.

"Did you eat Nick's lunch?" she asked Gus,

who looked sideways in a patently guilty way. "No more of that, please." She ruffled the wiry hair on Roger's head. "Imagine that—you're the positive role model today. Good job."

Alex ate an early dinner and curled up on the sofa to read. Tomorrow while Nick was there, she'd go into town, do her shopping, and maybe look at the local furniture and thrift stores to see if she could find anything that might start making her house feel like a home.

She'd just started for the stairs when her phone rang. She didn't recognize the number, but the area code was from her part of Virginia. A chill went through her.

It was early evening in Virginia, after business hours, so it wouldn't be an investigator... would it?

Get a grip.

It had to be a robocall. The kind that came from familiar area codes and tricked people into answering when they otherwise would not. Alex turned off the ringer and headed up the stairs, wondering if she'd missed an opportunity to extend a warranty on a vehicle, or if the caller was interested in helping her pay off her student loans. Or perhaps a million-dollar lottery win if she handed over her social security number for verification.

But even as the logical explanations marched through her brain, another part of her wondered if it might be the beginning of something more insidious than someone trying to trick her into giving her bank account number. Maybe it indicated that someone was tracing her. An investigator, or an investor...or perhaps the guy who'd broken into her apartment. Maybe that same person was responsible for the tracks at her gate.

Alex pulled the sheets up to her chin, doing her best to take comfort in the fact that she wasn't alone—that her two furry protectors were there to warn her of intruders. But if she had an intruder, just how much damage could she do with her Louisville Slugger?

It was a scam call. It had to be...

Unless it wasn't.

NICK WAS BROUGHT out of a light sleep by the soft sound of whimpering in the girls' room next door to his. He got out of bed and pulled on his sweats and hoodie before quietly letting himself out of his room and into his daughters'.

Kendra was sound asleep, her face relaxed,

her hand tucked under her cheek. He wanted to make sure she stayed that way. She put herself under a lot of pressure being Bailey's protector as well as her sister.

Bailey was still whimpering—nothing close to a full-on night terror, but he didn't want to take the chance of her waking Kendra. He scooped her up into his arms and then carried her out the door and into the living room, which was navigable due to the porch light filtering in through the windows. He settled in the recliner and, after tugging an afghan over his daughter, started rocking.

Bailey gave a small sigh and snuggled against him, then her little body went stiff as she made a low keening sound.

And it begins...

But it didn't. Bailey gave a couple of choking half sobs, then her eyes snapped open and her body jerked.

She blinked at him through the semi-darkness. "Daddy?"

"Yeah, Bill?"

She stared at him, then her little body relaxed. She loved to hate her nickname. "Daddy," she murmured as she snuggled back against him. "Why are we out here?"

"You were having a bad dream and I didn't want you to wake up your sister."

"I didn't have a dream," she said simply.

"I think you did, but you can't remember. Dreams do that sometimes."

"Oh."

They'd had this discussion before, because she never remembered her night-terror episodes, but Kendra did.

"You know what, Daddy?"

"What?"

Her little fingers curled around the edge of the afghan. "I think if Woger spent the night sometimes, I wouldn't have dreams I don't remember."

"Roger lives with Alex, and he helps her with her dreams."

"Alex has dreams she doesn't remember?"

"Everybody has dreams like that." He smiled down at her. "Maybe Lizzie Belle could help."

"No." Bailey shook her head against his chest. "Lizzie Belle pushes."

"You're right. She'd probably hog the pillow and push you out of bed." He leaned his head back against the chair cushion. "Maybe Tigger would sleep with you." He was Katie's big ginger cat, who spent the night in Katie's room when he wasn't out hunting.

"He makes my legs go 'sleep." Bailey yawned. "Ellie and Unicorn will help me."

"They always have," Nick agreed. "I don't think they'll let you down now."

Bailey gave a murmur of agreement, then a few seconds later she was out. Nick closed his eyes and continued to rock. He'd put her back to bed when he was sure she was sound asleep, tuck her in with Ellie the Elephant and Unicorn, and then go back to his own bed.

If he went to sleep right away, he'd have three hours of rest before he had to get up and go to work.

Nothing new there.

ALEX WAS AT the table drinking coffee when Nick let himself in the back door. Other than giving a rap on the frame as he opened the door if she wasn't in sight, he'd given up knocking.

"Hey," she said, getting to her feet and heading to the coffeepot. After the first few days of him refusing coffee because he brought his own, she no longer offered. She pulled in a deep breath as she filled the cup, and he noticed that she was holding herself oddly, as if she wasn't feeling all that well.

"Are you okay? Were there more tracks at the gate?"

She turned, and that was when he saw the shadows beneath her eyes. "I didn't sleep well." She frowned then. "You don't look like you slept, either."

He hadn't thought it was that noticeable, although, now that he ran his hand over his chin, he realized that he had neglected to shave. "I was up last night with Bailey."

"Is everything okay?"

"Yeah. How about with you?"

She started to say something positive, then abruptly stopped and pressed her lips together.

"Alex?" He took a few steps closer, taking care not to get too close. He needn't have worried, because after a moment of hesitation, Alex closed the gap between them and brought her cheek to rest against his chest.

"What's wrong?" His arms closed around her.

"I know I said we shouldn't touch." Alex's cheek pressed harder against him as she spoke.

"It's okay." More than okay. It felt right.

"I had a phone call last night. It was probably a scam call. I didn't answer it, but what with the tracks at the gate, well, my mind kind of went wild. Needless to say, it was a sleepless night."

He pulled her close again, running his hand over her back, soothing her, wishing he could fix everything. Now. "It'll take a while for that to stop happening."

"I know." She whispered the words against the front of his shirt, and he pulled her closer, his fingers coming up to thread through her hair, loosening the knot so that it threatened to come undone.

He felt her swallow, then she brought her hands up to his chest and eased herself out of his embrace. "Nick… I'm not going to make any hard-and-fast rules here, because I don't know if I can keep them."

"Understood."

"I'm glad you're here, and I can't promise not to touch you."

He curled his fingers into loose fists to keep from touching her. "I get it, Alex. You're not in a position to make any kind of promise."

"Not until I feel like everything is behind me."

"It might already be behind you."

She managed a quick smile, then it was gone. "My logical side tells me that. My other more cautious side isn't so sure. It's going to take some convincing."

And he would be there while she figured things out, in more than a physical way. He lifted a hand, holding it out to her, palm up. Alex stared at it for a moment, then put her hand in his and his fingers closed. A sign of trust. That was all he needed.

She pulled in a deep breath and then exhaled again. Her grip tightened ever so slightly, then relaxed. "All right."

He wasn't sure what was all right, but he nodded. "We'll...go with the flow."

The faint smile returned. "No pressure."

"Just...flow."

She laughed then and pulled her fingers free. "You're a good guy, Nick Callahan."

He wanted to be more than that, but for the moment, he'd settle for good-guy status.

THE NEXT SEVERAL days passed in a flurry of activity as Alex helped Nick work on her house, repairing and replacing trim, painting cabinetry, and finally giving the okay to replace the worn kitchen floor. They took care not to touch, talked about ordinary things, but Alex couldn't shake the feeling that she was growing closer to the man with each passing day. He was there for her. She knew it as certainly as she knew he'd drive the quarter mile to lock her gate before turning around and heading back to his family at the end of the workday.

There had been no more calls—robo or otherwise—and Alex's paranoia ebbed as she put the situation into perspective.

She was *so* ready for the next bad thing to happen that anything out of the ordinary, even a phone call with a Virginia area code or tracks at her gate, made her believe that disaster was about to strike again. But that wasn't necessarily true. She'd been in Montana for weeks and nothing had happened to make her believe that the incident that had driven her across the country wasn't over and done.

She could take back her life. She just had to take care not to take it back so quickly that she made mistakes, and that was why she was keeping things between her and Nick at a low simmer. She didn't want to make a mistake. Heaven knew she'd made enough of them with Jason to fulfill her quota for the next several years.

As promised, Alex brought the box of quilt tops and lace to Rosalie's shop when she went to help make gift baskets. She also brought Roger and Gus after Rosalie assured her that the dog play area Nick had partitioned off from the rest of the backyard earlier that spring was inescapable. Alex half wondered if Roger was the litmus test for the inescapabilty of the construction prior to the official opening of the shop, but she decided that it was for Bailey's sake that the little dog was coming to town.

"You must be Alex!" A woman wearing a bright multicolored tunic over skinny jeans beamed at Alex as she started up the walk with both dogs on leashes. "I'm Gloria. It's so good to meet you."

"Nice to meet you. I'm looking forward to seeing all the wonderful stuff you make."

"I can say the same. Rosalie tells me you make an excellent buttercream frosting, but she won't let me get my hands on any of the eats."

"All in good time." Rosalie's voice came from inside the open front door, then she stepped out onto the porch and reached for Gus's leash. "I'm glad you brought them. Bailey speaks highly of both."

"She's definitely a dog person, and Kendra seems to prefer cats."

"I'm a goat woman myself," Gloria said, "but since my Lizzie Belle is having so much fun on the ranch with her beau, Wendell, I can't see bringing her back to town, even if we win the zoning fight."

Alex smiled at the mention of the goat who'd playfully knocked her into the mud puddle. "She does seem to enjoy herself on the ranch."

"Let's get these guys in the doggie playpen. They're the first to try it out." Rosalie looked over her shoulder as she led Gus around the house and through a gate leading to the backyard. "I'm hoping to get a dog. We've missed having Lizzie Belle here, and I don't think our neighbor can come up with a zoning issue for a dog."

The dog area was roomy and grassy, with a cute house located in the shade of a leafy tree. Water and food dishes were under a small shelter, and the areas that weren't grassy were newly graveled.

"I put some toys in that wire basket." Rosalie pointed to a bushel basket near the house, and sure enough, it was loaded with rubber chew toys.

"Roger will have those spread out in no time."

"As he should." Rosalie released Gus from his leash, and he made it three or four steps before lying down in the cool grass. Roger, on the other hand, immediately began exploring his surroundings. He passed the basket, stopped, went back, sniffed, then picked up a chewy hamburger and continued his exploration.

"Did you bring the quilt top and lace?" Rosalie asked.

"I did. I hope you can give me some tips on getting the stains out of the lace."

"If I can't, Gloria can. And if she can't, then we'll run it to the quilt shop to see what they think."

Katie showed up with Bailey and Kendra a half hour later, while Alex was loading gift baskets that were to be given away as hourly prizes over the course of the two-day event. The girls immediately came over to inspect the finished baskets, which contained a variety of small lotions, packets of potpourri and dried herbs, pretty gardening tools, candles, salt scrubs and gift certificates.

"I like the ribbons," Kendra said. "And the ballerina stuff." The ballerina stuff being the tulle wrapping around the baskets, holding the contents in place. "Bailey and I took ballerina lessons."

"But we didn't get on our toes," Bailey explained. "It hurts. I tried." She demonstrated how she tried to get on her toes, making an exasperated face when she failed to achieve a pointe position in her sneakers.

Alex gave an approving nod. "Nice try, though."

"Ballerinas wear special shoes," Kendra explained seriously. "And it takes a *long* time to get your feet ready to wear the shoes."

"Ah."

"Where's W-r-roger?" Bailey asked, drawing the name out and coming very close to getting that *r* out. Kendra must have been working with her on her pronunciation—and apparently winning the battle.

"He's in the dog yard in the back, honey." Rosalie came into the room, and both girls rushed to hug her. "Let's let him play and explore until after lunch, okay?"

Katie gave a nod. "You can each have a cupcake after you eat your sandwich." She met Rosalie's gaze. "I brought the ones we mangled with me."

"How about me?" Gloria asked from across

the room. "Do *I* get a cupcake if I eat my sandwich?"

Kendra and Bailey giggled.

"Yes," Katie said with exaggerated patience. "You get a cupcake, too."

For the second time in a matter of days, Alex was immersed in girl time—something she hadn't experienced since boarding school, when she and her closest friends had been inseparable. They'd essentially been one another's family, and the bonds had been tight.

And then they'd gone their separate ways.

Things had changed, life moved on, making Alex wonder if anything lasted. She glanced at the two older women and her question was answered. Yes. Some things lasted. Both women had been married for more than fifty years before losing their spouses. That was inspiring, to say the least.

"Alex!"

She looked up to see Bailey standing in front of her. "Can you let me into the dog cage?"

"Yard, honey. Dog yard," Rosalie said absently as she tied ribbons on vases. In addition to the door prizes, the first fifty patrons would receive a daisy bouquet in a cute vase.

"I'll let you inside and you can play with him if you want, but we can't let him out."

"I'll go, too," Kendra said. "So Gus doesn't get jealous."

When Rosalie came back, the conversation continued as Gladys Knight and the Pips, the Eagles, and Linda Ronstadt played in the background. Alex had just finished tying the last bow on the last basket when Bailey came racing into the room, Kendra hot on her heels.

"Woger got out!" Bailey announced on a half sob. "I wanted to go to the house to go to the bathroom and he ran right out when I opened the gate!"

"He did," Kendra said breathlessly. "And that mean man is yelling at him."

Gloria and Rosalie exchanged a quick glance, then Rosalie said to Katie, "Please keep the girls in here."

Katie took Bailey into her arms, and Gloria reached for Kendra's hand, pulling her closer and wrapping a comforting arm around the little girl. Alex hesitated, then purposely followed Rosalie through the room that had formerly been the kitchen and out the back door.

WHEN ROSALIE GOT to the backyard, Gus stood alone in the fenced dog yard, and Roger was indeed missing. And, from the commotion sounding on the other side of the fence, Rosalie knew exactly where he was. Disembodied voices floated over the fence, giving terse, hissed directions.

"Go that way."

"No, the other way."

"Grab that little mutt before he gets into the house again."

It was only when she'd started toward the front of the house, intending to gain access to Vince Taylor's property in the most legal way possible, that she realized that Alex had left the house and was following close behind her.

"He's my dog," she murmured as she caught up with Rosalie.

"It might be better if I handle this alone."

"I'm responsible. I brought him."

Since she didn't have time to talk sense into Alex, Rosalie simply continued on her way, letting herself out of the gate onto the sidewalk and then heading down Vince's walkway to the porch, where she rang the bell. A harried-looking woman answered.

She forced a smile, then realized who was standing on the porch.

"We've come for the dog," Rosalie said.

"I'll…" The woman turned, smiling at the couple sitting in the small parlor, holding glasses of wine while their gazes bounced back and forth as if they were watching a tennis match. The woman then took off through the house, and Rosalie and Alex followed, skirting a puddle of red wine.

"Mr. Taylor. The dog's owners are here," she called in a falsely bright voice. The couple with the wine followed, apparently not wanting to miss a minute of the action.

Vince had done a spectacular job renovating the interior of the house. Everything was top grade, from the flooring to the countertops. Too bad he didn't have that many guests to enjoy it.

When Rosalie stepped out into the backyard, Roger was holed up beneath some barbecue equipment and looked as if he had no intention of ever coming out. Vince had just finished a phone call. He gave Rosalie a hard look, then palmed the phone.

"Animal control will be here in a matter of minutes. They will take care of the matter."

Rosalie let out a breath and simply regarded the dunderhead in front of her for one very long moment. "What are you?" she asked at last. "Some kind of cartoon villain?"

Vince's face went red, and he shot a quick look at the guests standing on his back step before bringing his glare back to Rosalie. "Excuse me?"

"You stole my fence last year in the boundary dispute between our properties, made us give up Lizzie Belle." She nodded at the guests who were watching wide-eyed. "Lizzie Belle is my business partner's adorable pet dwarf goat. She now lives on a ranch instead of with us, thanks to Mr. Taylor." Rosalie turned back to Vince, whose color had risen to the point that he now resembled an heirloom tomato. "You've managed to turn the county commission against us, and now you are picking on small dogs." She heard a choked laugh but didn't know if it came from Alex or from a guest.

It had to have come from a guest, because Alex was now on her knees, trying to coax Roger out of his hiding place.

"That 'little dog' raced into the house and upset Mrs. Jennings, which resulted in a broken bottle of wine and probably a laundry bill."

"I'll pay for the wine and the laundry bill,"

Rosalie said. "And you do realize that this dog once lived in this house, and that his owner moved, leaving him behind? He spent months here waiting for his owner to return."

She heard a small "oh" and turned to nod at the guest holding the wineglass. There were small red stains on her skirt that Rosalie hadn't noticed before. "It's true."

"Got you." Alex climbed back to her feet cradling Roger against her. "I'll pay for the wine and the cleaning and any other damage Roger did. He's my dog now."

"I'm glad he has a home," the female guest said.

Vince gave a tight smile. "I was unaware of these circumstances," he said stiffly. "Forgive me. I thought he was some stray off the streets."

"He isn't," Rosalie announced. "So perhaps you can call animal control."

"Yes. Of course." Vince brought the phone to his ear, and Rosalie thanked her lucky stars that the wine-drinking guests had followed them to the backyard. Otherwise the Roger episode might not have had such a happy ending.

"How much do I owe you for the wine and the cleaning?" Alex asked.

Vince smiled, but Rosalie could see the deep anger in his eyes. "Don't worry about it. We're neighbors. These things happen." He turned to his guests. "Mrs. Jennings will open another bottle of wine. Compliments of the house."

Alex and Rosalie quickly made their way back through the beautiful house, out the door and down the walk to The Daisy Petal. After the front door was closed, Alex put Roger on the floor, and he was instantly surrounded by two little girls patting him and making certain he was okay.

Alex turned to Rosalie. "I am so sorry."

Rosalie held up a hand. "Not another word."

Alex nodded, then asked, "Roger really lived next door? Nick told me his story, but I didn't realize he was your neighbor."

"Wanda caught him a few weeks after we first moved in," Gloria said as she handed both women glasses of chardonnay. "So we didn't know him well. Just his name—and only because the animal-control guy kept driving up and calling him." She made a sputtering noise. "Like little Roger would fall for that."

ROGER SPENT THE remainder of the afternoon quietly lying between Bailey and Kendra in the dining room as the girls worked on a puzzle and then played a board game. Alex had brought Gus inside shortly after they returned from their adventure next door, but Roger stayed where he was, parked between the sisters, instead of greeting his friend with his usual exuberance.

"He'll snap back," Rosalie said when she caught Alex studying the terrier through the arched entrance of the dining room.

"I know," Alex replied before starting to tie one of the last vase ribbons into a fancy bow. "I think he's flashing back to his past." And she knew what that felt like.

"No doubt." Rosalie sent her a warm smile. "He'll feel better once he gets home again."

Home.

Alex liked the sound of that. She *was* making a home, for her and her dogs. And honestly? She'd never had a living arrangement approach home status before. Her apartment had been nice, but she'd never felt like she belonged there…in fact, she'd never felt as if she'd belonged anywhere until she'd moved to the dilapidated Victorian house near the Callahan ranch.

Alex gave the bow a tug, tightening it around the vase. She hadn't realized how good it could feel to be greeted with sloppy canine kisses, and to have real neighbors and a sense of community.

She shot another look at Roger nestled between the girls. Roger wasn't afraid to accept comfort and closeness now that he trusted his people.

And she was beginning to feel the same way.

CHAPTER TWELVE

NICK WAS FINISHING up a patch on the bathroom wall when he heard Alex's car in the driveway. He finished smoothing the joint putty, then headed into the living room as Alex let herself into the house, a dog on either side of her.

"How was it?" he asked as she bent down to take the leash off first Gus, then Roger.

"Well, Roger got out and caused mayhem with the neighbor—that jerk who lives next door to your grandmother."

"I know the guy you're talking about."

"Roger recognized home and escaped from the dog yard, broke a bottle of wine and basically enraged Mr. Taylor."

"It doesn't take much."

"Then your grandmother asked him if he was a cartoon, and then he got all nice when he realized that some of his guests were watching. I caught Roger, and we all went home."

"Sounds like a full afternoon."

"And we got all the gift baskets done."

"Well done."

"I like your family," she said simply. "They're like something out of a movie."

"I hope you don't mean *The Addams Family*."

The dimple showed in her cheek as she took another step forward and surprised him by taking a light hold of the front of his shirt. "I do not."

"Loosening up, are we?" he asked with a heart-stopping smile.

"I'm working toward it."

He gave in to temptation and leaned down to lightly kiss her. "I'm not going to get anything done if I do that again," he muttered. Alex hadn't backed off, and he needed to kiss her again, but he'd promised himself to take it slow.

"Then I won't pay you." She grinned at him and stepped back.

He headed back into the bathroom, then called out, "Would you like to go out Friday evening?"

His question was met with silence—to the point that he had to lean out of the room to make certain she'd heard him. Oh, yeah. She had. Suddenly there was a rock in his stomach. He'd moved too soon. "You don't have to go."

"*Where* would we go?" she asked cautiously.

He held her gaze, watching her reaction as he said, "We would go to the Shamrock Pub. Brady, Katie's fiancé, is coming home, and we're going out to celebrate his getting done with his welding course. If you don't come, then I'll go along as the much appreciated third wheel."

"You can't stay home?"

"No. Not an option. Katie made it clear that I need to get off the ranch. She says going to your place and the building supply store doesn't count."

"I'll go."

She made it sound like she'd agreed to face the firing squad, and she seemed to realize it. Her expression relaxed and she stepped forward, coming to stand a few feet in front of him. "Thank you for being patient."

Funny thing. He thought that when he decided to date, he'd be the one asking for patience as he worked through the obstacles that came with being a single dad devoted to his daughters.

"Just a warning. I'm going to be over-thinking."

He grinned and reached out to smooth the hair away from her temples. "Me, too. About you."

Her lips parted, then she closed her mouth and tilted her head to one side. "Fair enough," she said softly. He had no clue what she meant, but it didn't seem to be anything bad.

Cool. And he was about to go on his first date in over a decade.

ALEX STOOD AT the window watching the taillights of Nick's truck disappear before heading upstairs to bed with Roger and Gus trailing behind her. When she turned on the water to brush her teeth, the pipes no longer sang—thank you, Nick—and when she climbed into bed, easing Gus aside so she had room for her feet, she no longer felt the clutch of anxiety.

Thank you, Nick, Gus and Roger.

She was happy and secure for the first time in months, but she couldn't silence the small voice that wondered how long it was going to last.

There's no reason it can't last for a long time.

She had some stuff to tell Nick, sure. He

already knew the bare bones, but he didn't know that she'd come within a hairbreadth of being arrested. And while she was innocent, there were a lot of people who hadn't believed her—and still didn't.

She'd lived honestly, done the right thing and found herself in big trouble, all because she'd been too trusting.

And here she was—about to trust again.
This time it's different.

Alex put her feet against Gus's heavy body and pried a little bit more space free.

Different. Yes.

Alex fell asleep almost as soon as she'd levered enough legroom from Gus, waking to find sunlight streaming in through the window. She hummed to herself as she padded downstairs in her slippers and robe and made coffee. No Nick today because he was helping his grandmother set up the display in her booth, prepping for the big picnic the following day.

She'd just let the dogs back in after their morning romp and settled with them in the living room when her phone rang from where she'd left it charging in the kitchen. Expecting Nick, she nearly dropped it when she saw that once again someone was calling from the Virginia area code.

Biting her lip, Alex took a chance and answered.

"Alex…is that you?"

She didn't recognize the male voice, although there was something about the tone and timbre that seemed familiar.

"It's Lawrence. Lawrence Stoddard."

Alex almost hung up. Almost. But curiosity overcame caution and she said, "How are you?"

"I'm doing well, all things considered, but to tell you the truth, I've been worried about you."

That was…touching.

"There's nothing to worry about, Lawrence. I've been cleared and I'm doing okay." *Rebuilding my life one brick at a time.*

"I'm sorry for what Jason did. He screwed me over, too."

It was on the tip of her tongue to ask how, but instead she said, "I'm sorry to hear that."

There was a brief silence, then Lawrence said, "I don't suppose you'd like to meet for coffee. I wouldn't mind talking to someone who is, you know, going through the same thing. Even though I've worked to keep my head held high, the way people talk is getting to me."

So he wasn't doing all that well, and apparently he didn't know she was a couple of thousand miles away. *Thank you, Mom, for not letting the cat out of the bag.*

"I can't, Lawrence." She spoke gently. "I'm sorry."

"I understand."

"How did you get my number?"

"It was in some of the stuff Jason left behind. I've got a key to his old apartment. I'm selling everything."

"Good, Lawrence. It's best to get rid of the bad memories."

"My feelings exactly. I'm sorry to have bothered you."

"No. I'm glad you reached out. And if things get rough…well, call."

"Thank you, Alex. Take care of yourself."

Alex hung up the phone, her heart breaking a little at the sadness in the man's voice. She retraced her steps to the sofa, and when she sat, both dogs took their protective positions, Gus leaning against her leg and Roger on her shoe. She hugged a pillow to her middle and stared across the room. If she'd been in Virginia, would she have met with him?

Maybe, even though it would bring every-thing she was trying not to think about rag-ing back to the surface. Maybe that was where it needed to be so that she could deal with it. It would have been helpful to talk to someone who truly understood what it was like living under a cloud. And it would have been satisfying to explain to her mother that, no, Lawrence wasn't weathering the storm of his brother's betrayal any better than she was.

She wasn't weak for seeking out a new life in a new area. She was dealing with mat-ters differently than Jason's brother, and it sounded like her way was working better than his. She had friends in her life and a man...

She blew out a long breath.

She'd continue that part of the conversa-tion with herself later, because she didn't know what she was going to do about the fact that she'd fallen in love with Nick Callahan.

ROSALIE BREATHED A sigh of relief when the vendor tent she'd ordered for June in Bloom finally arrived several days after the prom-ised delivery date. Thankfully, they still had time to practice setting the thing up before the big event.

Some vendors made do with sunshades and folding tables, while larger businesses set up tents or built structures that mimicked their actual storefronts. Rosalie and Gloria had decided to hit the middle ground, purchasing a sturdy screw-together metal frame with a colorful canvas cover. The directions touted ease of setup, stating that all one needed was a screwdriver and a combination wrench.

"And apparently an uncanny ability to read between the lines," Gloria muttered as they attempted to connect two pieces that looked as if they should go together as per the instructions, but clearly didn't. Gloria dropped the heavy cross piece and sat down on the grass beside it, leaving Rosalie holding an upright.

The components were unwieldy, and some pieces were difficult to identify, even after laying everything out on the grass in the backyard, which annoyed Rosalie, who could usually put together anything simply by looking at a picture.

"There are steps missing," Rosalie muttered as she stared at the minimalistic directions.

She lowered the directions and gave Gloria a long look. "I should call Nick, but I hate to bother him while he's working on the Dunlop ranch." After all, Alex was paying him for his time.

"Is there anyone else you could ask?" Gloria inquired in a voice which clearly indicated that she had someone in mind.

Rosalie cut to the chase. "Do you think I should ask Will?"

"Yes. It's a matter of needing a third pair of hands, and I know that Will is still at the co-op coffee klatch since it's not yet nine o'clock. He's in the vicinity."

Given Gloria's reasoning, it seemed reasonable to ask Will for some assistance. They were, after all, friends. That didn't stop Rosalie from having to clear her throat twice as she called the co-op and asked to speak to Will. It was allergies, of course, not nerves.

Rosalie closed her eyes, wondering at the need to lie to herself. It was clearly nerves making her voice feel thick.

"Hi, Will," she said in response to his cautious hello. Apparently not many people called the co-op and asked for him. "If you have a few minutes, I need some advice as to how to put together the framed tent that Gloria and I bought for the June in Bloom—"

"Would fifteen minutes be okay?"

"I…uh… That would be lovely."

Ten minutes after her call, Will pulled up in front of the house and Rosalie met him at the door. After thanking him for coming she handed him the directions that had come with the tent.

"I think they left out every other step," he said after putting on his glasses and reviewing the directions. "This doesn't make a lot of sense."

"I agree." Thank goodness it wasn't just her.

Rosalie ushered Will through the back door into the yard where Gloria still sat on the grass, her face turned up to the sun. She smiled at Will as he came down the steps. "Thank you for coming, Will. I've been working out, but these frame pieces are heavy."

"Glad to be of service." He studied the pieces laid out on the grass, then looked over his shoulder at Rosalie. "Do you have a cordless drill?"

"Of course."

"I think we'd find that to be a real time saver."

"I'll get it." Rosalie turned and trotted up the steps. She liked how Will didn't make her feel like he was a man coming to the rescue. He made no secret about the fact that he found the directions as confusing as she did. He'd probably also built more things in his life than she had and was therefore more well-versed on what went where and why.

Will tended to move stiffly, the result of more than one encounter with a bronc back in his younger days, but as he held components of the frame in place so that Rosalie could fasten them with the rechargeable drill, he seemed to loosen up, and he also started to whistle under his breath as he worked. He seemed to enjoy the puzzle of the tent.

While she and Will constructed the frame, Gloria laid out the cheerful pink, green and white striped canvas cover, then they all gathered around to debate the best way to get the heavy material up and over the frame.

"Maybe I should call Travis to help," Will said. The frame was eight feet tall at the highest point. "He's in town for a couple hours."

Gloria gave her head a shake. "We grab these ropes and throw them over the frame and drag the canvas over the top."

Will grinned at her. "Like tarping hay."

"If you say so," Gloria responded. She shot Rosalie a look and came this close to winking. Rosalie was certain of it.

Well, she would let Gloria have her fun. She wasn't going to worry about where her friendship with Will was heading, because she'd made it very clear that all she was interested in was friendship. Will seemed fine with that. Like her, he was looking for companionship. A different kind of companionship from what he got at the morning co-op coffee meetings.

Rosalie couldn't say it was exactly easy-peasy getting the canvas up over the frame; however, they managed to get it into place after a few false starts.

It fit like a glove, and Gloria beamed. "It's perfect."

"It looks nice," Will agreed. He turned to Rosalie. "Do you need help taking it down?"

"We're going to leave it up for a couple of nights to see if there are issues with the wind and such."

"Good idea. If you ladies no longer need me, I promised Travis I'd meet him for lunch…he's paying."

"You don't want to miss that," Rosalie said

on a laugh. "Thanks so much for the help, Will. I'll walk you to your truck."

She'd spent so much time dodging the man that it seemed odd to want to prolong her time with him, but life was odd sometimes.

Will stopped at his truck and looked down at her. "I have a question, Rosalie. And I trust that you'll feel free to say no."

Her heart started beating faster. "What question is that?"

"Would you like to come out with me on Friday? Nothing fancy. I was thinking we could go to the Shamrock Pub. Just…casual like."

So that she didn't feel pushed or pressured.

Rosalie smiled. "I'd like that, Will. Shall I meet you there?"

"I could pick you up."

"Eight o'clock?"

"Eight it is."

NICK BROUGHT HIS hand to the small of Alex's back as they stopped just inside the door of the Shamrock Pub, his touch warm and reassuring through the thin cotton of her simple chambray blouse. Before her lay a classic Irish pub and a sea of cowboy hats.

"It's busy," Alex murmured. Almost every

table was filled, and two bartenders were working behind the beautiful antique bar that graced the far wall.

"It's a popular place." Nick pointed to one of the few free tables. "Why don't you commandeer that table and I'll see if I can round up a couple more chairs for Katie and Brady."

"Will do," she said, noting that another couple had come in through the back door and were also looking for a place to sit. She reached the table and settled into a seat that allowed her a view of both doors and the bar, putting her purse on Nick's seat.

Then she closed her eyes for one brief moment, doing her best to center herself.

She was on a date, and there was no reason she should be so uptight...except that this date mattered.

The drive to town had been quiet, with her and Nick staring out the front windshield, both lost in deep thoughts. It had been Nick who'd broken the silence as the lights of Gavin came into view.

"Scary, huh?"

Alex had slowly turned to meet his gaze. "Totally."

Although, honestly, Nick had more on the line than she did. Any decision he made in his life affected his daughters, whereas Alex had to worry only about herself, her own peace of mind. And not alienating the family she was truly coming to care for. A family that, even though she'd known them for only a short time, was more of an anchor to her than her real family had ever been. The call from Lawrence had helped her to realize just how well she'd landed and how many blessings she could count. She could still be in Virginia, living with her mother, letting the paranoia about her apartment break-in and the investigation eat her alive.

"The first date is the hardest."

Will there be more?

Alex hadn't voiced the question aloud. Instead she'd given Nick a sidelong look, hoping he didn't realize she was studying him. There was so much about him that she admired. The way he kept his word and cared for his daughters and was there for his family. And he'd been there for her, helping her deal with her fears, simply by his presence, if nothing more.

Nick spoke to a couple sitting at a nearby table, then grabbed two chairs and headed back to their table. He'd barely set the chairs down when the rear door opened and Katie walked in, looking dazzling in a pink tank top and dark denim jeans, holding hands with a breathtakingly handsome dark-haired cowboy.

Nick got to his feet and waved them over to the table before sitting down again. He wasn't quite seated when something caught his attention across the room. Alex followed his gaze and spotted Rosalie sitting at a table with a rather dapper older cowboy.

"Huh," Nick said as he settled all the way into his chair.

"Is it unusual for Rosalie to go out?"

"No…but…" He pressed his lips together thoughtfully, then met her gaze. "I don't usually see her in the Shamrock."

"She seems quite comfortable," Alex said.

"Yes," he said musingly. "She does."

"Grandma's here," Katie announced as she pulled out a chair. "And I think she is purposely not looking at us."

"I think you're right," the dark-haired man with her said with a smile. He held out a hand to Alex. "Brady O'Neil."

"Alex Ryan."

"We are poor hosts," Katie said to Nick, "making people perform their own introductions." She gave him a cheeky smile. "My excuse is that I'm kind of stunned to see Grandma out with Will McGuire. What's yours?"

"They have been spending a lot of time together," Nick said before raising his hand to flag down the server, a young cowboy with a towel tucked into his belt. He ordered two pitchers, then adjusted his chair so that his back was to his grandmother and put a hand on the back of Alex's chair.

She gave Nick a quick glance, and he met her gaze with a smile in his eyes before shifting his attention back to Brady. He seemed more relaxed now that they weren't alone. Or maybe he'd come to some kind of reckoning, because he started casually caressing Alex's shoulder with the tips of his fingers as he spoke to Brady, messing with Alex's peace of mind, albeit in a good way.

"Are you doing okay?" Katie asked.

Alex gave her a perplexed look. "Yes."

Katie shrugged. "You seem a little nervous, but you don't need to be. Nick's nervous enough for both of you."

Alex glanced at Nick, who was deep in

conversation with Brady, then back at Katie. "How can you tell?"

"Sister superpowers." She leaned a little closer, lowering her voice. "I know you guys are taking it slow and all that, and rightly so, given the situation, but I just want to tell you that since you've shown up, Nick is different. He's happier. So maybe you guys are just friends, but whatever you are…good work."

Alex blinked, not certain what to say after that rather amazing speech. "Uh…thank you?"

Katie smiled and raised her beer, and Alex couldn't escape the notion that Katie had just accomplished something she'd set out to do.

"By the way," Katie said more loudly, "Bailey and Kendra are cooking up plans to have a sleepover at your house."

Alex automatically glanced at Nick, who said, "Don't be puppy-eyed into something you don't want to do."

"No. You don't understand," Alex said. "It sounds like fun."

"Hey. I could come, too," Katie said. "We could play games with the girls, make popcorn or fudge, then watch something fun and mindless after they go to bed. I have a stack of old DVDs that—"

"Do you have *Bridesmaids*?" Alex interjected.

"Yes!" Katie held up a hand and Alex high-fived her. Brady and Nick exchanged looks, then tipped up their beers.

"We'll set a date tomorrow or the next day," Alex said.

A few minutes later the band started, and Katie and Brady exchanged a look, then got to their feet and started for the small dance floor. Rosalie and Will also got to their feet, but instead of heading to the dance floor, they went to the door, Will's hand hovering protectively at the small of Rosalie's back.

"Smart move on their part," Nick said. "It's more like a mosh pit than a dance floor out there." He gave Alex's fingers a small squeeze. "But if you want to brave it, I'm game."

"I don't need to dance." She was happy sitting there with Nick's hand on top of hers.

"Your grandmother looked like she was having a good time."

"Yeah. It's kind of strange to see her out on a date, but more power to her. By the way, just so you know, my sister is under the mistaken impression that she can whisper."

Alex bit her lip but smiled, anyway. "I

wondered if you'd heard the part about you being nervous and...the other stuff."

"How could I not?" His expression sobered and he leaned closer, putting his hand lightly on her knee. "But she's right. I am nervous, and I am happier."

Alex nodded, not knowing what to say.

"And, now that my grandma is no longer here to witness, I'm going to kiss you, Alex."

Her heart hit her ribs, but her voice was even as she said, "Here?" with a lift of her eyebrows. "In a crowded public place?" It had been a long time since she'd flirted in a bar, but judging from Nick's expression, she was holding her own.

He smiled, sending a plume of warmth curling through her. "Unless the lady has an objection."

She leaned closer, bringing her lips close to his. "No objection."

His lips met hers and her eyes went shut. She'd thought the place was too busy for anyone to notice, but she heard a couple of small whoops before Nick leaned back and smiled at her.

"Sorry about that," he said in a voice that kind of rolled over her, making her skin tingle.

"For the kiss or the response of the crowd?"

"The crowd, Alex. I don't for one moment regret the kiss."

CHAPTER THIRTEEN

TWO DAYS HAD passed since Nick had kissed Alex in the Shamrock Pub and then again on her front porch after taking her home. Two days since he'd whispered that she brought something special to his life before opening the front door for her and then declining her offer of coffee.

Instead, he'd framed her face with his big hands, giving her the sweetest kiss before bringing his forehead down to rest on hers. "I think I'd better go home, so that I am not tempted to stay."

Alex's stomach still did a little free fall when she thought about the regretful note in his low voice. But Nick was the kind of guy who had a code, and that code included not rushing things out of respect for her and her trust issues, and out of concern for his daughters.

Speaking of which...

Alex turned in her seat to smile at Kendra

and Bailey, who were already in the process of unbuckling their booster seats.

"Okay, girls. Do you have everything?"

"Except the stuff Bailey left on your table," Kendra said as she helped her sister lift the armrest of her seat.

"I'll get it at the sleepover," Bailey announced.

Nick had dropped the girls at Alex's place early that morning before he'd taken a trip to Missoula to pick up a lathe he'd bought via social media. Katie and Brady were meeting with a wedding planner and Rosalie had been tied up until noon, so Alex had the girls all to herself until she dropped them at Rosalie's gorgeous Victorian house, where Nick would pick them up.

"We had fun," Kendra said as she scrambled out of the car.

"I liked the pancakes best," Bailey agreed.

Alex had made chocolate chip pancakes using one of the giant cast-iron skillets Juliet had left behind, and then the three of them had taken a walk, with Kendra pointing out all of the plants her Aunt Katie had taught her to identify and Bailey picking flowers.

Looking back, her life had been so empty before the Callahans had come into it. Alex was as in love with the girls as she was with the father.

Rosalie opened the front door and waved at the girls, who raced for the front gate. Alex undid their seats from the seat belts and followed with a seat in each hand.

"Is that glitter I see on your hands?" Rosalie asked Bailey, who turned her wrist so that the glitter caught the sun.

"We made pictures with the stuff Alex's aunt left when she moved out," Kendra explained.

Rosalie met Alex's gaze with a warm smile. The woman approved of her, and that was huge. Alex smiled back. "We had fun," she said simply.

"Do you have time for a cup of tea?"

Alex shook her head. "I have some shopping to do." She waited until the girls were in the house before saying, "I'm hosting a sleepover in a few days, and I wanted to get some special food and a few odds and ends for some games we used to play at boarding…"

Her voice trailed, and Rosalie laughed before putting a reassuring hand on Alex's shoulder.

"I know that you went to boarding school. It's not a crime."

Alex let out a sigh. "I know." She smiled wryly. "It's just that my background is so different from that of the people around here. I want to fit in."

"I think you fit in in the best way," Rosalie said with a knowing look. "Now I'd better go see about my crew. We'll see you soon, Alex."

Alex blew out a breath as she walked back to her car, then spontaneously smiled as she opened the car door and a bubble of happiness rose inside her. She was living a life she hadn't imagined possible when she'd first arrived in Montana. A life full of warmth and a sense of belonging.

ALEX'S SENSE OF well-being lasted until she drove through her unlocked gate and parked in her usual spot near the old barn. That was when she noticed the top of Roger's head showing momentarily above the backyard gate and then disappearing. Her heart stopped.

Roger wasn't supposed to be in the backyard…but Bailey had gone back into the house at the last minute. She might have let him out or left the back door open.

Alex let out a shaky breath. She was so looking forward to the day when things out of the norm didn't trigger a panic attack. When she could accept that she wasn't being hunted down by people who wanted their money, and that the guy in her apartment had been a run-of-the-mill burglar.

She forced a wry smile as she gathered her purse and bags of groceries, nudging the car door closed with her hip. The fact that she was happy to be robbed by a normal burglar spoke to how crazy her life had been before she'd fled.

"What are you guys doing out?" she asked as she shooed the dogs back and managed to open the gate latch with one finger. A true urbanite, she hated to make two trips, so all of her bags were hanging from her arms.

Sure enough, the back door was open, and the dogs had made their way out by pushing on the unlocked screen door.

"Well, sunshine is good," she murmured, and maybe it was time that she allowed herself to believe that Roger would stay put if she left him in the yard, even though she knew for a fact he could get out if he wanted.

A few days prior he'd taken a running leap and was able to lever himself up to the top of the pickets. He would have gone over if Alex hadn't seen him. But even if he did, would he leave Gus?

No.

Alex nudged the screen door open with her foot and stepped inside, dropping the bags onto the table and pulling her arms free of the handles. Roger made a beeline for the living room, and then she heard him race up the stairs. Alex stared after him, then noticed that Gus, who hung by her side, was also staring intently.

He's waiting for Roger to come back.

Of course.

But as she looked around the kitchen, she realized that some of the drawers weren't fully closed, as if someone had opened them and hadn't quite gotten them shut again.

Alex's heart started thumping against her ribs, and since her Louisville Slugger was upstairs, she picked up a short piece of two-by-four lumber that Nick had left leaning against the wall after making repairs in the cellar. The second that she set foot in the living room, she sensed that someone had been there. Her laptop was not on the coffee table, where she was certain she'd left it, and again, the single desk drawer wasn't quite closed.

Alex stood stock-still and listened.

Despite the blood pounding in her ears, the house seemed quiet. If someone was still there, then they'd hidden their vehicle, which would have been something of a trick, since there were no good hiding places when the only buildings were a small barn, an unused chicken house and the house she was standing in.

Roger trotted down the stairs and sniffed around the living room, interested, but not agitated. Alex gripped the two-by-four more tightly and made her way up the stairs, swallowing dryly as she crept upward.

The scene that met her in her bedroom had her stumbling backward. Her belongings were strewn everywhere. The mattress had been pulled off the bed and box spring knocked askew. The contents of the dresser drawers had been dumped and the drawers themselves overturned, as if someone had been looking for something taped to the bottom.

Alex raced back down the stairs and out the back door. Once clear of the house, she dialed 911, explained that she'd had a break-in, then called her dogs and loaded them in her car.

There she waited for the deputy to arrive, fighting nausea as she realized what might have happened had the person who'd ransacked her house arrived while she and Nick's daughters had been happily making chocolate chip pancakes. The girls she had grown to love could have been innocent victims of the trouble she'd brought with her to Montana.

She pressed her hand to her forehead, squeezing her eyes shut. Was this really trouble that she'd brought? Could this have been a coincidence? Could she be the victim of a random break-in, in a relatively crime-free area so soon after suffering a similar incident back in Virginia?

Possible, but not probable.

Another wave of sickness swept through her when she thought about Kendra's and Bailey's happy faces and what might have happened to them if the person who'd committed the robbery had been dangerous. If he'd wanted answers from her about Jason that she wouldn't have been able to give.

She reached out for Roger, who sat on console, and rubbed his wiry head, doing her best to calm herself before the deputy arrived. Gus poked at her from the back seat and she awkwardly turned her hand to pet him, too.

"We need to get out of here for a while, guys." She knew she was teetering on the edge of shock and that her thought processes were muddled because of it, but one thing was crystal clear—she needed to put distance between herself and the Callahans until she had answers. She would not allow the family to be hurt because she'd blithely allowed Jason Stoddard to use her as his patsy.

As Nick approached the Dunlop ranch road, a sheriff's vehicle pulled out in front of him and turned in the direction of Gavin.

Odd, and, given the fact that only the Dunlop ranch and his ranch were accessed by that road, more than a little unnerving. He reached for his cell and punched in Alex's number after making the turn, but he got no answer, and when he reached the gate, it was locked.

He undid the padlock, pulled through, then stopped and locked it again.

When he got to Alex's house, she was in the process of loading a suitcase into her car.

Nick stopped the truck and got out without bothering to turn off the motor.

"What are you doing?"

Alex didn't meet his gaze as she said, "I'm leaving for a night or two."

"Why? What happened? Where are my girls?"

"Safe with Rosalie." The mention of his daughters seemed to shake something loose, and Alex pulled in a shuddering breath as she finally met his eyes.

"They weren't here."

His stomach tightened at the odd statement. Something was very, very wrong.

"Here for what?" he growled, needing answers. What had put that look on Alex's face and what hadn't his girls been there for?

Alex shut the rear door of her car. "The break-in."

"What?"

She straightened her spine and her jaw muscles tightened before she said, "I dropped off the girls, went shopping, came home and…someone had taken my house apart while I was gone."

A low curse escaped his lips and he reached for her, but Alex jerked back out of reach. Slowly he dropped his arms, staring at her. Her face was pale, and her eyes had an odd blankness to them, as if she wasn't allowing herself to feel.

"You're in shock."

"No. I was in shock. Now I'm engaging in a plan of action that I worked out with the deputy."

He noticed then that the dogs were in the back seat. She really was leaving for a night or two. "I don't feel safe here for obvious reasons, so I'm going to stay where there are people nearby."

"Come to the ranch," he said in a low voice. He needed her there, where he could calm her, protect her, find out what had happened. Then he'd find the person who had done this and take them apart.

"No."

"Why not?"

She lifted her chin. "I need to go somewhere where I can think."

"You need to be somewhere you feel safe. You said so yourself."

"That isn't with you."

Nick's chin jerked as if she'd slapped him. "What does that mean?"

Alex glanced down at the gravel between them, pressing her lips together so hard that they started to turn white. "I didn't mean that to sound so harsh, but it's true." When she looked up again, she wore an expression of stony determination. "I let myself believe things that weren't true, because I wanted to believe them, but when things got real—" she gestured at the house, making him believe that she was talking about the break-in "—I came to my senses. I don't belong with you, Nick. I have too much baggage to be involved with your family."

She reached for the car door handle, and Nick had to close his fingers into fists to keep from pushing it shut again after she opened it.

"That's not true," he said in a low voice.

"You have no idea of what's true. And as long as you have little girls and a grandmother to keep safe, you need to let me go."

He needed to keep her safe, too, and he had no idea how to do that, short of wrestling her into his truck and driving her to the ranch, which he had no right to do.

"Where are you going? At least tell me that."

For a moment, he thought she was going to simply get into the car and drive away, but then she relented enough to say, "The local deputy suggested a place that I can stay. I'll be back in a day or two. When I come back, I'll be changing the lock on the gate. You can drive through the property until then."

"*Are* you coming back?"

He had a strong feeling that she wasn't. That, after she got to her safe place, she'd spend a night or two, then head out for parts unknown, attempting to stay one step ahead of whoever she thought was after her.

"I said I was."

"Do you know for certain that this is related to your past?" He gestured at the house. "That this has something to do with your boss and the missing money?"

"I'm not willing to take the chance that it isn't," she said. "For all of our sakes."

"Alex—"

"I have to go." She got in the car and shut the door, leaving Nick staring helplessly through the window. Helpless wasn't his normal mode of operation, but he had no idea how to handle the situation. Alex was right— if her presence put his daughters in danger, then they had to think of a different way to tackle this. But they needed to tackle it. He couldn't simply allow her to drive out of his life…which she was doing.

He stepped back automatically as she put the car into gear, then drove toward the gate that had originally brought them together.

Then he turned and stalked to his truck, his jaw muscles so tightly clenched that his temples were beginning to throb.

He thought about following her, then instead turned in the direction of his own ranch. The deputy had told her where to go. She had a plan and it sounded as if she was going to follow it. Unfortunately, her plan involved removing herself from his life. He hit the steering wheel with the palm of his hand before putting the truck in gear.

Alex wasn't the only one who had some serious thinking to do.

"GREAT. THANKS, COLBY. I owe you." Nick hung up the phone and turned to his sister, who was leaning against the kitchen counter, staring at him. Now he could add relief to anger, frustration and confusion.

"Well?"

"Colby can't tell me where Alex is, but she checked in with the sheriff's office in case they had information, so they know she's safe. And I imagine, given the time frame, she didn't travel too far."

"So she's in a pet-friendly motel some-where in a hundred-mile radius." Katie folded her arms over her chest. "What now?"

Nick gave her a frustrated look. "I have no idea. She made it clear that she thinks she's putting our family in danger."

Katie scowled. "Is she?"

Nick swallowed. "I don't know." And it was killing him. "But if she's in danger, I need to figure out a way to help her without getting the girls involved."

Bailey came into the room holding up a pink nightgown covered with tiny metallic stars. "I'm wearing my Wapunzel dress to the sleepover."

Nick met Katie's gaze over the top of Bailey's head, then knelt down to deliver a hard truth. "Honey. Alex had to go away for a few days. There won't be a sleepover."

Bailey's eyes went wide. "But…"

"No sleepover!" Kendra practically skid-ded into the room.

"Alex had to leave for a while," Katie said.

"We can have it when she comes back." Kendra had a determined edge to her voice.

Nick thought about lying to ease the blow, but what would it get him in the long run? If he wanted his girls to trust him in the future, to believe him when he warned them about the dangers of life, then he couldn't give them false hope now.

"I don't think we'll be seeing much of Alex anymore."

His statement was met by stricken looks.

"Wh-why?" Kendra asked in a small voice. "Did something happen?"

Oh, yeah. Something had happened, and this was the reason Nick had feared diving back into the dating pool. Why he'd sworn to himself that if and when he did start dating, it would not affect his girls. Yet here they were, both hovering at the edge of a meltdown.

No... Bailey had just gone over. Big crocodile tears started rolling down her cheeks.

Nick gathered his girls to him, and once his arms were around them, they both dissolved. His fault. He'd gotten too involved. And Alex...he was angry with her, but he was also sick with worry.

"Hey. Sometimes people come into our lives, but it's only for a little while. Then we have to let them leave."

"But I love her," Bailey whispered against his shoulder, and he felt Kendra nod in agreement.

Yeah. Me, too.

And he didn't know what to do about it.

An hour later, after he'd put the girls to bed, Nick joined Katie at the table.

"Cassie called while you were gone."

"How's she doing?" Nick asked, assuming that she had to be doing better than he was.

"She sounded kind of tense. I worry about her." Katie fixed a sad gaze on him. "But I'm more worried about you."

"I'm fine." He wasn't. "It's the girls I'm concerned about."

"Kids are resilient."

"Then why are there all those articles out there about how kids get warped by small incidents?"

"Your daughters have four stable individuals watching over them. Me and you, Brady and Grandma. They have a solid base."

"Yeah. I guess you're right." He studied the woodworking scars on his hands, which were loosely clasped on the table in front of him. "Colby said she'd call me if she finds out anything about the break-in that can be passed along."

"Aren't you glad you dated a future deputy back in junior high?"

He gave a short grunt of acknowledgment, then raised his gaze. "I don't know what to do."

"Do you love her?"

His heart twisted inside him. Despite being angry and worried and frustrated, there was no getting around the fact that he loved her. He wanted to be with her and to protect her, but he couldn't turn his daughters' lives upside down.

Katie must have read his answer in his face, because she said, "I like her a lot, too."

"What am I going to do?" he said more to himself than to his sister.

"I imagine you'll do what you always do," Katie said, raising her eyebrows in a thoughtful way. "You'll find a way."

ALEX KNEW SHE wasn't exactly invisible living on the ground floor of a motel near the freeway in Dillon. It was difficult to walk two dogs regularly without having people notice, but the important thing was that she wasn't alone. If someone came after her here, she'd have help nearby, something she didn't have at the ranch.

Alex peered through the slit between the closed curtains. The sun was setting, and soon she'd walk the dogs again and then eat yet another granola bar. The dogs were actually eating better than she was, because when she'd stopped at the local store before checking into the motel, she'd had no trouble figuring out that the dogs would want to eat dog food, but in her stressed-out state she didn't feel like eating at all. Finally, she'd bought a couple of boxes of granola bars and a bag of apples. Subsistence food. And even though no one had followed her on the highway, she still felt like she was being watched, just as she had after the assault in her apartment.

After pulling the curtains tightly shut again, Alex sat on the bed. Roger instantly jumped up to sit next to her and put his head on her lap. Both dogs stayed close to her, and when they weren't actually touching her, they watched her closely, sensing that all was not well.

Understatement.

She kept having the nightmare thoughts about what might have happened if Kendra and Bailey had been there during the break-in. What if Nick's daughters had been hurt because of her?

The thought of people she loved becoming collateral damage ruined her. The Callahans had opened their hearts and homes to her, and she would not have them hurt because of it.

Tomorrow she had to make a move—
either go back to the ranch or…she had no
idea. She'd thought that once she was off the
ranch and in a safe place, she'd be able to
calm her nerves to the point that she could
think straight, but so far that hadn't happened.

If she went back to Virginia, she'd have
to give up her two canine best friends. She
couldn't take them with her without actually
adopting them—not legally, anyway—and if
she found herself in a situation where she was
hiding out somewhere else, then there was
no way she could have two dogs with her.

Which raised the question—did she need
to hide out?

It was possible someone had simply broken into her house to steal things, but how
could she accept that as fact without any sub-
stantiating evidence? And until she knew for
a fact that she was safe, she wasn't about to
have contact with Nick and his family, because she needed for them to be safe.

This was her issue and she would handle
it alone.

Now she had to figure out how.

And she needed to stop thinking about
Nick, because that, too, was ruining her.

IT WAS NEARLY midnight when the text came in, startling Alex as she lay in bed with a dog on either side of her. It said simply, "I need to talk to you. Please don't shut me out."

Alex stared at her phone, stunned that he'd reached out to her, and stunned at how badly she didn't want to shut Nick out. She'd said horrible things to him, but everything in her cried out for contact with the guy who made her feel whole again. Made her feel safe, even though that had obviously been an illusion.

Did she go with honesty or another hurtful lie to push him away?

I have to.

There. A painful middle ground.

Alex pulled in a shaky breath. She was doing the right thing in the wrong way. The least she could do was to tell him the full truth instead of handling things the way she had, out of fear and protectiveness. Her phone buzzed again.

I have news.

Alex's brow furrowed. News?

Deputies caught kids breaking into a house tonight.

Alex was still processing that bit of news, and the fact that Nick knew, when her phone buzzed again.

I need to see you.

Another buzz and another text.

I need answers.

True. He did. She owed him that.

Tomorrow morning? Harrington Inn. Dillon.

She replied, I'll be there.

Maybe it was because of the news about the kids being caught breaking into the house, or maybe it was sheer exhaustion, but Alex fell asleep shortly after Nick's last text, waking with a start when her phone rang. She pushed herself up onto one elbow as Roger jumped off the bed and flopped down next to Gus near the chair beneath the window.

The room was dark, but she could see a sliver of light shining in from beneath the curtains as she pushed her hair back. The phone rang again, and she snapped on the light to check the number on her phone against the number on the card the deputy had given her before answering.

"This is Deputy Lauren Colby. We made an arrest for breaking and entering at a rural residence last night. They had a car trunk full of stuff. Some of it might be yours."

"Was there a laptop?"

"Several."

Could it be that simple?

"Thank you for telling me. What's the next step?"

"We have to process the items," the deputy continued, "so we'll give you a call and make arrangements for you to identify anything that belongs to you. Will you be in the area?"

"Yes," Alex said. She would. "You can reach me at this number regardless."

She hung up the phone and got out of bed, again wondering if the question of who had broken into her house had been solved. A part of her whispered no.

The thieves had laptops, but was one of them hers? And if these people were thieves, then why had they taken her laptop, but ignored her jewelry, which had been scattered across the bedroom floor along with the other items in her drawer and jewelry box.

Even a rookie thief should have recognized the value of her pearls and the gold-and-diamond tennis bracelet.

Maybe it was too hard to fence jewelry.

Maybe she was afraid to believe it was over, or that there'd never really been an issue. The other thief in her life had also been a random occurrence, and she'd crossed the country for no reason, met a family she'd fallen in love with and then hurt them. Because she had hurt Nick last night, and if he explained matters to his girls, she was certain she'd hurt them, too.

Alex pulled on her jeans and tugged a sweatshirt over her head. The instant she touched the leashes, Gus and Roger were on their feet, ready to meet the day.

"I'm ready, too," she murmured to her dogs as they surged out of the door ahead of her. They headed to the trail near the undeveloped land by the freeway, both taking care of business as soon as possible so that they could commence walking. Now that she was outside of the dark room with the cool morning air moving over her face and the traffic sailing back on the freeway several hundred yards away, the world seemed different. Less frightening.

Would she feel the same way when she went back to her house to clean up the mess?

She could hope, because she hadn't been herself when she'd left the place. The overwhelming sense of déjà vu, coupled with her protective instincts regarding Nick's daughters, had caused her to operate in fear mode. She'd needed to get to a safe place, and she'd needed to make sure Nick didn't follow so he didn't get sucked into her drama.

Except that he had followed—or was about to.

Nick didn't see Alex's car when he pulled in to the parking lot of the Harrington Inn. Had she strung him along, only to run again? His jaw tightened, but he gave her the benefit of the doubt and parked before shooting her a text asking for the room number. He got an answer within seconds, and he closed his eyes, willing his tight muscles to relax.

She was still there, and she trusted him enough to see him. Talk to him.

He had some things to say to her, but mostly he had questions. And once he got the answers, he'd know what his next step was.

The door opened almost as soon as he knocked, and Alex stood aside to allow him entry into the dimly lit room. Roger and Gus jumped to their feet to greet him, and he took a moment to gather his thoughts as he rubbed heads and ears. What he really wanted to do was to pull Alex into his arms and assure her that she was safe. That he would take care of her. And he wanted her to trust him in return. But if she couldn't do that, then they would have to part company.

"I'm…sorry," she said as he got back to his feet.

"Me, too." The tension in the small room was growing by the second, and he was having a hard time diving into the things he'd come to say. "You ran instead of trying to work with me."

Pain shot across her face. "I want you safe," she said fiercely. "I want the girls safe. They were at my house mere *hours* before that person broke in."

"Yeah." He wasn't doing too well with that circumstance, either, but he didn't blame Alex because someone had marked her house as an easy target. "That makes me want to take the guy apart, but are you responsible for his actions?"

"I don't know."

She was still hung up on the fact that she'd

had a previous break-in, that people who'd lost money thought she knew where her boss was.

"They caught the guy that did this, Alex."

Her frown deepened. "How do you know that?"

"I dated the deputy in charge of the investigation." Her eyes went wide. "In seventh grade."

She rolled her eyes, the first sign that she was relaxing, then the tension came back into her face as she said, "They didn't take my jewelry. Just my laptop."

"Maybe it's hard to get rid of jewelry." He could see by the way she shifted her eyes that she'd come to the same conclusion. "What will it take to convince you that you are safe?" The words came out slowly as he locked his gaze onto her face, half-afraid that if he looked away he'd lose her.

"I've been asking myself that question."

"What will it take to trust me, Alex? To know that you can depend on me?" He hesitated, then asked the question foremost in his mind—the one that had been haunting him since she drove away with her dogs. "What will it take for you to love me?"

Her eyes jerked up to his. "I do love you.

You have to know that." Her voice was barely more than a whisper, but the impact of her softly spoken words rocked him to his core.

"Alex…" He reached out and she closed the distance between them, sidestepping Gus and almost losing her balance. Nick caught her and waited until her feet were under her before drawing her into his arms.

"This is what people who love each other do. They catch one another." He smoothed the hair away from her face.

"I didn't want you to be hurt," she murmured.

"I don't want you to face your fears alone."

"It's hard to let other people in…even special people."

"I know." He'd faced his own fears alone after losing Kayla. "And I do love you." He touched her lips with his fingertips, then leaned down to kiss her. When he raised his head, he said, "We have stuff to work through. I need to be careful about the girls. They were pretty devastated by your departure."

"I'm so sorry," she said.

"We have challenges ahead of us." There was no sense pretending they didn't. "But if we can talk, if you can tell me what's going on instead of doing the brave thing to spare me, I think we can build something."

He knew she wasn't wired that way—that she'd been raised to deal with matters on her own rather than to share—but what was the use of having someone who loved you if you didn't allow them to face life with you?

Alex lowered her gaze to focus on the buttons of his shirt, studying them for a long moment before she tilted her head back to meet his gaze. "I will try."

And instead of going Yoda on her, Nick smiled and drew her closer. "That's all I ask."

NICK FOLLOWED ALEX back to her ranch, and he stopped to lock the gate after them. The person who'd ransacked her house might be in jail, and she believed Nick when he said she had nothing to fear, that he'd be there for her, but she still felt better locked in. And he understood that.

"You ready for this?" he asked after she'd let Gus and Roger out of her car. They instantly started snuffling around, checking for new smells.

"I pretty much have to be." There was no way to avoid facing the mess in her house, and the sooner she sorted through things, the better.

He put an arm around her, and she gave him a let's-do-this smile.

"I'm here," he said simply.

She leaned into him, then eased herself out of his embrace. Now that she knew who was behind the crime, she could face it without ruining herself wondering if she had to start running again. And she could let Nick help.

She wanted Nick to help. He understood and accepted things about her that *she* had trouble accepting. They went in through the backyard and allowed the dogs into the house first. Neither seemed to notice anything out of the ordinary, and Alex's anxiety shifted into anger as she started sorting through the debris in her bedroom.

Nick pulled the mattress back onto the bed and helped her put on clean sheets, bundling up the old ones and taking them to the laundry. When he got back, she was folding her clothing and replacing it in drawers.

"I don't understand why, if he was looking for small electronics, he tore this room apart."

"Looking for drugs?"

She grimaced at him. "Should I be concerned about you being so tuned in to criminal motivations?"

"I read a lot."

"And you dated a deputy."

"We played video games at her grandmother's house." He waggled his eyebrows and she laughed. "I think you should stay at the ranch tonight."

The laughter died on her lips. "The girls—"

"Love you. I think it's too late to do anything about that." A shadow crossed his face. "I hope that doesn't make you feel trapped. If so—"

"No," she said quickly. "It makes me wonder what I've done to deserve something so special." She propped a hand on her hip and surveyed her room. "But I think it's best if I take back my house."

She could do this. The gate was locked. The thief was in jail. Her past had not caught up with her, and there was really no reason to believe it ever would. Jason was sipping top-shelf rum on a beach, and instead of taking the fall, she'd found a new life, with a man and little girls who loved her.

"You're sure."

She turned to slide her hands up his chest and curl her fingers around his solid shoulder muscles. "I need time to process. I just ran like a scared rabbit, giving in to instinct. Logic tells me I'm wrong."

"Do you want me to sleep on your sofa?"

She gave him a grateful look. "Actually, if the girls wouldn't mind…"

He smiled down at her. "The girls are spending the night with Grandma in town because tomorrow is the kick off of June in Bloom."

"Oh, my gosh. I forgot."

"I'm not allowed that luxury," Nick said with a smile. "I'll text Katie and let her know what's going on, then leave early to help Grandma with the June in Bloom setup. The girls will never know."

"Just this one night. After that, I need to tackle things on my own."

ALEX SLEPT BETTER than she'd slept in weeks, knowing that Nick was downstairs. True to his word, he tapped on her door just as the sun was rising, then poked his head in to tell her he was leaving.

"I'll see you at the park later this morning, right?"

"Right around lunchtime." If she hadn't needed a shower and felt an incredibly strong need to scrub every inch of her house in an effort to purge all traces of the thief, she would have gone along to help. Nick assured her that he could handle matters.

"I sometimes get too much help, believe it or not." His eyes crinkled. "And conflicting advice. It's…fun." Roger jumped off the bed and trotted to the door where Nick stood, and Gus ambled after him. "I'll let these guys out."

"Thanks, Nick. I'll see you later." Alex rolled over, pulling the sheet over her and listened as Nick made his way through the house, opened and closed the back door, then started his truck. There was no way she was going back to sleep, but she allowed herself to lie in bed until Gus started scratching at the door as he did every morning when he wanted his breakfast.

Three hours later, the dogs were sleeping in the shade, and Alex had finished washing her last floor. The scrubbing had been cathartic, and, after her shower, she did something she never looked forward to doing—she called her mother to touch base. But it was time.

"Alexandra. What a surprise."

"How is everything?" Alex asked in a bright voice. She was actually feeling bright and hopeful, an unexpected side effect of a thief breaking into her home. The guy was in jail, and she and Nick were closer because of what had happened.

"Going well, actually. Margo Peterson's son was just arrested for dealing a large amount of cocaine."

"Dear heavens, Mother."

"And I made an error where Lawrence was concerned." She made it sound like her error was Lawrence's fault. "Which has also been a topic of conversation."

"Oh?" Alex couldn't explain the sudden tightening of her stomach. "What kind of error."

"Well, he just abandoned his job. Walked away."

An odd chill went through her.

"He never did like to work." Alex spoke absently, but her brain was racing as little bits of disjointed information started sliding together. She'd always thought it was odd that Lawrence had found her number in Jason's apartment, when Jason had kept everything in digital form. He was not a hard-copy kind of guy, but she'd accepted Lawrence at his word.

Until now…

"You wouldn't by any chance have given Lawrence my phone number?"

"Why do you ask?"

"He called me a few days ago. He wanted to go for coffee. I'm wondering how he got my number."

The silence on the other end of the line made Alex's stomach slowly clench into a hard knot.

"I did not give him your phone number," Cécile said in the voice she used when she was working things out. "But I did lose my phone recently."

The blood started pounding in Alex's ears. "Did you lose it? Or was it stolen?"

"I don't know. It was the DeYoungs' garden party. A total crush. So many people there."

"Was Lawrence there?"

"I caught a glimpse of him. But my phone has a passcode."

"Passcodes are easily broken, Mom."

"I have a hard time believing that Lawrence would steal my phone. I mean, why would he do such a thing? He seemed so thrilled to be free of his brother and putting his life back together." Cécile let out an audible breath. "So commiserative concerning the way you were used."

"It might have been an act, Mom." Alex closed her eyes. "Does he know that I'm in Montana?"

Cécile let out a small laugh. "I make it a point to tell people, Lawrence included, that you are in the city, staying with a friend while you interview for new positions."

"So if he went looking, it would be in New York."

"Trust me, Alexandra, I did not tell anyone that you went to Montana."

Alex believed her. She could almost see the curl of her mother's lips as she said *Montana*.

"Thanks, Mom."

She was about to hang up when Cécile said, "Alexandra."

"Yes?"

"You will keep me posted. If he calls again, I mean. You can ask him how he got the number and then you can tell me."

She rubbed a hand over her forehead. That almost sounded like parental concern. "I will. And if you see Lawrence again, please let me know."

"Of course."

"Thank you. Goodbye, Mom. I'll talk to you soon."

CHAPTER FOURTEEN

ALEX AUTOMATICALLY WENT into the living room to open her laptop, only to stop at the kitchen doorway and put a hand on her forehead. Her laptop had been stolen and was now in the evidence locker at the Gavin Sheriff's Office.

She hoped. She'd yet to be invited down to identify it.

Laptops had information on them, and if someone wanted information concerning someone else, what better way to get it than to hack into their laptop?

Don't get ahead of yourself.

Alex put her car keys into her pocket, then went upstairs to look out the windows. There was nothing out of the ordinary. Gus and Roger were sound asleep in the cool dirt next to the porch, and a little chipmunk ran along the top board of her fence. If someone was lurking, the chipmunk wouldn't be there.

You're okay.

She went downstairs and took a seat on the top step leading to the back porch and began researching on her phone.

How to trace a phone without the owner's knowledge. How to locate a phone. Can I find a phone via the phone number alone?

The results were chilling. There were a number of shady ways to track someone with a phone number, and a guy who would steal her mother's phone wouldn't hesitate to use an illegal process to track her down.

Alex took a deep breath, tamping down the instinct to run. Instead she turned off her phone so it wasn't a beacon, as it could well have been while she was here in Montana.

What now?

Call Nick. She'd promised not to handle this alone.

She reached for her phone, then went still as a thought struck her. If Lawrence could hypothetically trace her via an app, could she trace him?

Alex turned her phone back on and, after waiting the millennia it took for it to come back into service, typed Lawrence's number into the box on the Locate Your Buddy screen.

Maps flashed and then began zooming in

on the western part of North America. The zooming continued, zeroing in on Montana and then dropping a pin in a nebulous region between Gavin and Dillon.

Alex fought to breathe.

She needed to get out of there. Get away from her house and Gavin and find a place where she could hole up and think without worrying about Lawrence waltzing in on her.

Instead, she did exactly as she promised and dialed Nick.

"Hey," he said with a smile in his voice. "Are you on your way to town?"

"I…uh…have discovered that Jason's brother might be in Montana."

"What?"

"I'll explain it all when I see you. Right now… I just want to get out of here."

"Do you have any reason to believe he's there?"

"No. It's quiet and the dogs are the opposite of being on alert." But they were also lethargic from the heat. Neither of them had done more than lift his head over the past couple of hours.

"You're leaving now?"

"Yes. I'll see you at the booth."

She called the dogs, who slowly rose to their feet. Even Roger was moving in slo-mo.

"Hey, want to go for a ride?" Alex jingled the keys and they both perked up. Roger even went so far as to give a half-hearted jump.

Alex opened the back door and they jumped in. She quickly rolled down the windows to give them air, then started the car while Gus blew hot breath in her ear.

She'd stop at Rosalie's and slip the dogs into the kennel, then continue on to the park so that they wouldn't have to sit in the hot car. And then she was going to keep her word and allow Nick to help her deal with the issue at hand.

Nick and quite possibly his seventh-grade main squeeze who was now a deputy.

And she wanted to see the evidence from the thefts as soon as possible. If her laptop wasn't part of the loot, then it was very possible that the local burglar hadn't been the one who'd stolen it.

NICK PACED AROUND the booth that he'd helped put together prior to the kickoff of June in Bloom, watching the parking lots at either end of the park and willing Alex to drive into one of them. He wanted to know exactly how she knew that her ex's brother was there in Montana, and he wanted to know just what that meant.

She'd been upset, so it obviously meant something bad, but he had no facts, and not knowing was killing him.

"Nick…is something wrong?" Gloria asked when they had a break in customers. The booth had been swamped during the early hours, and they were almost out of cupcakes and had only a few more gift baskets to raffle off. The girls were having a ball charming customers and eating things that they were going to regret later.

"He's waiting for someone," Katie said with a knowing smile before Bailey took her by one hand and Kendra by the other.

"We want to play the duck game," Bailey said.

"Duck game it is," Katie laughed.

Nick smiled at his grandmother, who'd been watching him closely. Like his sisters, she had some kind of radar, and the last thing he wanted was for her to start trying to work information out of him. He glanced at his phone, noting that it'd been only five minutes since Alex called him a couple of miles from town to tell him she was dropping the dogs at the kennel at her grandmother's house. He understood why she'd brought them and agreed that the kennel was a good idea. They weren't allowed in the park, and it wasn't a fit day for anything to be in a car.

"Nick," Gloria said, pointing up at the quilt that was working its way free from the clip that held it in place as a backdrop. "Could you re-clip that? I'm not tall enough."

"Sure." He reached over her head to fasten the quilt more securely.

"That's one of Alex's quilt tops that she got from her aunt," Gloria explained.

"Very nice." And speaking of Alex… "If you have everything under control, I need to make a call."

"Totally under control," Gloria said as she shifted a gift basket to make room for another.

Alex's phone didn't ring through. She was either in the dead spot just out of town, or she'd turned it off. That was it. He was going to look for her.

Nick worked his way along the colorful displays toward the parking lot and had just spotted Katie and the girls near the plastic pool filled with yellow ducks when Emmie Cooper called his name. He raised a hand to acknowledge the greeting, then shifted course when he caught sight of the serious look on her face.

"What's up?" he asked as he approached the building-supply booth.

"I was about to ask you the same," she said. Jenna appeared from around the back of the tent.

"Some guy has been asking about your neighbor's spending habits."

"What?"

"Yeah," Jenna said. "He's like an inept private eye according to Reggie, asking questions in an awkwardly casual way."

"When?"

"Yesterday for sure."

Nick ended the conversation with a nod. Katie and the girls were no longer at the pool, so he turned and headed back to Rosalie's booth. "I have to go," he said. "I'd like to leave the girls with you and Katie."

"Where are you going?"

"I have to check on Alex."

"Where is she?" Rosalie asked.

"That's what I need to check on. She's supposed to be here, so I want to make sure she hasn't had a flat or something."

Roger and Gus sniffed around the dog yard while Alex waited for her phone, which had frozen, to come alive again so she could call Nick and ask him to meet her at Rosalie's, if possible. The quiet Victorian house was a much better setting for her to discuss what might be happening in her life than a crowded park, although she really didn't mind the idea of a crowd.

The house was locked, but she'd been able to access the kennel through the side gate she and Rosalie had marched through on their way to rescue Roger. Had that been only a little more than a week ago?

Her life, her perspective, had changed so much over the past few hours that it seemed like weeks had passed. Was Lawrence dangerous? Was he simply obsessed with her because of her relationship to his brother?

The screen finally lit up and Alex made a couple of attempts at touch ID before giving up and typing in the pass code. The home screen appeared just as the sound of the gate squeaking open brought her head snapping up.

"Hey, Alex. Long time."

For one horrifying moment, Alex's entire body froze, just as it did in the dreams she'd had after the assault in her apartment, where danger was coming, and she couldn't get out of the way because her legs wouldn't respond to her brain.

"Lawrence."

He smiled, and she couldn't say that it was a particularly evil smile. He looked like he had every other time she'd met him. But the fact that he was there, in Rosalie's backyard, led her to believe that his intentions were not pure.

"There's no need to look alarmed, Alex. All I want is the key."

"What key?"

"The safety-deposit box key," he explained, as if spelling something out for a child.

"I... There's nothing in the safety-deposit box. The police checked."

A shadow crossed his face and his mouth tightened. "Not that safety-deposit box."

Alex looked past him to the gate, judging the distance. "Do you think that Jason gave me a key to something?"

"Yes." He said the word in a deadly tone. "You know, *as planned*."

Alex knew nothing about the plan. She also knew Lawrence would never believe that.

"Just give me the key, Alex. Because I swear, if you don't—"

Alex rushed him, knocking him sideways as she dove for the gate. Behind her, Roger and Gus went nuts in the kennel, roaring and yipping frantically. She was almost to the gate when something hooked her ankle and she went down hard, her chin hitting the ground and sending stars shooting in all directions. She kicked frantically and started screaming.

The gate burst open, and in the part of her brain that worked in slow motion, she wondered how Nick had gotten there so fast. But when her vision cleared, it was Vince Taylor who pushed his way into the yard, the picture of outrage.

"Leave this woman alone!" he demanded.

Lawrence's expression went blank, but he slowly released his grasp on Alex's ankle. She scooted toward the fence as he then rose to his feet, reached into his pocket and calmly pulled out a small gun. "I want you to close the gate and go stand next to the kennel."

Vince didn't move.

"Now." He waved the gun and Vince slowly closed the gate. Alex met Vince's gaze, and he gave her a desperate look before starting to move toward the kennel as commanded. Lawrence turned, keeping the man covered as he walked.

"The young woman and I are going to continue this conversation elsewhere. Now open the kennel and get inside."

Vince lifted the latch and edged the door open. Roger shot out, heading straight to Alex and taking a stand in front of her, bristles standing up on the back of his neck.

"Get. In," Lawrence repeated. Once Vince was inside, he snapped the latch in place—a latch Vince wouldn't be able to get at from the inside due to the fine mesh of the chain link.

"If you climb out of that pen before I'm gone, I'll make sure you regret it." He waved the weapon at Alex. "*She* will really regret it."

Vince held his chin high, glaring at Lawrence through the mesh. Lawrence laughed, then shook his head.

"Come on, Alex. Let's get that key and I'll be on my way."

No, he wouldn't. She knew it as certainly as she knew that the sound of the engine coming down the street was that of Nick's truck. How many people were going to be put in jeopardy because she'd chosen to hide in this community? To try to become part of it?

She got to her feet while Roger held his stiff-legged position next her, his lips pulled back menacingly, the effect totally ruined by his bat ears. She met and held Lawrence's gaze in a challenging way, hoping he wouldn't know that the truck coming down the street was destined to pull in right behind her car.

"Think, Alex," Lawrence said in a reasoning tone.

Oh, she was thinking all right. She was thinking that there was no way he was going to hurt her or someone she loved. Or Vince Taylor, for that matter.

She pulled in a deep breath and said, "Let's go."

CHAPTER FIFTEEN

NICK CAUGHT SIGHT of Alex's car parked in front of his grandmother's house as soon as he turned the corner onto High Street, and a wave of relief rolled over him. He would not have to go looking, and now they could get down to the business of figuring out exactly what was going on with the embezzler's brother visiting their fair state and apparently asking questions about Alex's finances.

He drove past Vince Taylor's impeccably restored Victorian house and was about to pull to the curb behind Alex's car when a flash of movement in the side yard caught his eye. His neck tightened and he realized that whatever he'd seen, it hadn't been Alex. He rolled on by, as if looking for an address, then parked a few houses away and picked up his phone to dial 911.

"Nine-one-one. What is your emergency?"

He was pretty certain it was Dora Mellow on the other end. "This is Nick Callahan at 455 High Street. There's a trespasser on the premises and I think he's threatening someone."

"Do you know who it is, Nick?"

His hand tightened around the phone as Alex and a man he didn't recognize came out the side gate. The man was holding her arm in a seemingly congenial way, while little Roger walked stiff-legged behind her, his lips curled back, his eyes trained on Alex.

Son of a... "It might be a kidnapping, Dora. Get someone here fast."

He dropped the phone and opened the truck door just as Alex tripped and went down, making a valiant effort to knock the man's legs out from under him. He wobbled but kept his balance and then tried to jerk Alex to her feet as Nick raced down the sidewalk.

The man turned to stare stupidly when he heard the sound of Nick's boots on the concrete, then Roger sprang into action, leaping into the air and biting the man first on the thigh and then on the belly. The guy howled and clutched at his leg as Nick launched himself, knocking him sideways.

Nick grunted as a small weapon slid across the grass, then he jerked the man's arm up between his shoulder blades, not caring in the least if he broke it, and put a knee in his back. Meanwhile, Roger kept darting in, biting the guy anywhere he could reach, accidentally getting Nick a few times in the process.

The man writhed and jerked beneath him. He was strong, but Nick had spent most of his teen years wrestling calves to the ground, and after he took hold of the guy's hair with one hand and pulled it back, he quieted.

That was when Alex grabbed the gun and threw it over Vince Taylor's fence.

Nick gave her an incredulous look. "I don't want him to get it again," she said. "He almost got away the last time Roger bit him."

"Makes sense," Nick said through his teeth as the deputy sheriff drove up.

Lauren Colby got out of the SUV, bent over Lawrence and, without a word, cuffed him. "You can get off him now," she told Nick, who rolled onto the grass and sat with his forearms on his knees catching his breath. "Want to tell me what happened?"

An outraged cry came from the kennel, and Colby squinted as she peered through the side gate. "Is that Vince Taylor all kenneled up?"

"Yeah," Nick said. "I think it is."

"Huh."

A short time later, Lawrence Stoddard was in the back seat of the SUV, Vince Taylor and Gus had been released from the kennel, and the unloaded gun retrieved from Vince's yard. Another deputy had arrived, and he took charge of Stoddard while Colby took statements. Except for when she and Nick had given their statements, Alex had kept close to Nick's side, but it didn't seem to be because she was nervous about her safety or because she was in shock—it seemed to be because she felt protective of Nick. And he couldn't say that he minded.

"Does it matter that the gun was un-loaded?" Alex asked Colby.

"He's going to be in deep trouble regard-less," Colby replied. "I think we will have a kidnapping charge here, and who knows what else the DA might come up with. Out-of-towner threatening a local..." She wrin-kled her nose and shook her head. "It won't be pretty." She jerked her head toward the street. "We'll be in contact, and if you have any concerns, just call."

"Thank you," Alex murmured from be-side him.

A few seconds after Colby drove off, Will McGuire's truck pulled up and Will and Rosalie got out.

"What happened?" Rosalie demanded, her gaze bouncing between Nick and Alex, as if expecting them to hedge on the truth with her.

Nick filled her in on the essentials of the situation, and as he spoke, Will put an arm around Rosalie, pulling her to his side. And Rosalie, he noticed, didn't seem to mind.

"There's a lot more to tell," Alex said. "I'll explain everything later. I…uh… I'm sorry to have brought this to your home."

Rosalie gave her an affronted look. "Did you twist that man's arm and force him to do what he did? I don't think so," she said sternly. She reached out to put a hand on Alex's arm. "I always sensed something was bothering you. I hope this is the end of it."

"I'm taking Alex to the ranch," Nick said abruptly. "Can the girls stay with you tonight?"

Alex tensed at the mention of the girls but didn't argue about going to the ranch.

"Certainly."

"And…be careful not to say anything to upset them."

The corner of his grandmother's mouth tightened. "That is a given. Now go on home." She glanced at Will, then back at Nick. "Will and I are going to have a word with Vince."

"He tried to save me," Alex said.

"Yes," Rosalie said. "The villain redeems himself. I want to thank him."

"ARE YOU OKAY?" Alex asked as Nick drove past the Gavin city limits sign. He gave her a sharp look.

"I think that's my line."

She directed her gaze straight ahead, marveling at the sense of well-being that had settled over her after Lawrence had been handcuffed. "I'm good. Remarkably good." She bit her lip, then shot him a quick glance. "I feel like for the first time since Jason took off with all that money that my life is once again my own."

"Really?" He sounded pleased.

"I know." She now knew who had broken into her place in Virginia, and the fact that no one who'd investigated Jason's crime had contacted her since her move to Montana made her feel as if she truly was in the clear.

And if she wasn't, well, she had people she could lean on.

Speaking of which...

"You know that I like to do things on my own. Handle my problems alone."

He let out a short breath. "I kind of noticed."

"I want to thank you for helping me on this one. And I'm talking about more than the tackle and wrestling Lawrence to the ground. I also mean in helping me to understand that there are people who honestly are there for you. Through thick and thin."

In answer, Nick set his hand, palm up, on the gearshift. Alex put her hand in his and laced their fingers together before smiling at him, then turning her attention to the road ahead. Sometimes actions truly did speak more loudly than words, and she liked Nick's answer.

They rode in silence, holding hands until Nick needed both hands to make the turn off the highway onto Ambrose River Road. And then he surprised her by turning into a small picnic area along the river. Roger and Gus both crowded to the window in the back seat.

Alex gave him a curious look as he turned

off the ignition and then slid his hand along the back of her seat, leaning close enough to kiss her. But their lips didn't quite meet.

"You know that I am here for you through thick and thin."

"And me for you." She would do anything for this man and his family.

He touched his forehead to hers. "You know that I love you."

The utter sincerity of his statement warmed her.

"And you know that we're probably both going to have some kind of delayed reaction to what happened today," he continued.

"Probably," she agreed, unable to stop herself from lightly brushing his firm lips with her own. She knew all about post-trauma syndrome. "I'm hoping we can have our delayed reaction together."

He smiled and kissed her back, a little longer this time. "That was exactly what I was about to suggest. That we meet the challenges together."

Her hand slid up around the back of his neck as she whispered, "I can't think of anything I'd like better."

He gave her a smile that made her breath catch. "Through thick and thin."

She smiled back. "Through thick and thin."

EPILOGUE

"YOU BROUGHT THE GOAT?" Alex asked as Bailey and Kendra and Lizzie Belle emerged from the back seat of Nick's truck.

"She rode between our seats," Kendra explained.

"But…why?" Alex asked in an amused voice. Nick simply smiled, allowing his daughters to explain.

"Well," Bailey said, "it's a 'ganic way to get rid of weeds."

She glanced at Nick, reading the amusement in his gaze. "I thought you were bringing the weed whacker." After a few early autumn rain showers, the weeds were threatening to take over the area around her small barn and outbuildings.

"It's on the fritz, so Katie suggested Lizzie Belle. We can stake her out where we need her to eat, and she can spend the night in the barn."

"Just make sure the door is shut tight,"

Kendra said in a way that made it obvious that she was speaking from experience.

"Will do," Alex assured them. "Maybe you can tie her to that fence near the barn and she can get started."

Kendra pulled a long rope out of the truck. "Come on, Lizzie Belle."

The goat followed the girls to the barn, snatching at weeds as she walked.

"Tie her tight," Bailey said. "'Member what happened last time."

While the girls were busy with the goat, Alex jerked her head toward her house and Nick fell into step.

"I got some news," she said once they were out of the girls' hearing range.

"Yeah?"

"The investigator from Virginia called. The authorities found Jason and they're working to extradite him."

"That's fantastic," Nick said as he pulled her a few steps closer.

"It might finally be over." Lawrence had been charged with numerous offenses in Montana, but he'd also been named as Jason's coconspirator in the embezzlement scheme in Virginia, and Alex had a feeling that he would be more than willing to testify against the brother who'd cheated him as part of a plea deal. "I think they're both out of my life."

"Good. They're out. I'm in." Nick slid his hands up to her shoulders, looking down at her in a way that made her very glad that she'd chosen to hide out in Montana. Her running and hiding days were over, but it was good to know that they'd served a purpose.

"You are so in," she murmured back, nuzzling his chin.

"They're hugging again," Kendra said in a rather pleased voice, and Nick and Alex stepped apart, still smiling. They were careful not to show too much affection when the girls were around, but every now and again, they failed. No one seemed to mind—especially the girls.

"Good," Bailey said as she dragged her toes through the gravel. "I like hugging. Let's go play with Roger."

* * * * *

Get 4 FREE REWARDS!

We'll send you 2 FREE Books plus 2 FREE Mystery Gifts.

Love Inspired Suspense books showcase how courage and optimism unite in stories of faith and love in the face of danger.

FREE Value Over $20

YES! Please send me 2 FREE Love Inspired Suspense novels and my 2 FREE mystery gifts (gifts are worth about $10 retail). After receiving them, if I don't wish to receive any more books, I can return the shipping statement marked "cancel." If I don't cancel, I will receive 6 brand-new novels every month and be billed just $5.24 each for the regular-print edition or $5.99 each for the larger-print edition in the U.S., or $5.74 each for the regular-print edition or $6.24 each for the larger-print edition in Canada. That's a savings of at least 13% off the cover price. It's quite a bargain! Shipping and handling is just 50¢ per book in the U.S. and $1.25 per book in Canada.* I understand that accepting the 2 free books and gifts places me under no obligation to buy anything. I can always return a shipment and cancel at any time. The free books and gifts are mine to keep no matter what I decide.

Choose one: ☐ **Love Inspired Suspense Regular-Print** (153/353 IDN GNWN)   ☐ **Love Inspired Suspense Larger-Print** (107/307 IDN GNWN)

Name (please print)

Address   Apt. #

City   State/Province   Zip/Postal Code

Mail to the **Reader Service:**
IN U.S.A.: P.O. Box 1341, Buffalo, NY 14240-8531
IN CANADA: P.O. Box 603, Fort Erie, Ontario L2A 5X3

Want to try 2 free books from another series! Call 1-800-873-8635 or visit www.ReaderService.com.

#319 TO SAVE A CHILD
Texas Rebels • by Linda Warren

When a baby and the beautiful Grace Bennet wind up
unexpectedly in Cole Chisholm's life, the by-the-book cop
might just have to break his own rules to protect them...and
let Grace into his heart.

#320 SECOND CHANCE FOR THE SINGLE DAD
by Carol Ross

Rhys McGrath is no dancer, but he'll learn in time for the father-
daughter dance at his niece's cotillion. He's smitten by beautiful
dance instructor Camile—and he's dying to know if she feels
the same!

#321 RANCHER TO THE RESCUE
by Patricia Forsythe

Zannah Worth hates change. So her new business partner,
Brady Gallagher, has a tough time swaying her opinion with his
flashy ideas for the family ranch. He makes her feel too much—
frustration, anxiety...and something like love?

#322 CAUGHT BY THE SHERIFF
Turtleback Beach • by Rula Sinara

After her sister goes missing, Faye Donovan flees with her
niece to Turtleback Beach. But when Sheriff Carlos Ryker offers
a shoulder to lean on, Faye faces a choice—keep lying, or trust
him with all of their lives...

HWCNM0220

ReaderService.com has a new look!

We have refreshed our website and we want to share our new look with you. Head over to ReaderService.com and check it out!

On **ReaderService.com**, you can:

- Try 2 free books from any series
- Access risk-free special offers
- View your account history & manage payments
- Browse the latest Bonus Bucks catalog

Don't miss out!

If you want to stay up-to-date on the latest at the Reader Service and enjoy more Harlequin content, make sure you've signed up for our monthly News & Notes email newsletter. Sign up online at ReaderService.com.